CONNER

Hockey Royalty
Book 1

Victoria Denault

Editing: Brandi Zelenka at My Notes in the Margin

Cover: Winona Randall Designs

Proofing: OCA Proof Reading

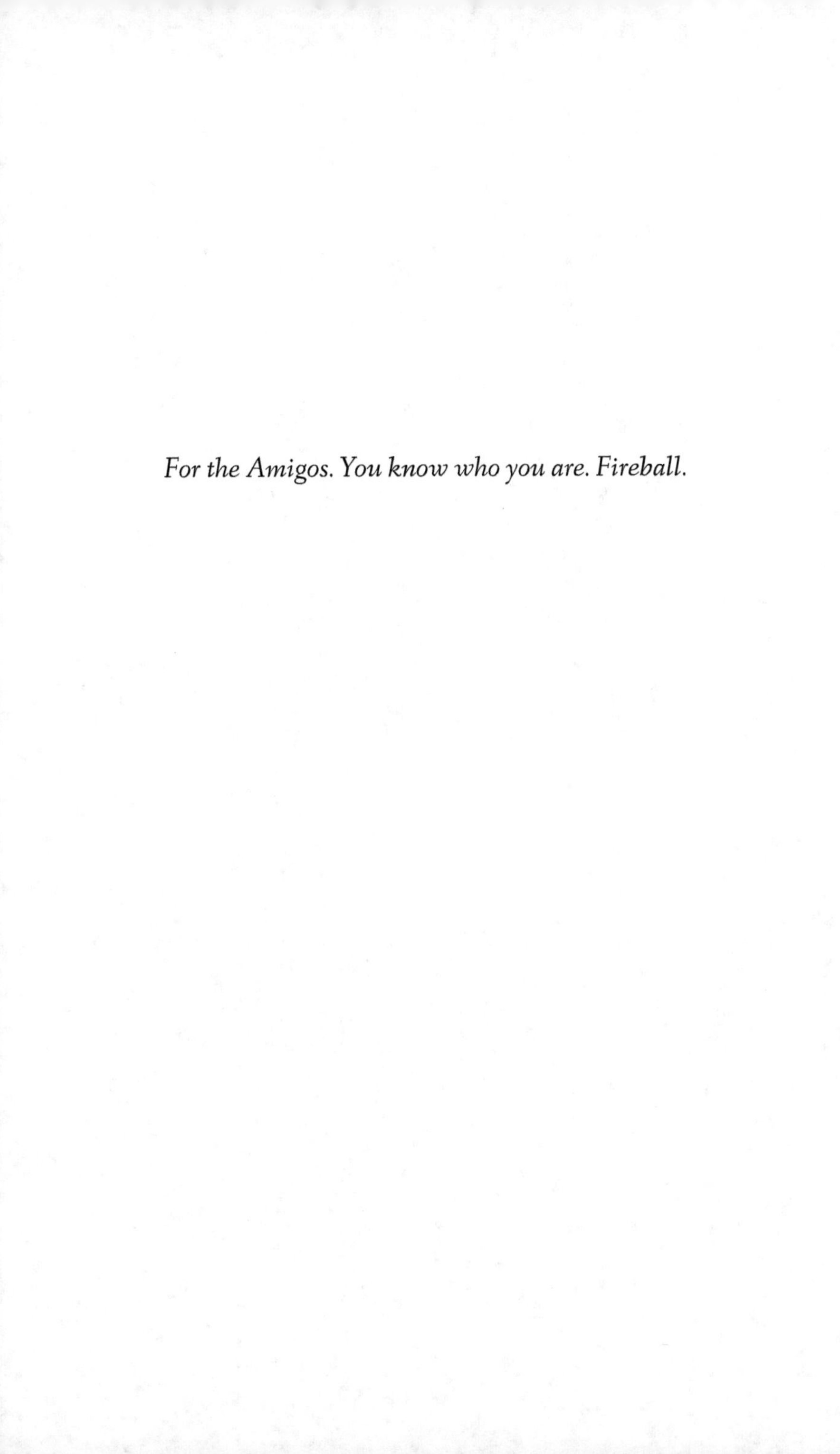

For the Amigos. You know who you are. Fireball.

Author's Note

Hockey Royalty is a 'next gen' series. The heroes and heroines in this series are the children of heroes and heroines from my previous hockey romance series Hometown Players and San Francisco Thunder. That doesn't mean that you have to go back and read those series if you haven't, although I would love that. I give enough backstory in this series that you won't be confused or lost. But if you have read the previous series, here's some things to keep in mind.

Time Jump. The first Hometown Players book released in 2015. Conner was about three in that book which means he would only be twelve today (2024). He's twenty-five in this book. Everyone has aged up.

The League. Some of the fictional NHL teams featured/mentioned in HP and SF Thunder are the same (Seattle Winterhawks, Vegas Vipers, Quebec Nationals, etc.) But I changed the name of some others. I've also included the Portland Riptide, a Maine-based team invented in the Ocean Pines series.

Tate. If you know my work you know I have a hero named Tate in Blindsided. There is a Tate in this series too because

Jordan Garrison and Jessie Caplan had a boy named Tate in the final book (Game On) in the HP series. I didn't feel it was a good idea to change it. So yeah, I have two different heroes, in unrelated books, named Tate. Sorry I didn't have better foresight.

Waivers. I know how I handle waivers in this book is not exactly how the actual NHL waiver rules work. The joy of creating a fictional league is fictional rules.

I hope you can understand the need for all these things and can lose yourself in this new world.

Hockey Royalty
Garrison Family Tree

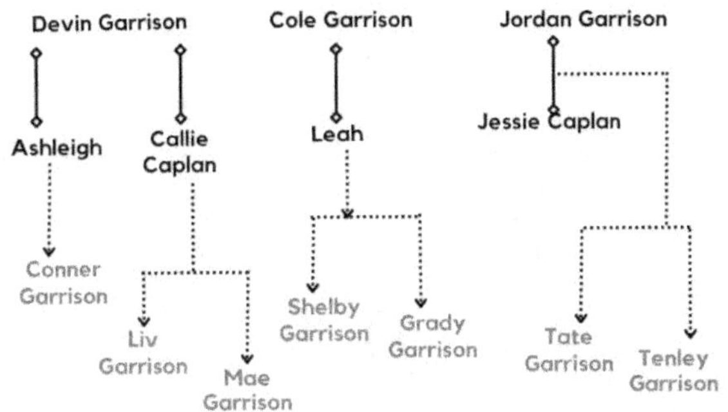

Jessie & Jordan are featured in One More Shot (Hometown Players #1)

Callie & Devin are featured in The Final Move (Hometown Players #3)

Richard Family Tree

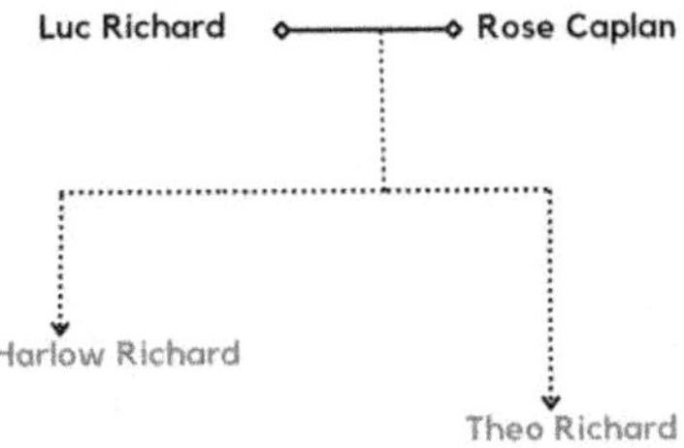

Luc/Rose are featured in Making a Play (Hometown Players #2)

Rose & Luc are featured in Making a Play (Hometown Players #2)

HOCKEY ROYALTY
LARUE FAMILY TREE

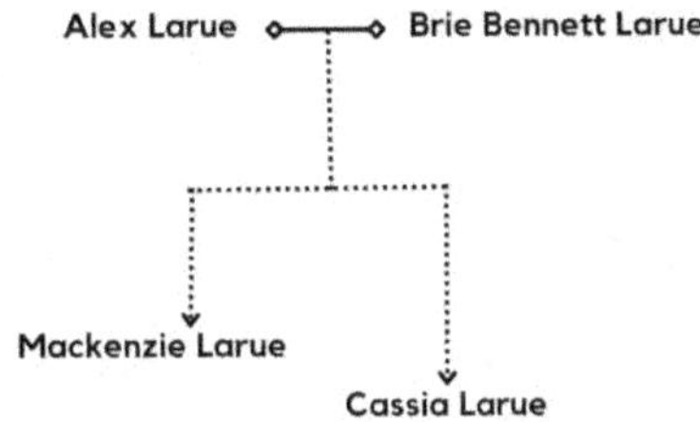

Alex/Brie are featured in Game On (Hometown Players #6)

Chapter 1

Conner

I stare at my empty locker, take a deep breath, and slam it shut. Someone clears their throat behind me. I turn and see Barry Owens, one of the alternate captains on the team, standing in the doorway. "Garrison, are you sure this is the way you want to handle this?"

I shrug into my coat and grab the bag with all my personal effects. As a last-minute spite move, I yank on my nameplate until it snaps off. Owens rubs the back of his neck and stares at me with big, sad brown eyes. "Maybe talk to your dad. Get his advice on this before—"

"Bye, Owens. Thanks for being a great teammate," I say and toss the nameplate across the room. It hits the wall and drops into the garbage below it. Maybe I should take up basketball since this hockey thing isn't panning out. "Sorry, I couldn't lead you guys better. Take care."

"Garrison..." Owens calls after me as I head out of the locker room. He follows me a few feet into the hall and then stops. "Conner! Man, I don't think this will help anything."

I don't argue with him because he's right. Walking out on my team isn't going to make my situation any better. It might, in fact, make it worse. But how the fuck do I keep playing for a team that's already dumped me? I can't. I won't.

Owens stops calling after me and I don't see another person until I'm pulling out of the private parking tucked below the Brooklyn Barons arena. I stop at the security booth and roll down my window. Maurice smiles at me, completely oblivious to what is happening within the team he's worked for for the last twenty years. I hand him my security pass and parking pass. "Can you return these for me please?"

"Are they faulty?" Maurice asks. "If you give me a minute, I can replace the magnetic strip on the back. Sometimes they crap out."

"No. I don't need them anymore, Maurice," I say.

He blinks, looks at the pass, and back at me. "Oh no. They traded you? The captain? Where to?"

"Take care Maurice and thank you for everything," is all I reply and then, with a smile and a nod, I roll up my window and drive away.

The drive back to Silver Bay, Maine, is almost six hours. And I spend every single second of it reliving the last, hellish, twenty-four hours of my life. God, how did this all go so wrong? I'm only twenty-five. My career shouldn't be on the brink of ending.

Hockey Royalty. That's what every media outlet in the country has called me since *before* I was drafted. Hell, since I first strapped on skates at three and teetered around the arena with my dad for his team's family skate. I'm the eldest son of the eldest Garrison brother. I was drafted second overall at eighteen. My father Devin, and my uncle Jordan were also both drafted at eighteen. My uncle Cole was actually even better than Uncle Jordan and Dad but he had a career-ending injury before he could be drafted and never got his shot. My uncle Luc —who isn't an uncle by blood but was essentially raised by my grandparents alongside my father and blood uncles—had also been a professional hockey player.

I'm destined to do great things with a black rubber puck a stick and some skates. It's in my bones, blood, DNA. And honestly, I've always believed that hype. I sailed through my junior hockey career. I scored the tough goals, I skated the fastest and was a born leader. It wasn't even hard. And I loved every minute of it. I wasn't just trying to follow in my dad's footsteps because hockey was our family business and I felt like I had to. I was trying to be better, stronger, and earn more achievements than my dad and uncles combined because I fucking *love* this sport. I do. More than anything.

Yet here I am, driving home for Christmas because I don't play for an NHL team anymore. This morning after practice the coach hauled me into his office, after yet another loss the night before, sat me down, and announced that he'd told management I had to go. I was shocked, to say the least. I've been with the Barons since I was drafted and have been the captain of the team for the last two and a half years. No, we hadn't won a Cup yet. Yes, last season we'd failed to make playoffs, but that wasn't *just* on me. Did they think it was?

They fired most of the management, and the coaches, at the end of last season, but when we started this season by losing the first three games in a row, the new coach—Coach Landry—decided to start pointing fingers at the team. At me. We did not get along, but I tried my fucking best to eat my feelings and just work even harder. But no matter what I did, it wasn't good enough for Landry. He, like the new General Manager Chance Echolls, seemed to have it out for me. Echolls, I get. He was from my hometown and his family and ours did not get along. But Landry? He had no reason to hate me, but he did. "You gonna live up to your hype one day kid or what?" he'd barked on just his second game behind our bench. He was an out-and-out asshole and a bully. And he pulled the biggest asshole bully move when he pulled me into his office today to tell me I wasn't even being traded, I was being *waived*. Coaches and management didn't tell players these types of things. They told agents and managers who then told players. That's how this terrible shit was supposed to work. But Landry was too petty for that. He wanted to see the shock and pain on my face.

Landry smirked smugly at me and leaned back in his chair in his office. "We're waiving you. Management, like me, thinks it's the quickest, easiest way. We don't want to waste time trying to sell you to another team. We doubt there'll be any interest."

And that's when he got what he wanted. A reaction. My face dropped and drained of color and his smug smirk deepened. I'll always hate that I gave him that, but I was too fucking shocked to hold it in. Being traded by the team that your father played for, was captain of, that retired his jersey, that was a slap to the face. But being *waived* by them, that wasn't a slap that was a knife. And not to the back. Right through the heart while they stared you in the eye.

"I'm worth something." I hate that I said that, but I did. It was weak and vulnerable and all the things I've never had to be and didn't want to be in front of this asshole.

He folded his arms over his barrel chest and exhaled sharply like he was dealing with a particularly delusional child. But I was delusional. I couldn't comprehend being *waived*. Waivers are when the team gives up the player and his contract to whoever wants it. They don't bother negotiating something, or someone, in return like they do with a trade. Waivers mean that they think the player isn't valuable and they just want to be rid of him. Like offloading a lease on a car they no longer like. Or putting an old piece of furniture on the sidewalk with a cardboard sign that says 'Free'.

"You know you're breaking rules by even having this conversation with me," I reminded him, finally finding a way to rein in my humiliation and turn it into anger. "Also, you can't waive or trade a player until December twenty-seventh, so why the fuck are you telling me this?"

"Because you're a fucking nepo-baby player and I fucking hate all you entitled little shits," Coach Landry snarled, his true nature finally unleashed. He uncrossed his arms and leaned forward, elbows on his desk. "You nepo-babies who coast into the league thinking you're better than everyone else because your daddy played. You always want an easier ride than everyone else and I'm not the one to give it to you. You haven't scored a goal in nine games. Your assists have been shrinking every year for the past three years, just like your face-off percentage. No one is motivated by you as captain. If they were, we wouldn't be last in the division."

"I'm contacting my union rep," I said while yanking open the door to his office. "Do not speak to me again about any of this."

"See you at the game tomorrow," he said, stopping me from the grand exit I was hoping to make.

"Excuse me?"

He shrugged. "You said it yourself, we can't waive you until the week after Christmas so you're still playing. Well, I mean, I fully intend to bench you, but you still have to be here."

"Really?" Now it was my turn to sneer. "Let's see how that works out for you."

I headed straight to the locker room. Most of the team had showered and gone home already, but Owens was still there because his wrist was acting up and he'd met with the trainer. He's the only other person who knows about this. They haven't even told my fucking agent yet or else he would have called me. And I really do need to call the union, but... I just want to get home first.

I don't know why. I don't know how I'll face my family right now, but staying in Brooklyn felt... well it made me want to puke. I am the first Garrison to ever be placed on waivers. Yeah, I still want to puke, even as I drive down the turnpike to the little town on the big lake, where every single member of my family grew up.

How the fuck was I going to face my family? My cousin Tate plays for Los Angeles. My cousin Theo is set to be drafted this summer. Grady Garrison, only son of Uncle Cole and Aunt Leah, is the backup goalie for the Seattle Winterhawks. Hell, my baby sister Mae, who we all call Mayhem, is on a full-ride hockey scholarship at Boston College. Everyone says she'll be the first female drafted by the NHL. And I'm the first Garrison to fail. I did not have that on my bingo card.

It's December twenty-first and all of the NHL players in my family are still playing. But Mayhem will be home from college, as will my sister Liv who is studying at UCLA, and a bunch of my other female cousins, as well as Theo who is in his last few months of high school. Worst of all my dad and my stepmom are most definitely home. But that's why I'm going home, I guess. Because I would rather tell them in person.

Although right now, as the lights of Silver Bay, Maine, glimmer in the distance, I'm beginning to think this wasn't such a hot idea. Because I don't know if I have the balls to see the disappointment on their faces up close and personal. And they *will* be disappointed. How could they not?

I pump the brakes as I descend the hill drawing me closer to town because it's been snowing like crazy for the last hour and this road is notoriously slippery on a good winter's day. Despite the precarious driving conditions my mind still wanders as I try to predict how this will go. My dad, two-time Stanley Cup winner Devin Garrison, will look like he's been shot. Like this is happening directly to him and not to me.

He's never pressured me about hockey, but I know he has a lot of pride in my career. Or he did. This will sting. But then he'll kick into supportive mode. *Way* too supportive. He'll try to give me a pep talk and offer to make calls to league big wigs and I'll want to puke again. Mom, well, she'll be the opposite. Ashleigh formerly Garrison-now-Milligan, will ramble on about how this is for the best and how maybe the universe is showing me I shouldn't have tried to copy my dad. That I should give up 'that brutal, stupid sport' altogether. They're divorced, can you tell? Mom hated being a hockey wife so she stopped being one when I was little. Too little to really remember much, which is probably a good thing. She's in Palm Springs for Christmas with her husband so if I'm lucky, she won't even know this is going on. She doesn't follow hockey at all. Has never even been to one of my professional games.

And then there's my stepmom Callie. The woman has never heard of the word boundaries, and normally I don't mind it at all. I absolutely adore it, actually. She's there for me, rain or shine, day or night. And I have had some of the most raw, honest conversations of my life with her. So she'll expect me to open up about this. She'll demand it. Truth is, I don't know what to tell her. I don't know what went wrong. I don't know when I lost my magic touch or why. I don't know how to stop sucking at hockey because I don't know why I started to suck at hockey in the first place.

A number pops up on my nav as a ringing sound fills the car. It's my agent Clark Abbott. I swear and punch *accept*. Before I can even say hello he's talking. "Want to tell me where the fuck you are and why the Barons general manager just called me to say you've gone AWOL?"

"They're putting me on waivers, Clark."

"What?" He sounds genuinely stunned. "They haven't

informed me, why are they informing you? You can't be on waivers until—"

"December twenty-seventh," I interrupt and grip the steering wheel a little tighter as I kick my wipers up a notch faster to deal with the snow pelting the windshield. "But that little bitch of a coach, Landry, pulled me into his office today and told me anyway. Calls me a bunch of bullshit names and then expects me to show up to the last game before they publicly humiliate me, even though they aren't even going to play me. Naw. Fuck that. If I'm going out, I'm doing it my way."

"First of all, you should have called me. Immediately," Clark barks, annoyance dripping from every pointy, stabby word and I can't even get uppity about it. I should have called him.

"I know. I'm sorry. I'm spiraling."

He sighs so loudly it rumbles through my car speakers like wind. His voice is soft when he speaks again. "This is terrifyingly egregious on their part. On Landry's part. I don't know what the fuck to do next, because no team has ever been this fucking stupid with one of my players, but I will sort this out and get back to you. I can't believe they're calling me up like you're the villain here and not even mentioning this waivers bullshit."

"They can do it, though, right?" I ask because I know they can, but I need someone with a brain not melting into an emotional mess to tell me. "They can dump me this way?"

"They can but it's one of the worst business moves I've ever heard of," Clark confesses. "You are still a hot commodity, Con. Yeah, your year hasn't been great but that team is a sinking ship and you are just one bucket. They can try to blame it all on you, but I won't let them. In the meantime... where are you and are you okay?"

I swallow and feel a lump in my throat. "As good as

expected. I kind of freaked out and got in my car and started to drive to Maine."

"Fuck," Clark sighs again. "There's a fucking blizzard."

"I know but I'm fine. Almost home." I swallow again. Fucking lump. "I can turn back around if you think I really have to go to the game tomorrow."

"Nope. Get home and stay safe," Clark advises. "And pick up the phone when I call, no matter the hour, okay?"

"Yeah. Promise."

"Bye."

The phone goes dead before I can thank him. The snow is a bit heavy now. Not exactly a whiteout but on its way to one. Luckily I'm going to be done driving before it gets too bad.

Seven minutes later I'm passing the sign that says **Welcome to Silver Bay. Home of Hockey Royalty.** And then underneath, on individual hand-carved wooden signs made by a local artisan are the names: Devin Garrison. Jordan Garrison, Luc Richard. Conner Garrison. Tate Garrison. Grady Garrison. There will be a ceremony to add Theo Richard's name after the draft this summer. I wouldn't be surprised if they just took my plaque off and replaced it with Theo's. They should. Maybe I'll drop the idea in the suggestion box outside city hall. I don't deserve to have my name up there anymore.

I used to think that sign was the coolest thing ever, but now it's humiliating. It's not long from the city limits to the lake, which is huge, and the town's main attraction. Callie and my dad built a big place on the lake, next to Uncle Luc and Aunt Rose's place, after Liv was born. Then, Uncle Jordy and Aunt Jessie bought the land right next to Dad and Callie and built a home there. It's a regular Kennedy Compound as the three homes take up a quarter of the lakefront.

I turn onto the long driveway and see the large, two-story, wood and river rock structure that is my dad and Callie's house loom into view. Even half-obscured by the thick sheet of falling snow, it's still imposing. They've hung their Christmas lights. Rows and rows of big, old-fashioned, multi-colored lights skirt every peak and roofline on the house and four-car garage. The two massive Douglas firs that flank the drive are also twinkling with lights. Callie supposedly was bah-humbug about Christmas before she married my dad. Everyone says it's because of me, Liv, and Mayhem that she became the epitome of Christmas spirit.

I loved how special she made Christmas my whole life. But tonight as the fresh snow crunches under my rolling tires and the house grows closer and closer, I'm filled with dread. Because my eyes are focused on the pile of cars in the drive. More than just the three that should be there—my mom's, my dad's, and the car Mayhem and Liv share. There's, like, four... no, five other cars here. I park behind them and turn to look out the passenger window, towards Uncle Jordan and Aunt Jessie's house. The gate in the middle of the fence that separates the properties is wide open.

When I turn back to look out the windshield at the house, I notice Mayhem is on the front porch swing. She's wearing her entire ski suit as well as a hat, mitts, and balaclava, but I still know it's her. She's the only one crazy enough to be reading a book outside in a blizzard. Her dark chocolate eyes are staring right at me, and she gives me a little wave. She's the only reason I get out of the car.

Mayhem is someone I never ignore. She's not my favorite sister, I love Liv just as much, but she's special. She's an old soul. She's always seemed wise beyond her years, like Yoda. It's kind of funny that we all call her Mayhem because she's the calmest, quietest of all the Garrison spawns. But she's also the quirkiest and she came into the world in a terrifying birth ending in an emergency c-section that almost ended both her life and

Callie's. I still remember that night as one of the scariest of my life.

"Welcome home, bro," she says in a deep voice like she's trying to imitate one of my teammates.

"Thanks, Mayhem," I say as I climb the snow-covered stairs, she lifts a mitten-clad hand up for a high-five. I give her one, and it almost makes me smile. "How many of them are here?"

"Many. So many. Too many."

I blink and stare down at Mayhem, who has shifted her gaze to the paperback in her hands. If she's not reading a book on her phone, it's one on her tablet, or a good old-fashioned paperback, like tonight. "Elaborate."

"Uncle Luc, Uncle Jordan, Aunt Jessie, Aunt Rose, Aunt Leah, Uncle Cole, Grandma, Grandpa, Dad, Mom, Liv, Tenley, Harlow, Theo, and Grady."

"Why is Grady home?" I ask.

"Grady is injured, Con," Mayhem explains and her brows pinch together enough to become visible through the eye holes in the balaclava. "Didn't you look at the family WhatsApp? Groin pull. He's out until the new year so the team let him come home for the holiday. Mom decided to throw an impromptu Christmas party. I was in there, with all of them, but they're so loud and distracting that I kept reading the same page over and over."

Mayhem frowns. I frown harder. I am *not* ready to deal with all of them at once. I run a hand through my hair and then scrub my stubbled chin. I haven't shaved in a few days and it's gone from five o'clock shadow to scruff, which isn't my normal look. Mayhem watches. "You need a shave and a haircut."

"Yeah," I mutter. "Actually, I'm going to go do that now."

I about-face and start back down the stairs. "What? Are you kidding? You just got here!"

"I know but... no time like the present."

"It's late and there's a blizzard, Con!" Mayhem sounds confused and maybe a little concerned. I open the door to my SUV and jump in as Mayhem stands up, the bench swinging behind her. "You live here! Where are you going?"

"I'll be back tomorrow, okay. Just... can you not tell them I'm here yet? I just... I'll be back. Just give me a minute."

She nods, but it's hesitant. Concern is still all over her pretty features. "Con-Con... are you okay?"

"Yep. Back tomorrow!"

I do a U-turn on the drive. Mayhem yanks off her hood and balaclava and I can see her sweet, confused face in my rearview, and I feel bad. But not bad enough to turn around and face all my relatives.

I drive aimlessly around Silver Bay as the weather conditions worsen and the roads get icy. I can't go back to my parents' but I don't know where else to go. And then it hits me. When cousins Tenley and Tate are in Silver Bay they share the old farmhouse Aunt Jessie and Uncle Jordan used to live in when they first got together. The old barn, which is a home gym the whole family uses, also has an apartment. Aunt Rose used to live there before she married Uncle Luc, but no one has lived there since. I'm pretty sure everyone has forgotten it exists. But it does. So I turn left and head to my new hideout.

Chapter 2

Mac

Someone is in my apartment.

I didn't realize it when I stumbled in after a long, grueling shift at the hospital, but I should have. The signs were everywhere. The bathroom door was closed, and I always left it open. The light was off in the kitchen and I always leave it on when I know I'm coming home after dark. I know better than to miss these signs. I'm street-smart because I used to actually live on the street. I'm a survivor.

But yet, the realization that I am not in this space alone feels like a dream... not real. Logic tries to stamp it down. This is Silver Bay, Maine. And my apartment is in the barn on Jordan and Jessie Garrison's property. The Garrison family is the closest thing this town has to celebrities. No one would dare break into this place.

The bathroom door swings open.

Fear floods my veins. I jump up from where I collapsed on the couch a few minutes ago, exhausted from twelve hours on my feet. Before my eyes can register more than a backlit shadow, I scream. The figure jumps and screams too.

"What the fuck?" a deep male voice yells. I hurl the only

thing I'm holding directly at him. My keys. They hit him square in the middle of his forehead. "FUCK!"

Both his hands shoot up to his face, which means he's let go of the towel at his waist. It's his only piece of clothing. It drops to the floor and now I'm face-to-face with a *naked* intruder. Well, naked except for the bubbles on his shoulders and chest. My serial killer was taking a bubble bath? God, I wish I was going to be around to see *that Dateline* episode.

My brain is screaming 'Help!' but all that comes out of my mouth is another blood-curdling wail. As I bolt toward the door, to run to freedom and safety and all those good things, I manage to get a good look at the face of my potential murderer. In the dim glow of the single string of Christmas lights I bothered to hang in the living room window, I see the light brown hair, the strong chin, and the sharp angle of his high cheekbones. I stop running. My intruder is... a Garrison. Conner Garrison?

"Oh shit!" I gasp and then take a step toward him. But he's still naked and so I spin around to face the other way, covering my eyes for good measure. "I'm sorry. I thought you were a murderer or something. Are you okay?"

"No!" he barks out. "Who the fuck are you?"

Right. I know who he is because *everyone* knows who the eldest Garrison offspring is, but Conner hasn't seen me since—I do the mental math—I was a freshman in college and he was still in high school.

"I'm renting this place from Jordan and Jessie while I intern at the hospital."

"You should be a pitcher in the MLB with an arm like that," he replies in a clipped tone and then he swears under his breath again.

"If you put on some clothes I can take a look at your forehead," I offer. "I'm a doctor. Well, about to be. My specialty is psychiatry but the first few years is general medicine and I'm basically a GP at this point."

"Wait..." The venom slips from Conner's voice suddenly. "Mac? Mackenzie Larue?"

"Yes!" I'm so excited he remembers me I make the mistake of spinning around. Oops. He's still naked. Shit! I spin back around so fast that I stumble into the coffee table and fall onto the couch. And then—thud—onto the floor. "Fuck! Ouch!"

"This is a nightmare," he declares, and I hear him stomp across the apartment as I rub my elbow and sit up and catch the back of his bare ass as he slips into my bedroom.

By the time I'm on my feet again, he's emerging from my room and he's clothed. Well, I mean he's got on a pair of sweats that are snug in *all* the right places. Conner Garrison is no longer a gangly teenager. He's all man.

My dad doesn't play hockey professionally anymore but he's still involved in the sport because he's moved into coaching, although he's in-between gigs right now. It's still his main topic of conversation when I call or go home, and so I'd heard how Conner was a big, elite hockey player now. Big, elite hockey players are *never* gangly. So of course he's standing in front of me all muscled, sculpted, and gorgeous. I feel heat creeping up my face because my brain keeps flashing back to the naked version I got a good look at, even in my panic. He is impressive on *all* fronts.

He scratches his light-brown hair sheepishly. "I had no idea someone was staying here. I didn't know you lived in Silver Bay. I thought you were in Syracuse."

"I was. For undergrad. Then I got a scholarship to the University of Maine for medical school," I explain and walk around the couch, focusing on the red welt forming in the center of his forehead. There's also a little trickle of blood. "Shit. I made you bleed."

"You did?" He pinches his eyebrows and immediately winces.

I take his hand. It's big, strong, and warm. A ripple of electricity courses down my spine but I ignore it. It's just a not-so-subtle reminder I haven't been with a man in almost an entire year. I pull him toward the bathroom, where I saw a first aid kit in one of the drawers when I moved in. "I need to clean it and put a Band-Aid on it before you go."

"I'm *not* putting a Band-Aid in the center of my forehead," Conner grumbles. "And I'm not going anywhere."

I freeze on the white marble penny tiles and turn to face him. "I live here. I told you. I pay rent. It's *my* place."

"Yeah. Okay. But there's a freaking blizzard out there," Conner argues. He points toward the oblong window at the top of the bathroom wall. It looks like it's got a piece of white Styrofoam blocking it but it's just the pile of snow on the ledge outside.

He shouldn't have to remind me about that. I just drove home from the hospital, white-knuckling it the whole way because of this blizzard. My eyes find his again. He looks sheepish as he adds, "Plus I don't have anywhere to go."

I make a face like he just skunked the room. "You're related to half the town. You have a million places to go."

His face twists in an emotion I know all too well—shame. But why? "My parents don't know I'm in town and I want to keep it that way right now. If I tell a single Garrison, other than my sister Mae, they'll all know by dawn. And I can't... I'm not ready for that. When the weather calms its tits I'll think about facing reality. But I'm not heading out in this storm, in the middle of the night to humiliate myself, okay?"

No. This is not okay. But he's right. The weather is horrible and I'd have to be a complete bitch to kick him out into it, especially if it's going to humiliate him somehow. And I guess I could insist he go stay in the main house, where his cousin Tenley lives, but he's trying to avoid every single relative he has. I've had glimpses of the Garrison family dynamic and they're as thick as thieves and wouldn't avoid each other if they had the plague. So Conner's reasons for ghosting them must be serious. Still, I point out a problem with this potential arrangement. "There's only one bed."

"There used to be a blow-up mattress in the closet of the empty second bedroom," Conner tells me. "From when we used to... hook up with girls up here in high school."

Classic. Of course, he and his cousins did that.

"There's no door on that room," I reply, pulling open the drawer that has the first aid kit. I grab the red canvas bag with the cross on it and put it on the counter.

"You've seen me naked. I think we're past the door stage," he mutters.

"I saw nothing," I reply hastily.

"Doubt that," Conner replies just as quickly. "I'm hard to miss."

I freeze and look up at him. He's wearing the cockiest smile. He chuckles as I ignore him and the blush traveling over my cheeks at the moment.

The tiny room still smells of my expensive bubble bath and when I tear open the antiseptic wipe, I notice all the bubbles still in the tub and the now nearly empty bottle of bubble bath. My jaw drops. "You used the whole bottle!"

"Yeah. I like extra bubbles," Conner says like it's no big deal. "I'll buy you more."

"It's from Paris. It costs more money than I care to admit and even if you order me more it won't be here in time for tomorrow, my day off and the day I intended to fill with self-care, including a bubble bath." I pout as I pull out the wipe and reach up to dab his forehead with it. Way up. Conner is a good four inches over six feet. It makes me feel tinier than my five feet eight inches.

"Sorry," he grumbles but he doesn't sound all that sorry. He sounds irritated like I'm the problem. "Ow! Shit that hurts!"

Conner jumps back from me like I just pressed a hot poker to his head. I smirk and make a poor attempt at stifling a giggle. His cheeks pink just a bit. "You know what? Maybe I should just face my family. It would likely be less humiliating than dealing with you."

"Oh, so this is *my* fault?" I don't know why I'm so offended right now. If he's actually going to leave, then I get what I want... right?

I follow him, waving the Band-Aid, as he storms into *my* bedroom. He's been here probably a couple hours and my room looks like a bomb went off. There's a duffle bag open on the bed with clothes hanging out of it. His jacket and winter boots are on the floor, leaving a puddle of melted snow on the hardwood. His toiletry bag is open on my desk, on top of one of my medical textbooks. "What the hell..."

Conner grabs his toiletry bag, zips it, and shoves it into the duffle bag. Then he stops and stares at me. "Also, for the record, this place looks barely lived in. How was I supposed to know someone was staying here?"

"I left a light on."

"Thought that was Theo last time he took a hook-up here," Conner replies with a shrug. "I didn't open the closet and you don't have, like, one single personal effect lying around. Except the textbooks, which I figured might be Aunt Jessie's old schoolbooks."

Right. His Aunt Jessie used to be a physiotherapist.

"Okay yeah, I guess I can see that," I admit. "I moved out of my last place rather quickly and left almost everything. Look, you don't have to go tonight. You should stay until the storm clears."

"No point," Conner replies and keeps shoving clothes back into his bag. "You tell your dad I'm here and my parents will know seconds later anyway."

"It's the middle of the night so I'm not talking to anyone," I promise. "Besides, my dad used to coach you on the Barons, remember? He's still got friends in the back office. I'm guessing whatever has you here instead of with the team, he may already know about it."

"Do former coaches get told when it's the end of someone's career? I would ask my dad but no one has ever dumped him from an NHL team. I could ask my uncles but they've never spent five seconds on a farm team. They're not failures."

"What the hell are you spiraling on about?" I demand because I'm confused as hell and too tired to process what sounds like pure and simple lunacy. "You're getting traded?"

He huffs out a short, bitter laugh. "I wish!"

"Look, my dad might have been a player, but I know very little about the business side of hockey," I tell him. "However I do know you were a number one draft pick. You're the Captain of the Barons, which your father was captain of, right? If hockey had a royal family, you'd be the crown prince. The sign entering town even says so. You can't just have your career taken away."

"Waivers," he says like I'm supposed to know what that word means.

"Wafers? What?" I blink and he heaves out a very aggravated sigh.

"*Waivers* is a process by which a player—any player regardless of contract—can be dismissed from their team and sent to the minors," Conner explains and when he steals a glance at me, his hazel eyes are filled with humility. "And my coach told me that they're doing that to me."

"Right now?" I'm confused. Conner is a great player. I remember everyone talking about how gifted he is.

"No one can waive a player between December eighteenth and December twenty-sixth. Guess they don't want players to go through that kind of upheaval around the holidays." Conner zips his duffle bag and slings it over his shoulder. "But my coach, being the prime-time asshole he is, decided to let me know that as of December twenty-seventh, I'm waived."

"What a dick move," I whisper because, as a mental health professional, I can see how this coach just defeated the purpose of the waiver freeze for Conner. He purposely told Conner to create emotional havoc. I really do want to call my dad now and discuss this with him. How can the league even allow that?

"Yep. So I pulled a dick move too and left," Conner explains. "They have a game tomorrow, the last one before the break, but fuck them. They can get used to playing without me."

"Can you do that?" I ask.

He shrugs his broad shoulders. "No. But I did. And my agent is handling it. I doubt the team will make a fuss publicly because if they make me look bad, no one will pick me up off waivers and they're stuck paying me. Not that anyone will want me anyway."

Okay, now I don't really understand what he's talking about, but I don't think it matters. He slips by me and shoves his feet into his boots, which are next to my bed. I realize he really is going to leave and now I feel guilty.

"Just... use the blow-up mattress or whatever. It's cool."

He looks over at me, his eyes scanning my face. "Are you sure?"

"I'm sure," I say even though I'm not. I'm honestly too tired to think about it anymore. I yawn, walk over, and pluck his duffle off his shoulder. I walk to the tiny, barren guest room and drop it on the floor in the middle of the room as he comes up behind me. "I'd love to talk about this more with you in the morning. If you want someone to vent to. But right now I need sleep. I'm exhausted. So see you tomorrow?"

He nods, but it's slow and hesitant. "Yeah. Thanks, Mac."

"Sure," I say simply as I cross the small distance back to my room. I close my bedroom door without another word. I manage to get off my scrubs and then drop into bed in just my underwear and sports bra. Yanking the covers up to my neck, I'm hit with a waft of a delicious smell. It's woodsy and warm, yet crisp... he must have lied on my bed. It has to be his cologne or deodorant or something. And boy, it smells *amazing*...

That's my last thought as I fall into a deep sleep.

Chapter 3

Conner

I don't sleep most of the night because my brain keeps bouncing between feeling humiliated and feeling guilty. Humiliated because I dropped my towel and screamed like a petrified child in front of Mac Larue, and guilty because I invaded her space and used up her fancy bubble bath. And she wasn't kidding about it being pricy. That shit is like sixty bucks for the smallest bottle I could find online. Plus fourteen bucks for international shipping. I ordered her some in the middle of the night as the air mattress deflated for the second time. The bubble bath won't get here until the day after Christmas, though, so her day of self-care is officially ruined thanks to me.

When the sun starts poking through the curtains, I get up and sneak out to get her some breakfast. Maybe that will help. Before this midnight misadventure, the last time I was in the same room with Mac was when she was in college. I remember back then she was a vegetarian.

So that's how I find myself in the Trader Joe's staring at the Meatless Magic section at eight in the morning. I'm like a toddler looking at a trigonometry textbook. Completely clueless.

"Why do they flavor meatless food like meat?" a female

voice from behind me asks. "It's like, hey cow, I won't eat you I'll just eat stuff flavored like you. That feels morally gray. Not that morally gray is a bad thing, necessarily."

I turn to locate the person speaking and, oh shit. It's Tenley. My cousin. I frown at her. She blinks her green eyes and her expression turns from flirty to utter horror. "Oh fuck! I thought you were a hot guy. Sorry. What the hell are you doing back?"

"First of all, I *am* a hot guy," I reply. She immediately makes a gagging sound, which I ignore. "Second of all, why are you cruising the vegetarian aisle at eight in the morning?"

"Because..." Tenley pauses, tilts her dirty blonde head, and smirks. "Never mind that. Why are *you* in a vegetarian aisle? In Silver Bay. Why aren't you in that baller penthouse loft of yours in Brooklyn?"

"I'm home for Christmas. I always come home for Christmas."

"Yeah... but you aren't home. I was at Aunt Callie's and Uncle Devin's last night. Everyone was there. They threw their annual tree-trimming party. And NYC is five and a half hours away in good weather, eight hours in the post-storm conditions we've got happening right now. You expect me to believe you woke up at like... two in the morning to drive here? So you could come to TJ's to make bedroom eyes at fake meat? Something you've never eaten a day in your life."

Tenley is not my most annoying relative, but she's in the top three. Why? Because she's too smart for her own good. Also, I used to have to threaten to fight my teammates to keep them from trying to bang her when we were kids. People say she's good-looking. Stunning, hot, and beautiful are the most common words people use to describe her, actually (but she's my cousin, so gross). Another tick in her annoying column is she actively flirts with any guy in skates. But my biggest pet peeve with Ten is she's afraid of absolutely nothing, which makes her terrifying.

"Tenley..." I could lie to her but it's no use. She's got her eyes narrowed in on my face, scanning it for any twitch or flicker of deceit. Did I mention she's minoring in criminology? Who minors in that, like it's a *hobby*? "I got back last night, but I saw all the cars at Dad and Callie's, and... I didn't feel like peopling, so I stayed elsewhere."

"Oh my God, you *totally* didn't lie!" Tenley whoops, the bright smile of victory so wide on her face her dimples are showing. "I'm kind of impressed. But it means I don't get to practice my more advanced interrogation techniques, which sucks. FYI, I knew you were in town. Saw your car hidden behind the barn late last night. I had to go out there with snowshoes to double-check the plates because the snow was like four feet deep and I thought I might get swallowed up by it, but yeah. I knew."

"You are a special kind of crazy, Ten."

She shrugs, neither confirming nor denying my accusation. "So why does your family's unwavering support annoy you?"

"Well, when you put it that way I sound like an asshole," I mutter and sigh.

She smiles. "Nah. I get it. We're a lot. And I know you're having a rough season and half the family will probably shower you with unsolicited hockey advice. All the ones with testicles for sure."

"Yes. Exactly." It's a win that Tenley doesn't realize the Brooklyn Barons still have a game to play before the holiday break. If she followed my team, her *Unsolved Mysteries* brain would be in overdrive.

Instead, she latches onto something else as a smile spreads across her wide mouth that she inherited from her dad, just like her light hair. "So...you're with Mac?"

"I'm not *with* Mac," I counter quickly, absentmindedly reaching up and rubbing the spot on my forehead where there's still a little cut, now all scabbed up. Tenley's eyes follow my hand, but she likely thinks it's a hockey incident and I don't explain otherwise. "I didn't know she was living there. I figured it was empty. And I knew the keys were hidden under the garden gnome."

Tenley and my cousin Harlow do pottery in their spare time and Tenley likes to make lawn ornaments. There are fourteen gnomes, fairies, rabbits, and other ceramic wild things peppered about the yard at her place. "His name is Sir Geoffrey Gnomeo," Tenley informs me.

"You are so fucking weird."

She slaps my arm at the insult, then wiggles her eyebrows. "There's only one bed in that apartment at the moment."

"Get your mind out of the gutter," I demand. "My team is dead last in the entire league and you think I'm out here trying to hook up with a woman I haven't seen in... like a decade?"

"It's a possibility. As for your team, it's only temporary, Con. You'll have them back on top soon, I know it," Tenley says, and she's completely sincere. She gives me a small smile. "You're a Garrison. You don't fail."

If only she knew what she was talking about.

"The whole pep talk thing is exactly why I'm avoiding family, remember?" I turn back to the vegetarian foods to avoid making eye contact. She's creepily good at reading expressions and I don't want her to realize there's more to my melancholy than a losing streak. I don't want to tell her I'm about to lose my whole career.

"You should talk to Mac about hating pep talks," Tenley suggests and moves to stand beside me again in front of the cooler full of fake meat. "She's about to be a full-fledged psychiatrist. She can figure out why your brain rejects support."

"*Psychiatrist.* Right." I suddenly remember Mac mentioning that. If Mac psychoanalyzed me last night, did she figure out why I'm suddenly unable to be good at the only thing I've ever been good at? Should I ask her? Do I want to know?

Tenley reaches out and grabs a package of meatless breakfast sausage off the shelf, and also the fake bacon. She puts it all in my basket.

"She's the vegetarian, not you," Tenley says, smiling. "And I think it's cute that you're trying to impress her with breakfast."

"Not impress her, just thank her for letting me sleep there." Tenley's eyebrows raise. "On the blow-up mattress on the floor in the second bedroom."

Tenley nods slowly, but it's a nod that basically screams a sarcastic *suuure*. Before I can tell her to stop it though, she switches gears again. "Also, for the record, you're not the only one going through a tough time. Mac just went through a nuclear-level nasty-ass breakup with a real cockwobble. She deserves a nice breakfast from a dude some women might say is okay to look at."

"Just okay? Yeah right." I snark at her pseudo-compliment. "Mac *just* broke up with someone? Who?"

Mac didn't mention it. Then again an about-to-be psychiatrist probably knows better than to spill her guts to some random hockey dude six years younger than her, who she hasn't seen in almost a decade, and who breaks into her apartment, flashes her, and pitches a bit of a fit.

Tenley's full mouth squishes up like she swallowed lemon juice. "Well, the breakup was almost six months ago now, but she had been with him for years. I refuse to tell you his name. It doesn't deserve to be on my lips. Anyway, it was the kind of bad break that lingers, you know? So treat her to breakfast... and maybe even a little of *something else*... if you're so inclined."

Tenley wiggles her eyebrows at me and then she gives me a big, pervy wink. I think I might puke. "Stop doing that! And also did you not just hear me say I do *not* need some kind of complicated romantic thing right now?"

"Who said complicated? Fucking is super simple if you want it to be, Con. And a little mutual orgasm might do you both some good. You do know how to make a girl come, right? Don't tell me you're one of those hockey jocks that doesn't have the intelligence or inclination to learn where a clit is or what to do with it." She sighs like she has first-hand experience with those types of jocks and I shudder at the thought, and this entire conversation.

"Leave. Walk away. Stop talking and pretend you never saw me," I mutter, my eyes closed because I can't even look at her after that TMI outburst.

She pats my shoulder and I hear footsteps so I peek and find Tenley trotting down the aisle toward the sourdough section. Over her shoulder, she adds, "Don't worry. I won't tell anyone I saw you. But you know Auntie Callie and Uncle Dev will be devastated if you hide your way through Christmas. We all love ya, Con, you big dummy. Now go slip Mac some sausage and I'll see you Christmas Eve."

It's ridiculous that Tenley thinks random sex is what I need right now. It's not. But she's got me thinking about Mac a little bit more. Mac mentioned last night she didn't have a lot of her things. She said she left her last place quickly...

I've never told a soul, but I used to have the biggest crush on Mac. I didn't see her much growing up, but every summer my dad and uncles would get together with their friends from the league. Their buddies would come to Silver Bay and spend three or four days on the lake with us. When they started settling down, their families would come too. I was the oldest kid in the group until Alex Larue married Brie Bennett and they adopted Mackenzie, aka Mac.

She showed up the summer I was eight. She was quiet and

wore indifference like it was a suit of armor. She barely spoke to anyone other than Alex and Brie. She'd watch everyone and everything with hard but beautiful blue eyes. I never spoke a word to her because I was an eight-year-old boy who couldn't fathom how to talk to the first girl to make me think of girls in *that* light.

Eventually, with each summer that passed, she grew more and more at home in her life and the annual summer vacation to Silver Bay. She started participating in stuff, like water skiing and volleyball. She'd go out on the row boats in the middle of the lake with just us kids, or go with us for post-dinner, parent-less walks to town to get ice cream cones. We'd talk and make jokes with each other. We were never what I would consider close, partly due to our age gap and also because I just found her intimidating. Every girl I'd ever met was impressed by me because of hockey, even ones older than me. When I was thirteen I once had a sixteen-year-old slip me her number. But Mac clearly didn't get impressed by my hockey skills, even when I mentioned how many trophies I'd won that previous season. And she always looked at me like I was a kid. Even worse, she made me *feel* like one. I was too insecure and immature to understand what to do with that. And when our age difference became less of a challenge, when I was eighteen and she was twenty-four, I felt like a timid kid around her. Getting over that would have been a challenge. Other girls my age from Silver Bay didn't take work. So Mac disappeared from my life without ever knowing about my crush.

Now, instead of being a guy who's too lazy to take on a challenge, I'm a guy whose entire career has turned into a challenge. So I better stop worrying and thinking about Mac Larue and this mysterious ex-from-hell. I have my own personal drama to attend to and even if Mac is still gorgeous, more gorgeous than ever, I need to focus on hockey.

Chapter 4

Mac

I don't hear a sound. Maybe Conner is one of those lucky adults who can sleep in. I yawn, stretch, and get out of bed. I strip and grab my robe off the back of the door. Then, I head into the rest of the apartment. Still no one and not a sound. I turn and glance toward the second bedroom. The blow-up mattress is half deflated on the floor, blankets tangled at the foot of it, but there's no sign of him. Maybe he decided to go to his parents after all?

I head into the bathroom and take a long, hot shower. My eye catches a glimpse of the remaining dollop of expensive bubble bath in the bottle on the ledge of the tub. I frown. Then I remember Conner naked and some of those expensive bubbles sliding over his hip and down to that soft but very formidable-looking cock. My cheeks flame so hard I have to turn the temperature down in the shower.

To be honest, I've never thought of Conner *that* way. Never wondered what he would look like naked, that's for sure. He is six years younger than me and at the time I met him, that was a big deal. He was a *baby*. The last time I saw him he was a teenager, and muscles had started to sprout on his long, lean limbs. He was stopped everywhere we went that summer. He got us free ice cream cones by taking selfies with the owner and his kids. He wasn't even an NHL player yet, but people treated him like he was. I was fascinated by that. By the way, he carried that attention like it wasn't a big deal. Like it was as natural as his eye color or height or any other part of his DNA.

And also, he had this way of smiling that was... Contagious? Enticing? Tender? I never did figure out the right word for it back then. And to be honest, I hadn't thought about his smile much since then. Now though... Now I'm thinking about it again. About *him*. He's definitely more intense than I remember. He's become a little bit grumpy when he used to be all sunshine. He's also a full-fledged man now. Naked Conner flashes across my brain again. I close my eyes and shove my face under the shower spray to wash away the memory with the soap on my face.

I remember the reason he was in my apartment to begin with. This waiver fiasco is obviously a big deal, and I'd like to talk about that with him some more. Maybe what Conner needed was to vent about it, or to strategize about what to say to his family. I'd be the perfect person to do that with because of my training. But Conner was gone, so it wouldn't be me helping him. Even though I kind of found myself wanting to.

I turn off the water, grab my towel from the rack, and carefully step out of the tub. After drying off and hanging my towel back on the rack, I slip into my robe and open the door. As soon as I step into the hallway, I know he's back. I can smell him. Is that weird? That's probably weird. But the rich scent of my pricey bubble bath, and that crisp, woodsy scent that lingered on my pillow last night permeates the air. And makes me much more aware of all the neglected bits below my belly button.

My head swivels and there he is, standing at the counter next to the stove. He looks up from whatever he's making. I yank off the shower cap that keeps my curls from getting wet in the shower. My hair is up in a pineapple-style pony and curls must be standing up all over the place, but it's less humiliating than the plastic fuchsia shower cap with orange flowers on it. "I thought you were gone."

"I was. To the grocery store," Conner explains. "Do you still want me gone? Like really gone?"

"No. I'm fine with you here in the light of day, not stealing my bubble bath of course," I say and smile. He smiles back.

"I have a peace offering." He holds out the plate with a breakfast sandwich on it. I eye the sandwich.

"I didn't know we were at war."

"We aren't, but I owe you a thank you and an apology," he reminds me, a sheepish smile playing on his lips. "I was kind of growly last night"

"I once lived on the street. I can handle growly," I reply and step closer to his outstretched hand holding the delicious-looking sandwich. "That smells incredible."

"It is," he replies confidently. "The guys all come over for my breakfast sandwiches if we have a day off on a weekend. I guess I mean they *used* to. Anyway, I usually use Spanish chorizo sausage for them but I know you're vegetarian so I bought veggie sausage and used sriracha mayo for the spice. I'm hoping you're still an octo-lacto veg head because if you aren't, this sandwich is worth converting back."

I lift an eyebrow at being called a veg-head but I'm sure he means it kindly so I just nod, and he grins. I can't believe he remembered I'm vegetarian? After all these years? Something about that makes my insides feel... lighter? Warmer? I guess I just never knew he paid that close attention. I take the plate from him and he grins like it's some kind of hard-fought victory. "Sit. Enjoy."

I sit on one of the bar stools at the small island. "You didn't happen to make coffee too did you? Do athletes do caffeine?"

"This athlete does," Conner replies. "But since it's your day off, I thought we'd start with something else."

He slides a glass of orange juice to me on the island. Only it's not in a regular glass. It's a wine glass filled with OJ. He grins again. It's such a good grin, equal parts mischief and kindness. "There're no champagne flutes so I'm using red wine glasses. It's a *big* pour. Sorry, not sorry."

"Mimosas?" I question even though it's quite evident with the open bottle of champagne on the counter. He nods. I contemplate not drinking it but he's right. It's my day off. And it's the holidays. I have to work Christmas Day so this is as close as I'll get to a celebration.

He tips his glass to mine and we clink in a cheers, then we drink. I take a bite of the breakfast sandwich and it's as divine as he promised. I can't help but groan as I chew and his hazel eyes twinkle with pride. "Told you."

We both eat and sip our mimosas in silence, which is more comfortable than it should be all things considered. But Conner's warm, welcoming energy I remember from when he was a kid is back. Maybe grumpy Conner only comes out when he's getting surprised, while naked, at midnight. The image of him naked flashes in my head again. I struggle to swallow the sandwich, so I grab the mimosa and take a big swig. When I recover from almost choking, Conner tops up my glass with more champagne than orange juice. I should object. I'm not a big drinker and one is more than enough. But I don't object. It's nice to have day drinks.

I think the last time I did this was Harlow Richard's bachelorette party two years ago. The hangover I had for two days was not fabulous, but I'll be more careful today. I move my eyes to his face. "This feels like liquid courage. For what?"

He takes in a long, slow breath. "Talking to my parents. If I just don't play today, without telling them why first, then Callie will freak out and assume I'm injured. Dad will start texting his hockey contacts and likely find out that I'm about to be dumped. Then he'll be freaking out that I didn't come to him first."

I remind him, "You're just essentially being traded. In a weird, stupid way that—as a psychiatrist—I find slightly emotionally abusive if I'm honest." The poor guy now gets to carry around the feelings of failure longer than he should. "The holidays are already a really hard time for many people and they go and dump this on you too. Fuck them."

"I appreciate you saying that," Conner tells me as he puts the last bit of his uneaten sandwich down on a napkin on the island. "Do all psychiatrists use the medical terminology 'fuck them'?"

I laugh. "I'm not a doctor, yet. I have a few months to go."

He nods, chewing thoughtfully, eyes examining me the whole time. At least it feels that way. "I didn't know you wanted to be a doctor when we were kids."

"When we were kids I just wanted food, shelter, and stable parental figures," I reply without thinking about it. My truths are always bombs. I sometimes forget that. Conner blinks his eyes, which have really cool flecks of smoke and amber in them along with a color I can only describe as terracotta.

"I never knew the details of your life before Alex and Brie adopted you," he tells me. "My parents said it wasn't cool to ask, and you never brought it up."

I sip my mimosa. "I wanted to just be past it back then. Once I let go of the trauma of it, with counseling and a lot of patience and understanding from my parents, I didn't want to tell anyone about it. I guess I still don't."

"Okay." Conner nods. "But you picked psychiatry to help kids who might need it, like you did?"

I catch his eye and let out a sheepish sigh. "I'm a cliché, aren't I?"

"Only the best possible kind," he returns with a wink. Man, this boy... now a man... went to charm school apparently.

"Yes. I wanted to be a psychologist to help kids, teens, and adults with addiction issues," I confirm. "And hockey players who are having existential crises."

He barks out a laugh, almost spitting out his mimosa. I grin at getting such a strong reaction from him. Wiping a dribble of champagne from his chin he cocks his head. "I appreciate that but I'm not into the idea of being your guinea pig."

"The term is patient," I correct him and take another bite of the dreamy sandwich. When I'm done, and have swallowed it down, I add, "Well speaking then as a daughter of a former professional hockey player, let me just remind you that the Garrison family is a well-respected institution in this sport. And *everyone* knows you're talented and destined for even more greatness than you've currently shown the sports world. The Barons' struggles are not your fault. I bet the team loses tonight. That will just prove their failure has nothing to do with you."

Spoiler Alert. The Brooklyn Barons win.

Chapter 5

Mac

It was an afternoon game because it was on a weekend. Conner didn't call and warn his parents that he wouldn't be playing because we got full-on day drunk on mimosas and lost track of time. We were catching up—laughing, sharing stories, and maybe, kind of, possibly flirting. I mean, I can't be one hundred percent sure because it has been *years* since I was flirted with, or did any flirting, but... our glances toward each other were too long, our smiles too deep, and we kept touching each other. A brush of hands, a knee pressing into a knee on the couch. I didn't know what to make of it, so I just kept sipping my mimosas until analyzing it seemed like too much work.

We only realized the game had started when his phone started blowing up. Call after call and text after text from every member of his family. Cousins, parents, sisters, even his grandparents called. He didn't pick up for any of them. And his mood, which had been upbeat, changed as the game went on. Grumpy Conner was back. With a vengeance.

It's been a very long time since I felt helpless, but I felt just that watching Conner watch his team play—and win—without him. I could do nothing but keep refilling his glass. We were out of orange juice now and by the time the buzzer went for the end of the third period, we were taking turns drinking straight from a second bottle of champagne.

"I guess it *was* me," Conner says as I click off the TV and his phone blows up beside him yet again. The name on the screen is Mama C, which I know is Callie Caplan-Garrison, his stepmom.

Once again he ignores it. "I don't know everything about your family but I know that Callie is not a woman who puts up with being ignored."

He glances over at me and shrugs. His handsome face is void of emotion, but I know his heart isn't. He's just putting on a stoic face because he doesn't want to break down or freak out in front of a woman he barely knows. Or probably any woman. Or anyone. That's why he's hiding. Conner is a prideful beast. Most professional athletes are.

He gets up and heads to the kitchen with the now-empty bottle of champagne. I stand to follow him but I'm a bit wobbly. Damn, I'm going to have a hangover if I don't get some Advil and water into me. But I don't head to the bathroom to grab the bottle of pain meds. Instead, I pause at the island and watch him clean up the kitchen.

He feels my presence and looks over at me. He smiles. His eyes, though, aren't lying. He's upset. "You look cute right now."

Well now... I was not expecting that to come out of his mouth. I look down at my outfit. I had changed into a pair of clingy, pale pink lounge pants and a white t-shirt before the game started, while Conner built a Boy Scout-worthy fire in the wood burner. I'd taken my hair out of the pineapple but hadn't beaten it into submission with product yet so the curls were wilder than normal. I arch an eyebrow. "You have champagne goggles on right now."

He chuckles. The sound is deep and robust, and sexy as all

hell. I start to tingle and it's not from champagne. "I've thought you were cute since I was nine so no, not the champagne."

"You... what?"

And then my phone goes off, filling the room with the sharp bell sound that is my text message alert. I'm off-balance internally from his little revelation so I walk over to the couch where it's balancing on the armrest. I reach for it, see the name across the screen, and freeze.

T.P.

"No. Fucking NO," I chant to myself and quickly open the message.

I'm downstairs.

What the hell is he talking about? I text him those exact words. He can't mean downstairs *here* because he doesn't know where I live. That's on purpose. I haven't told a single person at the hospital in case it gets back to him and the Garrisons are all sworn to secrecy as well.

My phone pings again.

Jordan Garrison's barn. I'm here.

"No fucking way," I say as I march right past the kitchen and Conner.

"What's wrong?" Conner asks because he's been watching me unravel, but I ignore him.

I head over to the two large windows right of the television. I see his car before I see him. It's a cherry red Ford F-150. His winter car. In the summer he drives a vintage Porsche 911. Not good vintage but, like, 90s vintage. A total douche-mobile. I frown. And then I see him. Well, the top of his head. He's walking around by the barn door, which is always locked. He tilts his head up and I leap back from the window like he's aiming a weapon at me.

My back slams into Conner's front. It's like hitting an actual wall and almost winds me. He grabs my shoulders to keep me steady. I hadn't realized he'd walked over. "What's going on?"

"My... he's... did you tell someone I was living here?" I demand, and there's no way to keep the panic from my voice. But it's easily misinterpreted for anger because my panic mode makes my voice hard and aggressive. That comes from the time I spent on the street. You couldn't show vulnerability. So I'm not at all shocked when Conner's relaxed, friendly expression starts to slip.

"No. I'm avoiding everyone, remember?" Conner replies. "Who's out there?"

He steps toward the window and I grab his arm and yank him back. Well, I try. The man is too sturdy and thick to be manhandled by the likes of me. My hand can barely grip his giant bicep. He continues moving forward without a problem. As he tips his head down to peer outside, his light brown hair tumbles forward, grazing the red mark on his forehead from last night. He bristles, which I know means he saw Beckett.

"Why is there an Echolls on Garrison land?" Conner demands and turns on me with a scowl.

This is not the time for my girl bits to get all warm, but they are. Angry Conner is very... *appealing*. I swallow and try to regain control of myself because this is definitely not the time and probably not the place. "He's my ex. And that sounded ridiculous. What are you two, Capulets and Montagues? Hatfields and McCoys?"

Conner's face twists in a series of expressions that include, but are not limited to, confusion, shock, disgust, and disbelief. "You dated an Echolls?"

"Yeah. Tenley has since explained the entire family is a bunch of assholes, but I didn't know that when I met him in med school," I mutter, and my phone dings again. Both of us tip our heads down to read the message.

I saw someone at the window. Just be an adult about this, please!

"Adult?" I repeat out loud in annoyed amazement. "Beckett's idea of adulting is convincing me to apply for the resident's program at his hometown hospital and then sleeping with his high school ex behind my back for an entire two years. Two years!"

"He did that?" Conner asks. His eyes dart down to my screen. "You named him T.P. in your phone? Why?"

"Toilet paper because he's a shit stain, toxic person, trash panda, it stands for a lot of things." I toss my phone on the couch like it's a hot potato and I'm a five-year-old. "And let's not even get into the ring I found in his sock draw. I thought it was for me."

My face heats at the humiliation because I had grinned like a lovesick puppy but as I shoved the ring back under his wool socks, I also found a box of condoms. Opened and half empty. And we hadn't used condoms since before moving to Silver Bay. But I don't tell Conner any of those gory details. Not in words. If I say it out loud, those tears building behind my eyes will fall. So I stay silent, but he can see the heat of humiliation reddening my cheeks. Can't hide that. "I don't want to see him. I left our apartment with nothing but my medical books, computer, and my suitcase of clothes almost seven months ago. I've managed to avoid him and his fiancée ever since, even though we all still work at the same damn hospital in the same tiny town."

"She's a doctor too?"

"Nurse. NICU, which luckily I don't have to deal with on

my psychiatric rounds," I explain as I pace the floor between the fireplace and the couch. "He's doing a cardiology specialty. And I confessed this drama to the admin who does the psych scheduling, your cousin Shelby, so she checks his schedule and makes sure we don't overlap."

"Gotta love Shelby," Conner murmurs with a small smile. Shelby is the daughter of his Uncle Cole and Aunt Leah. The big sister to his cousin Grady who also plays hockey, of course. . Conner turns back and peeks out the big window again. "What does he want?"

"He's been texting me to get my stuff out of the apartment and I've been ignoring him," I explain and reach for Conner's arm again. "Get away before he sees you!"

"Too late," Conner replies and my heart takes a swan dive in my chest. Conner lifts his hand and gives Beckett an abrupt, terse wave, but he isn't smiling at him, which I appreciate.

What I don't appreciate is that Conner then gives Beckett a 'one second' sign and turns and starts towards the door. "Conner! I do *not* want to see him!" I wail. "I can't!"

Anxiety starts to quake through my body, sobering me up. I don't want to be humiliated in front of Conner and nothing about seeing Beckett again won't be humiliating. Conner turns and grabs my shoulders in his wide, strong hands. His grip is firm but gentle. "Mac, I'll handle this, okay? I have a plan."

"A plan?" I squawk like a parrot as he marches to the door, flings it open, and starts down the stairs.

He stops halfway and motions for me to join him. "Come on. Trust me."

"I don't know you."

"Trust me anyway." He holds out his hand. I bite my lip and stand frozen at the top of the stairs. Conner's shoulders rise and fall on a frustrated sigh and then he reaches out and grabs my hand in his and pulls me toward the door.

He drags me all the way down the stairs. In the small square entryway at the bottom, he changes the grip on our hands. He's not holding my hand like you would a child while crossing the street anymore. Now he's got our fingers laced together, like lovers. I want to protest, or at the very least demand to know the details of this plan, but there isn't time. He flips the deadbolt and flings open the door.

Beckett Echolls is standing there holding a box. His girlfriend, Heather, is right behind him, also holding a box. And now this situation has officially gone from bad to worse. I don't have makeup on, my hair is everywhere, my eyes are likely glassy from the booze and I...

Conner squeezes my hand in his. I tilt my head up and he winks with the confidence of a King. Then he turns to face my ex. "Beckett, right?"

"Yeah. Hey, Conner," Beckett says like he's pleasantly surprised but his eyes are dull and flat. Not a bit of excitement in them. He looks irritated and confused. "Don't you have a game today in Brooklyn?"

"The Barons game just ended," Conner replies vaguely. He pauses to watch Beckett look at me, then back at Conner, then at our hands which are still joined. And then Conner says something that makes my brain explode. "I was scratched, so I came to see my girl."

I almost ask him who he's talking about, but I'm distracted by Beckett's jaw unhinging like he's an anaconda trying to swallow a truck. Heather leans forward and nudges him in the back "Beck! We can't stand here all day!" Heather snaps.

"Relax, babe!" he says but his tone is tight. He eyes us again, and I eye him back. Beckett looks the same as he always did. No weight loss from emotional stress. No bags under his eyes. No sad frown permanently creasing his forehead. He looks relaxed, unbothered, and even happy. I fucking hate him.

The top of the box in his arms isn't closed and I can see one of my picture frames on top of a throw pillow. A throw pillow? He's giving me back the throw pillows we bought together?

"Who told you where I was?" I ask Beckett. My voice sounds softer and less steady than I would like.

"Do you want your stuff or not?" Beckett replies tersely. He's got that look on his face which I know is pure annoyance. He has no use for me anymore. That doesn't sting as much as it used to, but looking past him, at the face of his pretty, thin, blonde ex-turned-current, does. She is nothing like me, inside or out, but he thinks she's the better option. "I could have just thrown all this stuff out, but I'm trying to be the adult here."

Again, this asshole tries to insinuate he's an adult. Maybe ignoring him and ghosting him wasn't adult, but I was in *pieces*. Conner squeezes my hands again and it gives me the strength to speak. "I believe the word you're looking for isn't adult but *adulterer*."

"Mackenzie..." He sighs and rolls his eyes.

"Mac," Conner interrupts and lets go of my hand only to wrap an arm around my shoulders and pull me forward so I'm snuggled into his side in the doorway. "She prefers Mac. Always has."

I feel myself relax a little into Conner's side. Beckett's big brown eyes widen even further. Behind him, Heather sighs impatiently and my gut rolls with humiliation. She's the reason he discarded me like week-old pizza. Conner looks over at her. "Heather, right? You were in my class at Silver Bay High."

"Yeah. Hi Con," she says with a flirty smile. She is flirting in front of her... my eyes move to her hands. No ring. That big, square-cut solitaire I found isn't on her hand. Yet. But Beckett is still definitely her boyfriend and she's flirting with Conner in front of him. Or am I overreacting? "How's the Big Apple? I love New York."

"I prefer Maine," Conner replies, and then, before I realize what's happening, he turns his head and presses his lips to my temple. "With my girl."

Oh no he didn't! Oh shit, he did.

Beckett blinks so rapidly that I almost ask him if he has something in his eye. When he speaks there's a stinging amount of disbelief dripping from his tone. "You're dating Macken... Mac? *You?* With her? Since when?"

Conner shoots him a look that says he thinks Beckett's an asshole but then he smiles. Not his usual warm, infectious smile, but this cool, intimidating one that's dipped in vinegar and wrapped in barbed wire. "Oh man, I don't know the date this all took off. Babe, do you remember?"

I shake my head unable to quickly do the math on a fake relationship I didn't know I was in until thirty seconds ago. But then glance over at Beckett and Heather who were sleeping together on and off for two years behind my back and suddenly, I'm furious Beckett would even dare ask the question. "I think, if we're going to put an official date on it, it would have been right before you left for the season. Not this September, but last. It was supposed to be a one-time thing but..."

I shrug. It's exactly what Beckett said to me when he told me about Heather. She was supposed to be a one-time thing. Getting each other out of their systems. A final official goodbye but... shrug. That's how he explained it to me. And now, Beckett knows those are his words. I can see it in the bitter look twisting his face. Then he actually inhales so sharply that I hear it.

But I pretend I don't hear a thing and turn my gaze up to Conner who is looking down at me with a *gorgeous* grin. He chuckles like we're sharing an inside joke. We kind of are. "Right. That time in my parents' boat house. I guess that's the official moment, huh? God, that was a fucking perfect night."

I nod, trying to imagine whatever he's imagining doing to

me in that boathouse. My face floods with heat. He leans in. "I love that it still makes you blush."

And then... Conner Garrison kisses me. Not on my temple or the top of my head or cheek, but on the freaking mouth. And not a peck. A real, adult, honest-to-toe-curling-God kiss.

The kiss is soft but intense. His mouth opens slightly and his tongue teases my lips. It has my heart pounding like an unlatched screen door in a hurricane. Beckett clears his throat awkwardly. Heather huffs out a breath impatiently. "Umm, can you just please take your stuff, Mac? I have a party to plan."

Conner pulls away and glances past Beckett to Heather. I'm fighting off a giant dizzy spell that's from the kiss rather than the ample amount of champagne still pumping through my veins. "Yeah. Sure," Conner says like it's no big deal.

He untangles himself from me reaches for the box Beckett is holding and hands it to me. It feels heavy like it's filled with not only physical things but emotional baggage as well. I turn and place it on the bench in the entry. Conner reaches for the box Heather is holding and gives her a cool smile. But his voice is light and cheery as he says, "I should be thanking you. In fact, I am. Thank you for taking Beckett out of the picture so I could finally get a real shot at Mac."

Oh my God, is he for real? I bite the inside of my cheek to keep from smiling as Beckett's face gets twisted grotesquely with... jealousy? No. Maybe? Conner keeps talking. "I've had a crush on her since I was nine."

"You've known him since you were nine?" Beckett barks.

"I was fifteen. He was nine," I clarify. "My father played with both Jordan Garrison and Devin Garrison and they were all friends off the ice. Didn't your dad make any friends when he played?"

Beckett glares at me but doesn't answer the question.

"Right. Cool. Well, you two better be going to plan that party," Conner remarks and reaches for the door.

"Do you guys want to come?" Heather asks.

Okay, this entire interaction has officially gone off the rails.

"To your party?" I ask, and I'm sure I look like I'm trying to incinerate her with my eyeballs. What kind of narcissistic, clueless monster invites the jilted ex to her party?

"It's not Heather's party," Beckett explains rolling his dark eyes. "She's on the committee that's organizing it for the hospital. It's a New Year's party for the staff. You've gotten the email. Guess you ignored it, like everything else."

"Beck, buddy, when Mac isn't at work I've been keeping her too busy to read emails. Sorry, not sorry." Conner shrugs that acidic smile on his perfect mouth again. "But yeah, we'll come to your little party. I'm sure she's allowed to bring her significant other, right?"

Beckett opens his mouth but nothing comes out. Heather nods. "Of course."

I reach behind Conner like I'm wrapping an arm around his waist but I pinch the top of his very firm, very round, butt. *Hard.* I feel his whole body flex as he absorbs the pain but he doesn't flinch. And he doesn't back down. "We really appreciate the invite, Heather. We'll be there. With bells on."

I am going to murder Conner Garrison.

Chapter 6

Conner

"Jesus, you are more ornery than a wet cat," I remark, which turns her into more of a hissing, spitting, angry little kitten. I have to bite my cheek to keep from smiling because Mac's super sexy this way.

"I am *not* going to a party organized by the woman my ex-boyfriend left me for. Why would you even think to say yes?" She sits on a stool at the kitchen island, plants her elbows on the counter, and drops her head in her hands.

I grab an open bottle of red that looks like it's been sitting on her counter for ages, yank out the cork, and pour some into the wine glass from our mimosas. "Drink this."

She uncovers her pretty but pained face to look at the glass in my hand. She shakes her head. I lean over the island with my arm extended, pushing it closer to her. "That's the wine I use for cooking."

"Still wine. Drink it."

"Alcohol doesn't fix anything."

"Sometimes you can't fix everything and it's a nice distraction," I reply, and she stares at me with a look on her face that says things she's too polite to say out loud. "Mac, I'm sorry. I just wasn't going to let him think he had an ounce of power. He thinks you're so upset you're running from him."

"Spoiler alert. I was. I *am*."

"Why?"

She looks like she might scream, and not in a good way. "Do I have to remind you of my origin story? I wasn't born into hockey royalty like you, Prince Conner. I was born to a drug addict and bounced around the foster system for over a decade until Alex Larue, hockey's court jester, and tough guy, found me and saved me with his girlfriend."

"FYI, I once heard Alex tell Callie you saved him," I reply calmly like that's not the most goddamn heart-melting thing I could have ever said. I know it is and I see her eyes flare and then get a little more watery than normal. I remember when I heard Alex tell Callie that. I was about fourteen, I think, and he was bragging about how Mac was on the Dean's list and she was paying for her own tuition. I remember thinking I hope I make my parents that proud.

She clears her throat and shakes off the soothing emotions I've just poured over her because Mac doesn't want to be soothed right now. She glares at me. "Okay yeah. Two-way street there, but my point is, I'm not like you. I wasn't born into the one percent."

"What does that have to do with Buttface Echolls?" I ask.

I sigh. "I worked really hard my whole life not to become the statistic I was born to be. And to heal. To be worthy of the luck that had come my way when my dad saw me in that alley in New York. And, most importantly, to fit in. I thought I had. Beckett... the way we broke up... made me feel like that was a lie. That I wasn't whole, wasn't worthy, and wasn't good enough to be a normal person or the girlfriend of one. Like Beckett. And before you tell me it's all bullshit, somewhere in my heart I know that, but it's a lot of emotional work to fight against those voices of past trauma and inferiority in my head. And I haven't had time to do that work because I'm busting my butt to finish this medical degree."

Her words have knocked the wind out of me. She's staring at me with such brutal vulnerability and it kills me that I look like someone who can't see his own silver spoon hanging out of his mouth. But also, that she thinks she's not worthy. This woman who has earned her place in life every damn step of the way. She's worthy of a hell of a lot more than Beckett Echolls.

"Well he isn't going to make you feel that way anymore," I announce as I sip straight from the red wine bottle I put in front of her. "You may have started broken Mac, but you put yourself back together, which makes you better than all of us. Frankly, I'm disappointed you don't realize that. Hurting you was the biggest mistake of Beckett's unremarkable, boringly average life."

"I don't know about that, but he definitely felt a sting today," she admits after a full thirty seconds of letting me do nothing but stare at her and hope she doesn't hate me. "The dates I gave Beckett for when we *allegedly* got together was before he broke up with me so... now he thinks I cheated too."

"Yeah. I figured that by the look on his face." I smile and watch her as she finally reaches for the glass and takes a sip of the wine.

I lift the bottle. "Here's to giving him a taste of his own medicine."

We both sip our wine, but my eyes are glued to her. I keep thinking about all the summers she would visit, and how every year, I'd sneak glances at her as much as I could. Looking at Mac is like being in a freezing cold lake and then hitting a patch warmed by the sun. She made me feel warm on the inside back then. As kids, I was smitten and it was harmless. Now... not so much.

I remember the kiss I laid on her in front of Beckett. It was chaste, and for show, so I didn't have time to enjoy it to its full potential. But I would like to do it again. And *really* feel it. The small taste I had set something on fire inside me.

"What?" she asks.

"I hope you don't mind that I kissed you," I say.

"I... mind? No. But it was a bit of an ambush," she replies. "I would have tried harder... I mean, like, participated, if I'd been able to anticipate it. But it sold the charade to Beckett, and pissed him off, so thanks for fake kissing me."

"You're welcome. I mean, it was a total hardship. Worse than a first day of training camp hungover, but I endured." She looks up at me, her blue eyes wide with horror for a split second before I wink and grin and then she blushes again. I take another sip from the bottle. More of a gulp really. "I'll likely have to kiss you again, at this party we're going to attend, so consider this your warning. Bring your A-game."

She stares at me in the most adorable, completely stunned way. But then she blinks and puts down her glass. "The party is New Year's Eve. You won't be here. You'll be waived on the twenty-seventh so by the twenty-eighth you could be on a team anywhere in North America. Seattle. San Diego. Las Vegas, Milwaukee. Canada. You could be in Canada!"

"The league doesn't have a single solitary game on New Year's Eve so I can get back here and leave right after the party. I don't care if I have to take a red eye or drive all night. Whatever. I'll do it," I say and walk around the island until I'm beside her barstool. I grip the back of it and slowly turn her to face me. "Besides I may not be picked up at all, in which case Brooklyn's farm team is in Rhode Island and they don't resume their schedule until January fifth."

"You looked at the farm team schedule?" Mac croaks, her voice uneven and breathy.

I nod. She frowns and puts a hand on my shoulder. "You're going to be picked up."

"Maybe."

"You will be."

She has such a look of unwavering confidence in her eyes now that I can't help but drink it in. I take a step closer and without hesitation, she parts her legs to make space for me in between them, which shocks me. I didn't expect her to fight me, but somehow I didn't expect her to be this receptive either. My ego gets an injection of confidence. I reach up and move the curls resting on her shoulder, pushing them back. "I'm taking you to that party, and you're going to wear a sexy dress, and even sexier heels, and hold that pretty little head of yours high because he has taken enough from you. And I'm going to help you take it back."

Her dark eyelashes flutter. I feel her exhale against the front of my thin t-shirt. "Did you really have a crush on me when you were younger?"

I smile. "Yes. And the last twelve hours make me think I still do."

She looks away, her eyes shifting downward, but her hands move up. Her fingertips run over my forearms and up my biceps, leaving gooseflesh in their wake. Mac subtly scoots closer to the edge of her seat. Her inner thighs brush my outer thighs. "I feel like I should practice or something... being your fake girlfriend."

"Practice does make perfect..." I murmur, and my hand reaches up to move back another wayward curl. God, her hair is *soft*. "You should probably kiss me now, so you don't have to worry about later."

"That would be crazy," she whispers as her head tilts up.

"Crazy can be good, Mac."

"And it can be terrible," she replies but her hands are

climbing up my shoulders, her tongue is wetting her bottom lip, and my dick is coming to life in my joggers. There's *nothing* terrible about that.

"A-game, Larue," I tease. "Bring it."

And boy, does she ever.

Her lips land on mine with intention. With purpose. And before I can even start to control this kiss, she's taken over. Not that I'm complaining. Her tongue sweeps into my mouth and her hands go around my neck. I loop my arms around her waist and yank her to the edge of the chair. Her legs twist around my back just above my butt, her core presses against my erection, and we both moan.

This isn't where I thought I would be today. When I drove into town with my proverbial tail between my legs, I had a million scenarios of how my time in my hometown might go. Mac Larue didn't factor into one of them. And now, it's the only place I want to be.

Chapter 7

Mac

If one of my patients was making out with a childhood friend, out of nowhere, after day drinking and being confronted by a cheating ex who triggers all their negative childhood trauma, I would have to assess whether their behavior was human error, recklessness, or at-risk behavior. Me taking the challenge and kissing Conner isn't human error. I purposely slipped my tongue into his mouth, and the way it was making my body wake up like it's been in a deep hibernation I didn't know about, well I don't regret it. At the moment.

This is fully and completely reckless behavior brought on by seeing Beckett and being submerged in those feelings of negative self-worth. I know it, but then Conner's tongue sweeps possessively into my mouth and I simply don't give a shit why I'm doing this. It feels fantastic.

I am kissing Conner Garrison. The scrawny kid I met when I was young is now a very bold, very grown-up, very muscled, and jaw-droppingly handsome man. My girl bits are going to set off the smoke detector.

What the hell kind of Christmas-time *Twilight Zone* did I tumble into? His hands are at my hips and they grip me tighter,

55

yanking me forward even more. I can feel the long, hard bulge in his joggers pressed right up against the space between my legs and it sends a shiver of desire racing through me. I haven't felt a man's want for me in a long time. The last six months of my relationship with Beckett were sexless. And before that... well, I don't remember feeling like he wanted me as brazenly and openly as Conner is exhibiting in this moment.

I hook my ankles behind that tight bubble butt of his, making sure the friction between us is uninterrupted. "None of this makes sense," I whisper against his mouth.

"But it feels good, doesn't it?" he asks, his lips ghosting my cheek as they move to my ear. Oh damn, not my ear. I love... he nips at my lobe, licking and sucking, and I let out the most unfiltered groan of my life.

"Yeah, that feels right." I let out a breath that's shaky with desire. "Is this the alcohol, though?"

He kisses me again, softer than before, and ends it with a tug to my bottom lip just before his husky voice whispers, "I wasn't kidding, Mac. You were my first crush. This... you... are a dream come true. And I fucking need that right now. A dream to come true. I think you do too."

"I do," I admit. I mean, he just watched me take my belongings back from a dude who ripped my heart out and, worse, dropped it into a vat of boiling humiliation. So yeah, I need a dream to come true instead of turning into a nightmare. Fooling around with the crown prince of hockey... definitely not nightmarish.

He pulls back again, and the heated look in his eyes cools a little. "If you aren't down, it's okay. I can—"

I wrap my arms around his thick neck and pull his lips back to mine. I want to be wild and free and I need to be wanted right now. "I'm down. Time for you to bring your A-game, Garrison."

And without another word, Conner Garrison uses all that muscle and height and power to pull me right off the stool, cup my ass, and carry me toward my bedroom. And I don't have a second to process that this is happening, that I don't intend to stop him, because there's a knock at the door. Actually, it's more of a bang.

"Mac!" a female voice bellows. "Is Conner in there?"

"I told you he was," Tenley's voice filters through the door next. "Guys! Open up!"

Conner stops walking and drops his forehead to my shoulder. "Ah fuck. That's my stepmom."

"Conner Garrison I have a key and I am not afraid to use it!" Callie Caplan-Garrison hollers.

I unhook my ankles from behind his back and he gently places me on the ground. I smooth my hair. Conner runs his thumb over his lips and adjusts the front of his joggers as he swears again.

"Legally, you don't have the right to enter," Tenley says loud enough so we can hear. "You haven't given notice to the tenant and you aren't even the landlord."

"Listen, Nancy Drew or Veronica Mars or whatever, I'm a co-parent and I don't care if he's twelve, twenty-five, or fifty-five, I am going to hunt him down when something is wrong," Callie tells her niece.

Conner sighs and crosses the short distance to the front door. He flips the lock and swings it open. In a blur, his stepmom and cousin barge right in. Callie reaches up and grabs her stepson's face between her gloved hands. "We love you."

"I love you too, Mama C." Conner's voice is soft and sweet and my girl parts start to melt again.

Then Callie lets go of his face and pokes him in the middle of his chest so hard he winces. Her brown eyes get harder. "But what the hell is going on and why are you ghosting your family?"

"I'm not ghosting you," Conner replies and turns to glare at Tenley. "You sold me out."

She raises her arms and her big green eyes move from Conner to me and back again. "I didn't *want* to tell her. She's better at interrogation than me."

"Spoiler alert," Callie says, pushing her brown hair over her shoulder. A few strands of silver reflect in the light. "I already knew he was here. Tenley just confirmed, under duress. Theo and Grady saw Conner's car drive by them this morning when they were on a donut run."

"Shit," Conner hisses.

Callie turns on him again. "Can we get to the explaining part? Are you okay? Why are you here and not playing with your team?"

"It's a long story." Conner glances over at me but I immediately look away. I'm... embarrassed? Shy? Overwhelmed? I don't know what I am. I'll unpack it later but right now, I just need to not look at him.

"I'll give you guys your space..." I suggest and start to back up, toward my bedroom.

Callie shoots me a soft, friendly smile. "Hi, Mac. How are you?"

"I'm good. How are you?"

"You know." Callie shrugs and motions toward her stepson. "Anyway, if you don't have plans for Christmas, consider yourself invited to our house."

"Thanks, but I'm working." I give her a grateful smile and slip into my room. I'm about to shut the door but a foot wedges itself in the way.

Tenley's blonde head pokes through the small space. Her

green eyes are pleading. "I'm sorry. I didn't mean to get involved in this."

I smile and let her push her way into my room. "I know. It's probably for the best that this is happening. He should talk to his parents."

"What is happening? I didn't realize when I saw him today he was bailing on a hockey game," Tenley says. "That's not at all like Con."

"You're going to have to ask him," I tell her and she pouts for a minute, but I can tell it's jokingly. Then Tenley gives me a quick, tight hug as I gently push the door behind her to give Conner and Callie some privacy. Tenley lets me go and plops down on my bed. "So..." She looks around the room. "You and Con have sex yet?"

My mouth drops open in an indignant O. My eyes flare like she's just asked the most bizarre, impossible, ridiculous question I've ever heard. But my cheeks turn red. Full-on, Rudolph's nose red. Tenley, being the Olivia Benson wannabe that she is, doesn't miss it. She grins, it's devilish and lights up her whole pretty face and it's easy to see why men do double-takes when she's around. Tenley is stunning. "You and Con! Oh my God, the dufus actually took my advice!"

"Your *advice*?" I repeat, and she stands up.

"I ran into him this morning buying you a breakfast feast and I may have said that you both could use a little naked ther-apy. Some sexy times, a hit of oxytocin," Tenley explains, and when I just stand there dumbfounded she moves closer. "Sex. I told him you two should have sex."

"I understood. I just..." Oh my God was that a pity kiss? Was I a second away from a pity fuck? Because Tenley made it sound like I was a sad, desperate scorned woman who needed it? I rub my forehead and close my eyes.

"Oh God.... Was it horrible? Does he suck in bed?" Tenley

asks and then squishes her pretty features together like she accidentally sucked a lemon. "Don't answer that. I do not want to know how my cousin is in bed. I'm sorry if it sucked. I have other cousins you could try."

"I'm sure he's fine at sex. I don't know because we didn't and I don't want to." I swallow and close my eyes again as humiliation burns through me hot and fast. "Not with Conner. My God, I don't even really know him. I appreciate you were trying to do me a favor but I don't want pity hook-ups, so don't ask men to give them to me, okay?"

"It wouldn't have been pity," Tenley argues. "If anything, you'd be the one doing him a solid. I mean, have you seen the tension knots in that man's shoulders? The crease he's developing between his eyes? The scowl that's almost permanently glued to his face this year? He's carrying the weight of the world on his shoulders, all because his team sucks. It's a bit much. He needs to unwind. I thought you could scratch each other's backs if you know what I mean."

"I know what you mean, and thanks but no thank you. I don't want Conner to scratch my itches."

Before she can argue there's a knock on the door, sharp and hard. I call, "Come in!"

The door, which didn't fully close when I swung it earlier, opens just enough for Conner to poke his head through. "Mama C is driving me home. Thanks for everything."

I nod because words don't want to form on my tongue. The tongue that knows what his feels like. Tenley's head is bopping from one side to the other, watching us like a particularly intense Wimbledon final. Conner stares at me, but something is off. He looks more than just tense. He looks angry. No... hurt? Maybe it's his concern over facing his parents presenting an odd expression on his face. But... I feel like it's personal. About me and him.

"Everything alright?" I finally ask.

He huffs out a hard, sharp breath like I just told a very sarcastic joke. "Thanks again, Mac. Sorry, I had to bother you. Take care."

"Umm... okay." I want to ask about the party. Is he still intending to go with me? It doesn't feel like it, but I also don't want to talk about this in front of Tenley.

Conner disappears from the doorway and I follow him out into the living room, Tenley right behind me. Callie is standing by the door and she looks worried, so I wonder how much Conner has told her about his hockey situation. She flashes both Tenley and me a quick smile. "If anything changes with your schedule, Mac, remember you have a place at our table."

Callie blows an air kiss, opens the door, and disappears down the stairs. Conner follows without even looking back before he firmly shuts the door behind them. Tenley looks as startled by his cold goodbye as I am. I mean, didn't he just have his tongue in my mouth less than five minutes ago?

"If you do come to Christmas, you won't have to even see him," Tenley promises and gives me a hug. "There's a ton of us, you can avoid him without making it obvious."

"Yeah. Thanks." I step out of the hug, still too humiliated to be consoled. "I'm fine. It was nothing. Clearly."

Tenley looks like she's going to challenge that statement but she doesn't. She shoots me a sympathetic smile and offers, "You wanna come up to the main house and have dinner with me? I'm making veggie lasagna."

I shake my head. "No I was hoping for alone time and a self-care day and now that my squatter is gone, I'm gonna do it."

Tenley nods and heads towards the door. "Okay, well offer's open all night. Or text me. Or whatever. I feel like... I should apologize for my relative."

"No. Don't. Honestly, it's fine. I'm fine," I assure her, hoping

I sound more believable than Ross from *Friends* even though I don't feel more confident in my words than him.

Tenley leaves and I stand there in my finally empty apartment. This is what I wanted, right? I walk into my living room drop onto my couch and lie there trying to wrap my brain around the last twenty-four hours.

Chapter 8

Conner

I 've never seen my dad look genuinely disappointed before, and I didn't even realize that until now. Because now, for the first time in my life, my dad is truly disappointed in me. And it feels way worse than I thought it would. I really shouldn't have come home.

"I'm gonna head back to Brooklyn," I announce when the silence in the kitchen is deafening. "I'm gonna have to pack up the loft and list it so I might as well start now."

"Con, wait!" Dad says firmly. I stop walking around the massive kitchen island but I don't turn back to face him. I can't keep staring at that look on his face. "Can we talk about how you handled this? Why did you refuse to play? Why did you avoid me and go day drinking with Mac? None of that is going to fix this."

"I never thought it would," I reply, still staring out at the great room attached to the kitchen instead of at him. "But that's the thing, Dad, *nothing* can fix this."

"A good fucking lawyer can fix this," Callie says from where she is leaning against the counter by the stove. "What they did, how they did it, was a violation of the league's policies. Your union should be all over this. That Landry asshole will be fined."

"She's not wrong," Dad adds. "What did your union rep say?"

"I haven't talked to them yet," I grumble, and I don't have to see his face to know I've disappointed him again because I can hear his sigh.

When I feel a hand on my shoulder, I know it's his. He turns me to face him. I avert my eyes. I look a lot like my dad, at least that's what everyone always tells me. His hair is lighter, especially now that there's gray at the temples and the blond has faded. But we have the same hazel eyes and dimple on our left cheek. His kind of disappeared as he aged, but mine is still deep. I'm taller than him but we, according to both my mother and Callie, have the exact same stubborn spirit. Now his mouth, also similar to mine with the full bottom lip and pronounced cupid's bow on the top, is set in a grim line. "I wouldn't have walked out with a game left to play. That will give them something to sue about."

"I'm not you," I reply. "And yeah you wouldn't have because you wouldn't have had to. No one would ever dream of waiving Devin Garrison."

"Conner..." Whatever he was about to say gets cut off by the ring of my cellphone. I pull it from my back pocket.

"It's Clark," I say, and I don't need to explain further. I turn my back to my dad again and answer my cell. "Hi."

"Hey. How are you?" Clark asks, concern apparent in his voice.

"I've been better," I admit and make my way out of the kitchen. As I turn the corner into the great room, I run directly into both my sisters. They were huddled up together against the wall by the bookcases eavesdropping, clearly.

They both jump back and try to act casual. Liv pulls out her phone and leans a shoulder against the fireplace like she is just casually cruising Instagram or something. Mayhem scrambles past her to the center of the mantle where she immediately starts examining the family photos there like she's never seen them before. I glare at both of them, flipping them the middle finger as I storm by.

"Well, here's the deal," Clark starts. "I don't think it will make you feel any better but they're going to pretend you had the flu. So this won't harm your value when you hit the market because you won't look like you walked out on your team. But that means you also can't rat Landry out to the player's union."

"What? No! I have to," I bark.

"They say if you do, then they'll claim contract violation for not showing up to the game," Clark sounds despondent. "Then they'll likely get away with handing you a suspension and no one will pick you up because you'll be labeled a problem child."

"Fuck," I hiss.

"What? What's he saying?" my dad asks, and I turn and shush him and storm into the dining room to get away from him. I mean shit, I am a grown adult, I should be allowed to have a private conversation. Why the fuck didn't I move out and get my own place?

Dad doesn't follow me, which is good, but I know, no matter how annoying it is, he only wants the best for me. So I kind of feel bad as I drop down into one of the dining room chairs. Almost as bad as I felt about storming out on Mac like we weren't just about to have sex. I stare out the massive bay window, at the snowy front yard and try to fight the guilt. "Clearly my team didn't need me."

"They won one game against a team that's circling the drain just like they are. It was dumb luck, not your absence that gave them that W," Clark replies tersely. "Anyway, I still say walking out was the right choice. Just shake this off and we'll regroup on the twenty-seventh, okay? Don't worry. That contract of yours is hefty, so it's a bit unattractive, but someone out there will know you're worth the risk. Your dad is buddies with a lot of ex-players who went into management or coaching. Have him give them a call and talk you up as soon as that waiver announcement is made. Not a second before, Con, or it's a violation. Okay?"

"Yeah." I rub my forehead. I am not going to beg my dad to help save my ass. I just... I can't. I have made a point of not needing his help. I'm proud of that. I don't want to give that up.

I also remember being so proud of that extension contract when I signed it twenty-two months ago. Five years and thirty million. It was the biggest contract anyone in our family had gotten. Definitely the biggest in my generation. And now it's going to be the thing people laugh about. Can you believe the Barons gave Conner Garrison all that money and they had to dump him because he sucked so bad?

"Con, don't spiral over this," Clark advises. "Please, just try and enjoy Christmas. I honestly think you have a good shot at being scooped up."

"Okay. I mean, I guess I don't have a choice," I say. Clark tells me to call him anytime if I need to talk and hangs up.

I don't see how I can enjoy anything in my life until this is settled. Then I remember how much I was enjoying being with Mac. How soft her lips were. How fierce her kiss was. Yeah, I guess I could find a distraction... but I overheard her telling Tenley *'Thanks but no thank you. I don't want Conner to scratch my itches.'*

"Con, what did Clark say?"

I turn around and my dad is standing there, arms crossed, looking serious and somehow older than his fifty years. Great, I'm aging my dad. "He said it's handled. The management is telling people I was sick. But they'll only stick to this story if I don't report Landry to the union."

Liv and Mayhem come walking in now, apparently done with pretending they aren't eavesdropping on my life imploding. "I don't know why they are dumping you instead of the goalie. Your goalie let in seven goals in the first two periods last month against Los Angeles and four in the first period last week against Washington. But they waive *you?* That's fucking bullshit. Your goalie is playing like Swiss cheese."

My little sister defending me should feel good, but it doesn't because she's trying too hard and it feels like she's making excuses for me. Liv reaches over and gives my shoulder a sympathetic squeeze, which I also hate. They both used to look at me like I was their hero. You don't console your heroes.

Dad sighs at Mayhem's language but we've never been the household that curbs swearing, if used with purpose, so he doesn't scold her. "Why does it feel like Landry's got a vendetta?"

"Did you sleep with his daughter or something?" Callie asks, walking up to stand beside Dad.

"Mom!" Mayhem and Liv bark in unison.

"What? It's been known to happen." Callie shrugs and points to my dad. "Hockey players are very sexual athletes. You two wouldn't be here if they weren't."

"Okay, baby," Dad wraps an arm around Callie and pulls her to his side as he almost smiles. "You don't need to traumatize your daughters so close to Christmas."

"I'm going to call my therapist," Liv announces and leaves, heading to the hall.

"Drama queen!" Callie calls after her, grinning.

"I'm going with her to see if we can get a group deal," Mayhem adds, but before she rushes off she hugs me, hard. I wrap one arm around her back and close my eyes for a second. "Love you, Con."

Wow. This must be serious if Mayhem is getting mushy. She lets go and darts for the hall after her older sister and a second later the house echoes with the sound of her feet up the stairs. I turn and look at my stepmom, who I adore. "To get back to the original question, I have no idea why Landry is such an asshole to me. And no, I didn't sleep with his daughter or anyone he knows. I've been really focused on trying to turn the team around and get my own game out of the toilet. I haven't even been on a date in six months."

"Well, maybe that's your issue," Callie suggests.

Dad rolls his eyes. "Don't start."

"I'm not going to tell him to go out and get laid," Callie says huffily like it's insulting he would even think that's how her brain works. But it's exactly how her brain works. Callie is very sex-positive and she's always told us, the kids, to be safe but curious. She made sure we were all vaccinated for HPV and had access to condoms by the time we were fifteen. She also always told us we could ask her anything. I don't think any of us have talked to her about our sex lives but there was still some comfort knowing we could, without judgment. "What I was going to say is maybe you should date. I mean, you're a lot like your dad and he is a serial monogamist. He needs the partnership and stability of a serious relationship. It makes him better on and off the ice."

"She's not wrong," Dad agrees and glances at her with this look on his face that I swear is more than love. It's always been inspiring, the way these two feel for each other. The older I got the more I realized I didn't even mind that my parents broke up because Callie was who my dad needed. She was his missing puzzle piece. He turns to me now. "Sometimes if you get the rest of your life right, hockey falls into place."

"It doesn't matter," I reply. "I'm being waived so my career is essentially over. I'm headed to a farm team."

"You don't know that for sure."

"Dad, my contact is huge," I argue. "I haven't lived up to it. Who the hell is going to take the chance?" He looks at me, unblinking, his expression somber. I nod tersely. "Right. I'm going to bed."

"It's only eight!" Callie calls out.

"I'm tired," I bark out and head up the stairs to my room.

I shut the door and lean against it, taking in the space I've spent most of my life in. I should have my own house by now. Lord knows I have the money to buy half of Silver Bay at this point, but I'm only here for such a short time—a few months in the off-season—and I like spending it with my family.

The room has been updated through the years. It's grown up just like I have. Gone are the posters of hockey players and the desk and bean bag chair. They've been replaced with a leather chair and footstool since I don't need to study anymore. And against the wall where the desk once was is a proper bookcase filled with trophies and memorabilia from my career, like the puck from my first NHL goal, the one from my first hat trick, and so on. I purposely move my eyes away from those things now, because looking at them stings, and cross the room to the king-sized bed. I grab the remote on the bedside table and punch a button so the music starts to play from my sound system.

Still holding my phone, I scroll through my contacts until I find Tenley. I pull up our texts. The last time she texted me was for my birthday months ago.

Hey Con, have a great one! Love ya, goof.

I stare out the window and debate how to approach this. But

it's Tenley, so I definitely don't need to be subtle. Tenley's mom, my Aunt Jessie, is Callie's sister. Yep. My dad and his brother Jordan married sisters. And Aunt Jessie is reserved and level-headed but her daughter Tenley inherited Callie's bluntness and lack-of-filter. So I just send the most direct text I can.

> I need Mac's phone number, please.

I wait. I see the bubbles that she's typing.

> Are you going to be nice?

> Of course. I swear.

More typing bubbles as I grow impatient and stare out the window. The Christmas lights are reflecting on the snow, casting green and red shadows everywhere. The lake just past the lawn is pure ice. On Christmas Day we'll all lace up. Everyone from my grandparents to my cousins will skate out there and play a game of pick-up hockey. I don't want to this year, I realize, and it used to be my favorite family holiday tradition. One of my first childhood memories is of my dad holding my mitten-clad hands as I slipped and slid on my tiny skates on Christmas Day on the homemade rink in my grandparents' backyard.

> Con, she's vulnerable.

I stare at Tenley's latest text. So am I! I want to scream, but instead, I just wait for more since there are still typing bubbles. It's clear Tenley knows a little bit of what transpired before she and Callie interrupted.

If you need to use someone or be used, no judgment. But not her.

My head tips back and hits the heavy oak headboard. I close my eyes. I don't want that. But what do I want? I don't exactly know, but I do know that I made a promise to Mac that I would go to that party with her. I want to permanently take away that look of inferiority she gets when Beckett Echolls is nearby.

She doesn't want to scratch her itch with me. I heard. Fine. Just want to help her get revenge on her ex. I swear.

Tenley sends me back an eye roll emoji. I have no idea what that's supposed to mean but before I can ask she texts me Mac's cell number.

Thank you!

Hurt her and I'll injure you.

Appreciate the threat, Ten, but you're the size of my forearm.

I'll emotionally injure you. Full-on psychological warfare. You've been warned.

Are you one of Mac's patients? You should be.

She doesn't respond.

Okay, I think as I add Mac's number to my contacts. Now I just have to figure out what the hell to say to her.

Chapter 9

Mac

I t's five-thirty in the morning and I just finished digging my car out of the snow when my phone buzzes in my pocket. That's odd, but sometimes my dad or mom is up this early and reaches out, but my dad texted me last night. We've had our weekly check-in.

As I get into the passenger seat I dig my phone out of my bag and pull down the scarf wrapped around my neck and the entire lower half of my face so it will recognize my face and unlock. The message, shockingly, is from Conner.

I hadn't heard a word from him since he left yesterday. I was still feeling the freezer burn from his abrupt change of attitude and so I read the message but I don't respond.

> Hey. It's Conner. Garrison. Wanted to say I
> hope you have a good day at work.

I drop my phone back into my bag, next to my lunch and wallet, and press the button to start the car. Only nothing happens. I press it again. I press it harder. I press it lighter. Wait... was that sound? I try again. I think I hear a faint ticking sound... or something. But that's it. No lights. No radio. No engine roaring to life.

I have to be at work by six. I can't be late. I mean, I think people would understand but... I'll kick myself mentally for weeks. I'm a perfectionist. I've accepted it. I'm never late. I always give one hundred percent and I don't accept my own excuses, valid or not. I twist in my seat and crane my neck to look at the main house. It's still submerged in complete darkness, which is to be expected. Tenley is not an early riser. She's a night owl and I don't want to wake her but...

My phone buzzes again.

I sigh and grab it.

Can we talk when your shift is over tonight? Please?

Fuck. Am I desperate enough to... yeah. I am. I punch the screen, my fingers telling my phone to call the number texting me. Conner picks up halfway through the first ring.

"Hey. You shouldn't use your phone while driving."

"I don't. I'm not. My car won't start."

"Oh. Shit. You're still at the farm?"

"Yes." I sigh and give my head a shake. "I hate to ask this but, since you're clearly awake at this hour, would you mind picking me up and driving me to the hospital?"

"I'm on my way."

And less than ten minutes later Conner pulls up in his fancy, reliable Range Rover. I hop into the passenger seat and give him a grateful smile. "Thanks."

"I owe you," he replies and a guilty smile flashes across his tired face.

As I do up my seatbelt and he starts back down the drive, I note he's in pajama bottoms and a big puffy coat in a bright yellow color that brings out the amber flecks in his hazel eyes.

The eyes that have dark circles under them. "Have you even slept?"

"Not a wink," Conner says as he turns onto the narrow rural road that leads away from the farm and to the hospital.

"So it went that well with your parents?"

He kind of shrugs. The radio is on. It's loud and I know he's using it as a distraction from his own thoughts and now probably to keep him from talking to me about this. So I reach over and turn it off. That gets his attention. He glances over, and our eyes connect. I raise one eyebrow. He sighs. "I've never seen my dad look so disappointed. Callie was full of unhelpful suggestions. My sisters both tried to console me, which made me want to crawl out of my own skin. I spent all night wracking my brain on how to stop this from happening but there isn't a way."

"Not everything can be fixed," I tell him as buildings start to pepper the sides of the road. "You're not used to having things not go your way so this is an... adjustment."

"I've had things not go my way before," he argues, like a reflex. It happens all the time. I see it with my patients. It's a knee-jerk reaction.

"You've had a seamless career, and that is not to say you didn't work for it. You did," I assure him as I feel my butt getting warm. I glance at his dash and see a little orange light. He has heated seats because of course he does. It's nice. "But you haven't had a real struggle until now."

"It's not a struggle. It's failure," he corrects me as he turns onto the main drag of Silver Bay, which is still void of traffic because virtually no one is up at this hour. "My whole career is going up in smoke. And you're right. I did work hard for it and that seems to mean nothing now."

"You're catastrophizing," I say, and of course, he takes it the wrong way.

"I'm not a drama queen." His voice is hard.

"Those words never left my mouth, Conner." I keep my voice even and calm. He's tired and he's stressed and unraveling. I think I'm making it worse, which sucks. I don't mean to. "I read up on this waiver process and you still have a shot at being picked up by another team. I know your brain is telling you that your contract is too big and your performance this year doesn't show your worth. I get that, but I also know that you are Conner Garrison and that name alone makes you worth more than any other player in your situation. Do you want my advice?"

Conner frowns as he slows the car to turn into the parking lot of the hospital. "Isn't that what you just gave me?"

"No. That was me giving you an outside opinion of your current predicament. For perspective," I reply, ignoring his frown and attitude.

He doesn't respond right away. He waits until he comes to a stop at the curb in front of the main entrance to the hospital. Then he puts the car in park and turns to look at me. Even tired and annoyed, Conner Garrison is the most attractive man I've ever seen in person. I shouldn't admit that, even to myself, but it's true. "Fine. Lay it on me. I know you're a shrink so shrink me."

"First of all, we don't like that term," I reply and undo my seatbelt. "Second of all, I'm not a full-fledged psychiatrist yet. Not for another few months. And lastly, I still think of you as a friend even though we irrationally went from not remembering each other to drunkenly sticking our tongues in each other's mouths."

He blinks rapidly at that and then, he kind of, almost, slightly smiles. And it's... *molten* so I look away to avoid him catching me blush. I take a deep breath and crack open the door so I can make my escape when I'm done talking. "You need to concentrate on the day-to-day. You aren't on a farm team. You haven't been waived, technically, yet. You haven't not been picked up off waivers. Stop feeling sorry for yourself and keep training. Live in the present, like you're still a professional athlete in the highest league in his field. Because you are. Oh, and be grateful for it. Thanks for the lift. Bye."

I make it to the front doors, which start to swish open automatically as I approach, but then he hooks my arm. I spin around and look up at him. He looks even more tired out in the rising sun than he did in the car. "I'm sorry."

"For what?"

"You seem mad at me."

I smile. "And you're sorry. Even though you don't know why I might be upset? What if you don't agree with the reason I'm annoyed?"

"It doesn't matter what the reason is, I would always regret upsetting you, Mac," Conner says so simply and with such earnestness that I melt inside.

"We're good," I assure him because we will be. I just have to rein in the attraction that bubbled up like the champagne we were drinking yesterday. Because he and I are a bad idea. Clearly. "Thanks again for the lift."

And I head inside, leaving him with a smile and a wave.

I make my way up to the psychiatry wing and run into Shelby Garrison in the elevator. She has her nose buried in her phone but she smiles and tucks it into her pocket when she sees me. "Speak of the devil."

"Hello and why am I the devil?" I ask with a friendly grin.

"You're part of the Garrison group chat gossip this morning," Shelby informs me, and I immediately groan and lean against the elevator wall.

"This has to do with your cousin, right?" I ask, and Shelby nods. "The idea of a Garrison family group chat is terrifying because that's half the town. But being a topic in it.... Shudder."

Shelby giggles. "You harbored a fugitive. What did you expect?"

I can't help but laugh at that. Shelby laughs with me as she flips the end of her long red ponytail behind her shoulder. "Seriously though, how did Con end up at your place? I didn't know you were close."

"We weren't," I reply and then catch myself. "We *aren't*. He thought the apartment was empty. And when I discovered him there it was late and there was the storm and I couldn't kick him out."

"You have a good heart, Mac," Shelby says as the elevators open on her floor and she starts to get out.

"Hey!" I say before she can disappear down the hall. "Did you tell TP or his insignificant other where I live?"

"No!" She looks genuinely shocked. "I know better. Why?"

"He showed up at the barn yesterday." Shock washes over her face and I can tell it's genuine, not that I doubt Shelby. She's always been nothing but authentic with me. "I'm fine. I got my stuff back and now I'm officially rid of him."

"Good," Shelby replies and shoots me a smile tinged with sympathy. "Time to move on to bigger and better."

I nod as the elevator doors slide shut and it chugs upwards again. I am ready to move on... right after I attend that stupid party with my fake boyfriend. If Conner is even going to follow through on that crazy idea.

Chapter 10

Conner

I tug on my winter boots as Mayhem walks into the hall. She's eating an enormous bowl of ice cream covered in caramel sauce, hot fudge, whipped cream, sprinkles, and what looks like crushed Oreos. I'm immediately jealous. Oh to have a nineteen-year-old metabolism again.

"Where ya going?" she asks before shoveling a mouthful of her snack into her mouth.

Mayhem is the tallest woman in our family at five foot ten inches, but much more slender than one would expect for a woman who wears between twenty-five and fifty pounds of goalie gear every day. She's the second Garrison to become a goalie, and she's better at her position than any of us are at ours. I'll gladly tell anyone who asks.

"Mac's shift ends soon and her car was frozen solid this morning and didn't start. I gave her a lift in so I'm going to pick her up," I explain and pull open the door to the hall closet to grab my jacket.

"Oh. So that's where you went at the crack of dawn this morning," Mayhem notes. "You drove her to the hospital?"

"You heard me leave?"

She nods and swallows down more ice cream. "You're into her?"

My brain flashes back to the kiss. How good it felt and the way my whole body came to life with something other than anxiety and dread when I lifted her off that bar stool and she wrapped those long legs around my waist.

"If I could be into someone, I would likely be into her," I confess because, of anyone in my entire family, I trust Mayhem the most with my secrets. It's weird because we're so far apart in age, and despite taking pucks to the face for a living and spending far too much time with sweaty vile male hockey players, and the misogyny they hurl at her on the daily, she's a very girlie woman. A T-Swift, Barbie, romance novels, frilly skirts, and blown-out hair type of girl. She's also an introvert and I've always been the family's biggest extrovert. I have three male cousins closer in age you'd think I'd be tighter with... but Mayhem is my go-to with secrets and fears and all of that.

Now, she takes that admission in stride and swallows another heaping spoonful of ice cream before asking. "And why, exactly, can't you be into someone?"

I stare at her. She genuinely doesn't get it. "What the hell do I have to offer someone right now?"

Mayhem's face goes slack. "Conner, you can't be serious."

"I am, and if you give me a pep talk like Mama C or Dad, I will leave Silver Bay and possibly never come back," I warn her. "At least not until this whole bullshit is settled."

"You are so much more than your career, Con," Mayhem tells me, completely disregarding my warning. I glare. "Sorry. I'll shut up. You just go and pick up the pretty girl you would be interested in if you hadn't tied your whole self-worth to a sheet of ice and a rubber disc."

I blink. She smiles, like she's an oblivious, sweet child and then she holds up a spoonful of ice cream, caramel sauce dripping from it. "Wanna bite? You have no reason to stay in shape now. Farm team is basically a beer league. Fuck it. Get fat."

"You're..." I can't even think of an expletive or adjective to explain how infuriating she is right now so I just shake my head. "Bye."

I storm out of the house. Mayhem stands at the open door and yells after me. "Love you loser! I can't believe I finally get to call you that and you won't argue. Merry Christmas to me!"

I know she's not serious. It's a Jedi mind trick. She's calling me a loser so I'll argue with her and pull myself out of this vat of self-doubt and misery. Well, I'm not falling for her tricks. I don't even acknowledge her as I get in my car and drive away. Fucking family.

It's an easy commute to the hospital and I'm only in the parking lot ten minutes when Mac steps out of the front doors. She's all bundled up with a thick scarf wrapped around her neck and the bottom half of her face, gloves on her hands, and a knitted toque shoved on over her curls, which are pulled back into a low ponytail.

She starts along the sidewalk that skirts the parking lot all the way to the road. Is she really going to walk to the barn? It's a good six miles to that place, and the road to it is basically all uphill, with no sidewalk and likely still coated in ice. I pull out of the spot I was in and drive into the oncoming lane to pull up beside her. My window goes down as she looks over. "Your chariot awaits, Ms. Larue."

"You're here for me?"

"You don't have a car," I remind her.

"No, but I have legs," she counters.

I look up through the windshield at the solid gray sky stuffed full of clouds that are slowly dropping flakes. The sun has set and if it weren't for the parking lot lights it would be pitch black. The narrow, hilly road that takes her to the farm doesn't have a single street light. "Are you seriously going to make me go all alpha asshole on you and order you into the car? I hate being that guy, but if it's your jam..."

She smiles and I can tell she wishes she hadn't. "I grew up on the streets of New York, Conner. I can handle an alpha asshole in my sleep. I can also walk myself home."

"You are the most stubborn woman I have ever met," I declare. "Too bad for you I'm chivalrous to a fault and have decided I'm spending this Christmas as your knight in shining armor so if you don't get in this car right now, I'm going to drive next to you, slower than a sloth if necessary, all the way back to your place."

Mac stops and folds her arms over her chest. Her big blue eyes are like icicles and not just because of their uniquely pale color. She's trying to murder me with her stare. Oh well. I give zero shits. I'm driving her home. She finally seems to realize that and, with a huff of disdain, opens the passenger door.

As she slips into the car I notice Heather is standing by the bushes, at the edge of the overhang by the front doors, smoking a cigarette and watching us like a hawk. A health professional who smokes seems ironic in the worst possible way, but whatever. I pretend I don't see her and as soon as Mac's butt is settled in my heated passenger seat, I lean in. I cup the back of her head to hold her in place. I can feel the muscles in her neck tense with confusion and shock until I whisper in her ear. "Heather is watching. Time for that A-game of yours, princess."

And then, I move my mouth to hers. The back of her head presses into my palm, as it takes a second for her brain to process what I told her. But as soon as it clicks, God bless her, she kisses me. Her lips press into mine, her right hand comes up and cups my cheek, and her mouth opens just enough for her tongue to tease my lip and wake up my cock.

She starts to pull back but my hand keeps her in place. I'm

not done yet. I open my mouth and she takes the hint and deepens the kiss. When our tongues meet I swear it's like *medicine*. I feel better, at a cellular level. And so I kiss her longer and harder than I need to for the charade. When I finally let her go we're both breathless and her lips are pink and swollen. Her eyelids flutter open slowly.

I pull my eyes from her in time to catch Heather glaring at my car as she flicks the end of her cigarette into the snow and disappears back inside the hospital. "Judging by the annoyed look on her face when she went back inside, she saw us."

"Oh. Okay. Good," Mac mutters. She runs a thumb along her plump bottom lip and I bite back a smile. I love how flustered it makes her to kiss me. "So we're still going through with this farce?"

"Why wouldn't we?" I ask as she reaches for her seatbelt and I pull away from the curb. "Did you call someone to take a look at your car?"

"Yeah. Tenley," Mac replies and settles back into her seat. She pats at her hair like I might have ruined her ponytail during our make-out session but I didn't. "She said it was just the cold. She jumped it and kept it running a bit then moved it into her garage to keep it warm. Should be fine tomorrow."

"If not, call me again," I tell her.

"Why are we still going through with this?" Mac asks. "I mean, Beckett thinks we're together, and that I cheated on him, that's good enough. We don't have to double down by actually going to that party."

I glance at her as I slow to stop at a stop sign, pumping the breaks in case it's still icy out there. "Honestly? I don't think we've done him enough psychological damage. He deserves to see more of you happy, moved on, looking gorgeous, and with your new and improved boyfriend who happens to be from the family his family hates. Because the Garrisons are just plain better than the Echolls."

"I won't argue that last point," she says as a smile flickers across her face again. "Except for Mallory. She's actually kind of great. The only one I bonded with in the years I used to have to go to Echolls family events with Beckett."

I scour my brain for exactly who Mallory Echolls is. "That's Beckett's youngest sister? I think she's the same age as Tate."

Mac nods. "She's living abroad right now as a nanny. She messaged me when she found out about the break-up. Told me that she thought Beckett was an asshole. Anyway, back to this, I'm not really into inflicting psychological torture. I'm a psychiatrist, remember?"

"Not for a few months," I counter, turning slowly onto the main road that will take us through the center of town. It's the longer route home, but the one that will likely have been plowed the best and have been salted. "Right now you're just a woman who deserves to live well. And rub her cheating ex's face in it."

"My God, Conner and I thought Tenley was the dramatic, shit-stirring Garrison." She laughs a little and looks out the window for a moment at the snowy landscape. "But seriously. I'm going to officially let you off the hook."

"I was never on a hook, Mac," I reply and clench my jaw in frustration. "I'm the one who hooked *you* into this situation."

I guess she really meant what she said and she wants nothing to do with me. That moment we shared, that almost turned into something I thought would be epic, she thinks was a mistake. A dodged bullet and that's almost more humbling than losing my spot on the Barons.

So yeah, the last thing I need. I pull onto the road that leads to the farm. "How about I let *you* off the hook? You don't have to go to the party with me."

"O... Okay," Mac says with no confidence or relief in her

voice, which I guess saves my ego a little bit. "I mean, I guess... thanks. No hard feelings or anything?"

"No. Never," I reply and force out a smile. The barn is in view on the crest of the hill just to the right. I can see the lights on in the farmhouse just to the left of it. And two vehicles out front. Tenley's and Tate's trucks are there now too.

"How was your day? With your situation?"

I glance at her and she seems genuinely interested. She's a psychiatrist. Of course, she's interested. I'm one hell of a case, I guess. But I don't want to be her case study so I just shrug. "Sucked, but in an unsurprising way. No need to talk about it."

"Well," she begins as I roll to a stop in front of the barn. Someone has shoveled out a nice, straight path to the door for her. I'm guessing Tenley with a snow blower. Or maybe Tate. "Thank you again for coming to my rescue. I'll... see you around."

"Yeah. Sure."

I have so many things I want to say instead, but I don't. I just let Mac Larue get out of my car and walk into her apartment without another word.

Chapter 11

Conner

I said the family lake hockey match was my favorite part of Christmas, and it is, but this is my second favorite part. Even tonight, when I've endured a lot of sympathetic pats on the back and words of encouragement so sugary and peppy that I swear some of my relatives should start a motivational poster company. Or print that shit on T-shirts and make millions on Etsy. But still, everyone gathered together Christmas Eve, getting tipsy on spiked egg nog and mulled wine, grazing over a dining room table full of charcuterie and appetizers, tucking away in little groups to share stories and laughs and memories of prior Christmases, while a cycle of classic holiday specials older than me and even my parents plays on the TV, that's my second favorite part of our family holiday.

So why am I not relaxed?

We always do Christmas Eve at Grammy and Gramps' house, which is the same modest three-bedroom seventies bungalow that my dad and uncles grew up in. Every single adult person in the family has offered to buy them something else and they refuse every time.

They have let Callie and Devin renovate the kitchen, Jessie

and Jordan put on a new roof, and Luc and Rose renovate the bathrooms, but they will not actually move. You could fit this entire house inside the garage of my family home, but I actually love it. I will admit though, I don't know how they raised my dad, Uncle Jordan, Uncle Cole, and Uncle Luc in such a confined space without someone being murdered.

Now, after stuffing our faces and getting tipsy, it's almost midnight. Gramps is asleep in his recliner, same as every year. Grams went to bed and told us all to lock up when we were done and she'd see us in the morning. Right before my dad wakes Gramps we do our usual family tradition. Tate, Grady, Theo, and I pose with an unaware, snoring gramps, making ridiculous faces, making rabbit ears up behind his head, and being idiots. We've done it every year since I was like ten and he first started dozing off.

Jordan and Dad chuckle as they snap the pic on their phones. "Definitely one for the Gram."

"Uncle J don't say stuff like that." Theo rolls his eyes. "It doesn't make you cool. It makes you weird."

Uncle Jordan flips his nephew the bird and we all laugh so loud that Gramps snuffles and his eyelashes flutter. Dad leans over and gives his shoulder a shake. "Time for bed, Dad."

"Right. Sure. Where's everyone?" His age-spotted hands grip the armrests as he starts to get to his feet.

"The girls are all on their way home already, with Luc. Jordy and I are gonna clean the kitchen before heading out," Dad explains. "The boys are probably going to end up passed out in your extra bedrooms."

"That's the plan!" Theo says and throws himself down on one of the sofas.

Gramps smiles down at him sleepily. "Love you idiots."

He turns and wanders down the hall, Uncle Jordy and Dad following him a little bit to make sure he doesn't sway too much.

Gramps had four spiked egg nogs, which is two more than his limit. When he's closed the door to his room, both my uncle and dad head into the kitchen.

Grady scoops up the last of the mulled wine and hands me a glass before keeping the other for himself. Theo has a Bailey's over ice in his hand and Tate is drinking a spiked egg nog. He's consumed much more of it than Gramps and his aqua-green eyes are glassy. He's sitting on an ottoman near the fire watching the flames dance.

I stretch out on the couch Theo isn't on, which leaves Gramps' recliner for Grady. He drops into it and the springs squeak in protest. "Don't break that thing you redheaded yeti."

He smirks at me. "Fuck you very much."

"I think he means Merry Christmas and may the spirit of the season fill your cup," Theo replies and lifts his glass in the air like he's cheers-ing the Christmas tree in the corner of the room.

"You're cut off," I mumble.

"Someone *please* confirm that Tenley didn't pull my name in the family gift exchange again this year," Tate groans, pulling his eyes from the fire. "I really can't handle another one of her ceramic monstrosities."

"I think she got Theo this year," Grady tells him. "I overheard her and Harlow talking about it."

"Fuck my life," Theo moans.

They all keep yakking about Christmas presents and who is going to score first in the family game tomorrow. I appreciate the discussion has steered clear of my career. But their efforts to not talk about the elephant in the room have kind of made the elephant feel like he's sitting on my chest, especially when it's just us because our careers and the game are usually all we talk about. I'm uncomfortable.

"The jet lag getting to you yet, Tate?" Theo asks him. "You look sad or tired. I can't tell. So it's either jet lag or you're a sad panda because your Silver Bay bunny didn't come home for the holidays."

"Neither. And don't call her that," Tate grumbles. "She's not a puck bunny."

"No. Of course not," Grady quips. "She just fucks you, a professional hockey player, every time she sees you."

"She falls on his dick, it's purely accidental," Theo adds.

"You need to stop," Tate grumbles. "Diana is officially out of the picture. She got engaged to some British dude and is staying in London. Mallory emailed me about it last week. I think I'm more upset Mal is staying with her. She's a good friend."

"She's an Echolls," Grady grumbles.

"Fuck off with that. She moved to England to get away from her family," Tate counters. "Now change the subject before I bolt."

"Well if we can't pick on you, and we can't pick on Con what the hell are we supposed to do?" Theo asks and then his brown eyes flare and he realizes his mistake.

"Why can't you pick on me?" I ask, raising both my eyebrows and letting my eyes scan the room. Grady is looking at Theo. Theo is looking at Tate. Tate is looking at Grady. No one is looking at me. "Fucking hell. Dad! What did you say to them?"

My dad's head appears in the entryway to the kitchen. "Me? What? Huh?"

"Oh for fuck's sake," I mutter and start to stand up. "Telling everyone not to pick on me isn't helping Dad. It makes it weirder."

"Well, I don't know what will help," he replies and the angst in his voice is another new thing, like the disappointment. Fucking great.

"Con, we don't know how to act. Not because of what's happening with your career, but because of how you're reacting to it," Uncle Jordan tells me as he, too, pops his head out of the entrance to the kitchen. He's holding a dish towel and wiping a wine glass. "You've never been so down."

"Do you blame me?" I ask like I've just been attacked but I know, deep down, that's not what my uncle is doing.

Theo, always the one to try and broker peace in the family, which I think he gets from his mom, my aunt Rose, sits straighter on the sofa. "Con, stop fighting with them so they can go back to cleaning the kitchen before they realize they forgot to ask us to help."

"Now that you bring it up..." Uncle Jordan starts.

"Nope! We're busy picking on Con because he doesn't want this to be weird" Tate tells his dad, standing up and walking over to me. "So, Con, time to tell me when you started hooking up with Mac Larue."

"Oh god," I moan, and Tate cups my shoulder and pushes me sideways so he can sit on the couch too.

"Dude, older woman. Nice score there," Theo says. "I had no idea Mac was even on your radar. Or that anyone was. You're a monk for hockey."

"I'm not a monk, Theo," I grumble as I sip my wine, which has cooled off almost too much. "I've had a few girlfriends in Brooklyn."

"Oh really? Well none of them were brought to Silver Bay so none of them were serious," Tate announces, because that *is* actually the standard for significant others in our family. If you bring them home to the madness, then they're special.

"And I'm not dating Mac," I explain as I sink into the comfy couch cushions, the wine finally loosening the knot between my shoulder blades. It only took six glasses. "I needed a place to crash and had no idea she was living in the apartment above the barn."

"Do you ever look at the group chat?" Theo asks me, his big dark eyes wide with amazement. "Ten explained how Mac had been screwed over by Beckett and needed a place to live and she offered the barn apartment, like, *months* ago."

"You people yammer so much on that thing I have it on mute," I admit.

"I thought you learned your lesson about muting us when you showed up at the church the day of Harlow's wedding," Theo says, getting up and heading over to the bar in the corner to pull out another beer, even though I cut him off earlier. I know Dad and Uncle J won't want him having a fourth. He's not legal and we look the other way on holidays but there are limits. I don't say anything though, because he won't listen anyway. "If you hadn't muted the group, you would have known she pulled a runaway bride thing."

Right. That was a good time. Being the only Garrison to show up to a church full of the groom's family five minutes after they found out Harlow had backed out. Zero stars. Do not recommend.

"Yeah well, you guys literally ramble on at all hours about garbage," I say, twisting the cap off the beer. "Last time I looked at the chat, your dad was asking for step-by-step instructions on how to hook up his new modem. And Shelby was ranting on about something to do with seafood killing us all."

"She watched a doc on how the fishing industry is destroying the ocean," Theo clarifies. "And my dad is absolutely useless with technology. Harlow ended up going over and fixing it for him. Also, both those threads were from, like, seven months ago."

"You must have terrified the hell out of Mac just walking into her place without warning," Tate says, tipping his head back into the cushions and closing his eyes. I reach over and take the half-empty glass from his hand so that if he dozes off, he doesn't spill it.

"Yeah well, it was worse for me than her, I think," I say,

placing his mug on a coaster on the coffee table. It's a coaster with a Barons logo on it, hand-carved out of wood. Gramps made them himself with all the logos of all the teams we play or played for. It feels good covering this one. I might throw it into the fire later. "I was naked when she got home."

The three musketeers all burst out laughing after the appropriate amount of stunned silence. Grady is the first to recover, and after a snort, he says, "Holy shit. So is that why she decided to date you? She got a look at the goods and decided, not bad, so why not?"

"I mean he's got to look better than Beckett naked, right?" Tate muses out loud like I'm not in the room. "That jackass is scrawny and probably a selfish lover."

"I do not want to think about Beckett in bed," I announce firmly and take a long pull of the beer. "Or Mac in bed *with* him."

The thought gets me really riled up for some reason. Must be the booze. Theo walks through the living room, dropping his beer on a side table before sitting on top of Grady on Gramps' recliner. There's the obligatory wrestling match that ends with a loud thump as Theo's ass hits the floor and Grady, too drunk to keep his balance, slips out of the chair and jostles the end table.

"Boys!" Uncle Jordan hisses, poking his head out of the kitchen again. "If you wake up your grandparents, I will cut a hole in the lake and throw you all in it."

We all grumble some sorries. Uncle J disappears again.

"How about Mac in bed with you? Can we discuss that? Was it a good time? Was it a one-night stand? Because Shelby says that the whole hospital is buzzing about how you and Mac have been an actual thing for a while. Beckett's girlfriend is telling everyone, acting like he's the victim now because Mackenzie cheated on Beckett with you."

I almost choke on my beer. "The hospital is talking about it?"

I give in and pull my cell out of the back pocket of my pants. I find our WhatsApp family chat, which I've named *Welcome to the Hellmouth,* and start to scan the latest messages.

> SHELBY: OMG why didn't anyone tell me Conner is dating Mac Larue!

> AUNTIE JESSIE: Excuse me? What now?

> TATE: Really? She can do better.

I pause to look over at Tate and glare. He tries to look innocent. "Is there an issue?"

"Fuck you, cuz," I snark and he grins because he knows exactly what I'm referring to. I go back to reading my entire extended family gossip about my life.

> AUNTIE ROSE: Leave Con alone. He's in a rough place and if Mac brings him joy, then good.

> MAYHEM: Love Mac! But when the F did this start?

> MAMA C: I thought I walked in on something!

> DAD: Why is the hospital talking about this?

> SHELBY: Because apparently her ex saw them together! His GF Heather is telling everyone Mac cheated on Beckett with Conner.

"Oh Shelby, I wish you'd shut up," I mutter and take a bigger-than-normal gulp of my drink.

Theo starts to pull himself off the carpet. His nearly jet-black hair, which he's growing out and is a complete mess, somehow looks slightly less askew than it has all night. Grady's hair is equally askew but not because he's in that awkward phase while trying to grow it long like Theo.

Grady has always had questionable hairstyle choices. At the moment it's kind of long and he fills it with product and makes it high and wavy. Earlier tonight Harlow aptly and hilariously told him he looked like he's just been fucked... by a tornado. "My sister isn't normally a gossip so this is a big deal."

"It's not a big deal. I pretended to be Mac's boyfriend because Beckett showed up at her place and she was kind of distraught about it," I explain as Theo crosses the living room to get himself another beer. "She got really crushed by the asshole and I thought it would give her some confidence if she could show him she's moved on to bigger and better."

As soon as the words came out of my mouth I knew I was in trouble. Tate starts to belly laugh. Grady gives me the deepest 'get over yourself' stare and mutters, "Egomaniac."

The good thing about this family is they will always keep your ego in check.

"Wait... I thought you said she saw you naked?" Theo muses with pinched eyebrows like he's really confused and not just being a sarcastic jack-off. "Pretty sure she knows that bigger statement is a lie."

"Fuck you!" I bark but I'm laughing.

My dad and Uncle Jordan emerge from the kitchen. "We're heading home. You losers sticking around?"

"Dad, you're not supposed to call your only son a loser," Tate reprimands him with a look of mock sadness like he's taken it personally. "My poor self-esteem might crumble."

"You'd have to actually listen to me when I speak to have anything I say affect you," Jordan counters and both he and my dad high-five each other over the burn, which instantly makes it less burn-y.

"I think we'll stick around for one more," Theo announces, and Dad immediately walks over and plucks his mostly empty drink out of his hands.

"Nope," Dad says simply. "But you all are welcome to stick around, crash in our old bedrooms, and wake up to the smell of cinnamon waffles like we did as kids."

"Sold!" Grady announces too loudly and we all shush him.

"Do not wake them up," Dad says, pointing at each of us so we know he means business before he walks toward the front hall. "See you kids in the morning."

We all wave goodbye. Jordan stops after he puts on his coat and catches my eye. "Mac Larue huh? You know her dad might be older than both me and your dad, but he can, and will, kick your ass. Just a friendly warning."

Everyone snickers. "Nothing is happening."

Unfortunately.

The adults leave and we let Theo have a beer and then raid the remnants of the charcuterie board Dad and Uncle J just finished wrapping and storing in the fridge. At about two-thirty in the morning, Grady is reclined in Gramps' chair, snoring away. Tate is passed out on a couch. Theo and I walk down the hall toward the bedrooms that used to belong to our parents. I hold his shoulders, walking behind him to keep him from weaving too badly. I deposit him in the first bedroom and he immediately nose dives onto the bottom bunk. I make sure he's in the recovery position in case he pukes, which I doubt will happen but... better safe than sorry.

"Con-Con?" Theo murmurs barely audible. He hasn't called me Con-Con since he was, maybe ten.

"Yeah, T?"

"Brooklyn is no longer my number one hope for the draft,"

he slurs, half his mouth unmoving because it's crushed into the pillow. "If they draft me, I won't sign."

Awe. Theo doesn't get to control what team drafts him, no player does, but we all have hopes. I honestly didn't know the Barons was his. "Don't do that, T. Sign with whoever wants you. It's okay."

"I just wanted to play for them because you were there," he whispers.

"Fuck, kid," I whisper to myself because he's clearly passed out now. That was a drunken punch to the feels I wasn't expecting.

I close the door and walk into the bedroom next door. My dad shared it with Jordan for about a decade until he moved into a room in the basement and Uncle Luc moved in with Jordan. I drop onto the bed left of the window, strip down to my undies, and pull back the covers. My phone is almost dead and I don't have a cable because I didn't know I'd be staying. I open up my contacts and stare at Mac's name. And then I hit record and leave her a voice message.

"I just wanted to say Merry Christmas. And let you know if we hadn't been interrupted the other day, I was going to give you the fuck of your life." I pause and think about how good she felt wrapped around my torso and all the things I would have done to her if we'd made it to her bedroom. My free hand slips under the covers and rubs my growing cock. "But I heard you tell Ten you didn't want me. So I guess you got what you wanted for Christmas, which is not getting the fuck of your life. From me. But, Mac, princess, you missed out because damn, it would have been the absolute most earth-shattering time you've ever had."

Well, even my drunken brain can hear how obscenely bold that sounds. I swallow and sigh and close my eyes. "Seriously, though, I wouldn't want you to regret anything. Regret *me*, so I am glad we got interrupted, for your sake. But can you please stop bringing your A-game? Because you kiss like you want me even though you said you didn't. It's confusing. Also confusing is the fact that your smile makes me forget my life is circling the drain. So anyway I'm gonna think of you tonight and do very bad things to myself. Ho. Ho. Ho, princess."

I hit end and pass out to the sound of my cousin banging on the door and calling me every name in the book for sticking him with the couch.

Chapter 12

Mac

I walk into the break room and don't see one familiar face. That's because none of the coworkers I've become friendly with have volunteered to work on Christmas Eve. They all have friends and family in town. So the faces staring back at me when I enter are either loners like me or new employees who didn't have the seniority to avoid the shift.

There's only one nurse two doctors and an orderly in there, but all of them stop chatting as soon as I open the door. They all stare at me, not a welcoming smile in the bunch. I mean no one is trying to eviscerate me with their eyes but the looks are cool, aloof, and slightly judgey. Apparently, even the skeleton crew tonight has heard the rumor Heather is spreading that I cheated on Beckett with Conner Garrison. A rumor I stupidly started myself.

I flash a brief smile at all of them, walk to the coffee machine, make a quick coffee, and then head right back out. I should have opted to be on call tonight instead of coming in. The head of the residents told me I could. But I didn't want to sit at home alone, so here I am, getting treated like the outcast in a high school dramedy.

There's a break room down the hall with two beds. If I'm lucky, I will find it empty. As it turns out, I am lucky and it's blissfully empty and dark. I put my untouched coffee on the small table, drop onto one of the cots, and close my eyes. But I can't resist the urge to re-listen to that drunken message Conner left me a couple hours ago. So I pull my phone out of the pocket of my scrubs and hit play.

His words bring heat to my cheeks, just like when I listened to it for the first time. And the seventeen consecutive times right after that. Now eighteen. There wasn't a single word in that message that didn't make my insides fizzle and pop.

Yes, he was drunk but... you could *hear* the authenticity in his words and the need in the way his voice quivered a little. I hit play *again*. When the message ends I almost fan myself.

Had I responded to that message at all, in any way? Nope. Because what the hell was I supposed to say? This whole thing was too much to process. Two weeks ago I hadn't thought about Conner Garrison for more than a hot second in years. Now I thought about him like he was my Roman Empire.

Before I can listen to his drunken confession again, I get a text from the ER telling me we have an ambulance arriving and it's all hands on deck.

My heart sinks, not because I can't indulge my Conner vice, but because no one should be in an ambulance on Christmas. I haul myself out of bed and out of the break room and rush to the emergency department. The thing about interning at a small-town hospital like Silver Bay is that, even though I have a specialty, I am still floating to any department that needs me sometimes, like on holidays.

It's a horrible situation. A seven-year-old boy tried to climb out his bedroom window and onto the roof of his house to prove Santa Claus was real. He fell. After the initial assessment, I'm asked to handle the parents as the two other doctors on staff stabilize the child and the nurses call Portland and prepare his transfer. He's going to need an orthopedic surgeon immediately and Portland is the place to do that.

Yes, I have the training to work through this kind of crisis with the parents and the child's siblings, of which he has three, which is why the other doctors assigned this task to me but prepared or not, it takes an emotional toll. Luckily the child should make a full recovery after several operations for his broken arms and legs. The parents take little comfort in that right now, which is fair. I make sure they've got a way to Portland and then when they head off to follow the ambulance with their son, I call child services, because it's protocol, so a social worker can meet them at the next hospital.

When that crisis is over, the sun is pushing through a bunch of gray clouds and my shift is about half an hour from completion. All I want is my bed. My phone buzzes as I head to the office I share with another resident and I pluck it from my lab coat.

Right. I promised the fam a moment. Might as well be now. I open the door to my office, flick on the lights, and FaceTime my dad. He answers immediately and his big, gregarious smile fills the screen. His face is, as usual, scruffy and covered in nicks and scars from his previous hockey career and his own rough childhood.

"Mac!" he exclaims and then turns his head away from the screen. "Baby, our baby is here. Christmas can start!"

"Oh, hey Mac! We miss you, kid!" My mom scurries over and after some commotion and a second where I'm looking at the ceiling of the kitchen in our Hampton's house, I see both their faces again. Mom is sitting on Dad's lap and if I squint real hard I can see the shoreline out the kitchen window behind them.

"I miss you guys too. And Cassia. Where is she?" I ask about my sister.

"Upstairs," Mom replies and then raises her voice to yell. "Cassia! Mac is on the phone!"

My sister, Cassia, came into the family five years ago. Even though I was long out of the house and a full-grown adult, I made it a point to go home lots that first year and try to bond with her. Cassia, like me, had been a runaway. But unlike me, her birth parents weren't dead. They considered *her* dead because she was transgender. They booted her out of the house at just ten years old. After bouncing around a foster system that isn't always safe for trans people for two years, she ended up at my mom's charity, which helps teens who have been failed by the system, live independently. Cassia was too young to enroll in my mom's program so Mom immediately fostered her, which led to adoption within the year. Unlike me, Cassia knew a good thing when she found it. She's fit in with our family like the link we never knew we were missing.

"You look exhausted, Mac. And thin," Mom notes. "Is everything alright?"

"Just work," I say.

"Mom! Don't tell your daughters they look like crap." I hear Cassia's voice as she enters the kitchen and walks into frame behind our parents. She smiles at me, but it immediately turns into a yawn. "I think you look *great*. Miss you!"

"Miss you too," I say with a chuckle as Mom looks horrified.

"I didn't mean it *that* way. I just..." Mom looks positively distraught.

"It's okay. I do feel like crap. It's six in the morning and I've been here since seven last night," I explain.

"Don't let her off the hook, Mac," Cassia says with a grin.

Then she leans in and kisses Mom on the cheek to prove she's just joking. "Also, I'm exhausted too. These two get up way too early. I need my beauty sleep."

"It's Christmas!" Dad argues. Cassia rolls her eyes and Dad turns the conversation back to me. "We wish you could have come home."

"Next year, when I'm an actual doctor, I can close my practice for a few days and be with you guys, I promise," I say and mean it, but the idea seems so far off. It's hard to believe I'll be an actual psychiatrist in less than six months.

"And we won't miss you so much because we'll see you all the time because you'll be back in New York City, right?" Dad goes on. "That's still the plan?"

It is not exactly the plan anymore. To be honest, I don't know where I'll set up my practice. I had gone into medicine intending to return to New York but now... Beckett aside, I really like Maine. I had started looking at Portland, which is a great, vibrant city a couple hours from Silver Bay close to the ocean and with a need for doctors of all kinds.

"Mac? Are you thinking of not coming back to New York?" Mom asks, and she doesn't sound upset, just shocked.

"I've been thinking of Portland."

"Oregon?" Dad gasps, and I smile. He doesn't want me all the way over on the west coast.

"Maine."

He actually sighs audibly in relief. Cassia laughs in the background. "I guess that means you won't be thrilled if I get into one of those West Coast colleges I applied to."

"I'll be very proud and happy," Dad responds without hesitation. "But not as proud or happy as I would be if you got into an East Coast school."

"Dad!" I bark and shake my head as Cassia laughs at his honesty.

"What? I don't want empty nest syndrome," Dad says. "I need you both close. And for the record, I'm good with Portland, Maine. I like the idea."

"Really?" I have to admit that shocks me a little.

"We have news too. Your father has gotten a call from a hockey team," Mom announces.

"What? Really? Coaching again?"

Dad coached for a decade after he retired. First with the Barons and then with the New York City Monarchs. He was actually an assistant coach with the Barons when Conner was drafted by them. "They haven't made an offer, but if they do... I'd consider it."

That's a big deal. He stopped coaching because the teams making offers were too far from New York and Mom's charity is tied there. "Mom? Cassia? You guys on board with this? What team? Are you leaving New York? All of you? What about your foundation?"

"Whoa! Hold up. I'm not going anywhere, not forever anyway. The foundation is my baby and I will always run it. And New York is our home, full stop," Mom tells me, and Cassia nods in agreement in the background while pouring coffee. "We'll figure out the logistics if it happens. We can make anything work."

I want my parents' partnership. I've always wanted it. They are a great example of unconditional love and open communication. They haven't always had it easy, and it's not that they don't have arguments, but they work at it. At all of it. I never had anything resembling that with Beckett, even though it's what I wanted to have. So why did I give him years of my life? It seems so obvious looking at it now, in the rearview, that we were never going to be the unit my parents are. How did I ignore that?

"Dad, if some player has a giant contract, what are the

chances they'll be scooped up from waivers?" Okay... why did I blurt that out?

"What?" Dad sounds absolutely gobsmacked because I don't talk about hockey, ever. He blinks as he recovers enough to give me an answer. "Well, it makes it very difficult. And it's rare a player with a big contract gets put on waivers because if the team is offloading them, they can usually find a buyer. They'd make every attempt to trade them first to get something more than salary cap room out of the loss."

I chew my bottom lip as I absorb this. "Can team management be vindictive? Like would they shoot themselves in the foot for no reason other than they didn't like a guy on the team??

"What's with fifty questions, hockey edition?" Cassia asks and she pops into view over Dad's left shoulder. "I thought you were like me—entirely indifferent about the sport."

"I was. I am." I chew my lip again. "It's just that I'm surrounded by hockey here. Silver Bay has kind of made the sport its entire personality because half the league is from here."

Dad snorts. "Yeah, there's something in the water over there."

"Anyway, never mind, I was just curious, and no better person to ask than our family expert." I smile at my dad. He grins back and gives me a wink.

"Okay well love ya sis but we gotta go open our gifts," Cassia says. "So I can get back to sleep."

Dad jerks his thumb in her direction. "Can you believe her? What kid wants sleep over presents?"

"Wish you were here, Mac," Mom says and blows me a kiss.

"Do you need anything?" Dad asks.

"You guys sent me my gifts and I opened them last night before the shift." I shake my head. "You spent too much. I told you I don't need anything."

They got me a subscription to a food box for gourmet meals,

a pair of durable yet somehow very stylish winter boots, and a hefty gift certificate to Sephora, which is where I get my fancy bubble bath from so the timing on that is perfect. My brain is thinking of Conner again as I tell my family I love them and end the video call.

I check the time on my phone. It's just a minute past seven. My shift is officially over. I open up the door to my office and jump. Because someone is standing in the hallway in front of the door—Conner Garrison.

Chapter 13

Mac

"Hey."

"Hi."

"So... Surprise!" He holds up a glass container.

I stare at it, unable to make out the contents. It looks like... bread or cake or something? When I slide my gaze to his eyes he says, "I couldn't bear the thought of you without a decent meal on Christmas morning so I brought you a couple of my grams' world-famous cinnamon waffles."

"Waffles?" I repeat dumbly, and my hands move to my hair. Do I look okay? Wait, why do I care? I let my hands drop to my sides. "You brought me breakfast?"

Conner nods and I step out into the hall to join him, the door to my office closing with a soft click behind me. "Yeah. I saw the way you kinda pass out as soon as you get home from a shift. And I also saw the pathetic contents of your fridge."

"Ouch. That's harsh," I mutter and he gives me a flash of a smile.

"I get it, you're busy." He holds up the container again and pulls a small one from the pocket of that puffy yellow coat of his. "Homemade blueberry syrup. Trust me, you don't want to miss this."

I look at the syrup in the second container, and then I glance down the hall where the nurse's station for the psychiatric ward is located. No one is there at the moment, thankfully. The last thing I need is an audience for Conner's Uber Eats impression. Crown prince of hockey bringing me breakfast? That would set the rumor mill on fire so intensely it would burn the hospital to the ground. "Apparently Heather has told everyone I cheated on Beckett with you. Hysterical he gets to be the victim in this suddenly, and it's my fault."

"Huh." Conner looks slightly confused, his thick eyebrows furrowed kind of adorably, I hate to admit. He looks sleepy and like he didn't even brush his hair, which is sticking up a little on the left side, but it's also adorable. And when it hits me that he went out of his way at the crack of dawn on Christmas Day to bring me something to eat... well, that is beyond adorable. It's downright thoughtful that Conner Garrison is taking care of me. "Well, then you should rethink letting me go to the party with you."

"Why? How would that help?"

"By the time the party rolls around I won't be a Baron anymore so people will be throwing you fleeting looks of sympathy that you hitched yourself to a faulty wagon." His strong, stubble-covered jaw flexes as he probably pictures it in his head. "They'll feel sorry for you instead of judging you."

I stare at him. "Is your entire self-worth attached to your skates? Because it seems that way, Conner, and that's something you should look into."

"It's not my self-worth," he replies, kind of annoyed. He feels attacked, I get it, but kid gloves won't work on him.

"Okay, so stop acting like it is then," I counter, and he frowns at me. "You think people are really going to be like 'Oh poor

Mac, she's stuck with a guy who still makes millions, is the eldest son of the most respected family in town, has a body that was built for sex, and a personality that could charm the venom out of a snake. But he isn't an NHL player anymore so none of that matters. She's better off alone."

We stare at each other under the fluorescent lights in the stark mint-green corridor. His expression hardens, muscle by muscle tightening in his face, and the look in those pretty eyes with all the warm colors swirled together turns cold.

"Here." He hands me the two containers. "If you don't like the waffles, I also brought a dozen donuts from Dick's for the rest of the staff. Just snag one of those."

"You brought everyone donuts? That's..." I can't find the word.

He shrugs, shoving his hands in his pockets and turning his attention to the nurse's station where one of them has returned and is smiling brightly, lifting the box of donuts up off the counter. "Dick's was opened when I drove by and I just thought that the people who gave up their Christmases to be here, helping others, deserved it. Anyway, have a good Christmas, Mac. Sorry to bother you."

He starts to turn away from me, and I instantly reach out. My hands are holding the containers, which are still warm, even the one with syrup. He literally rushed over to give me these while they were still warm. Oh, my heart... "I'm sorry. You are being really great and I'm being a bitch."

He stops trying to walk away and glances at me over his shoulder. "Bitch is a little harsh. And I'm being a bit of a grump now too. I don't like being psycho-analyzed."

"Nobody does," I reply. He looks truly humbled and a little bit lost. I resist the urge to reach out and hug him, mostly because I can't figure out how to do it with the food containers in my hands. "Have you been doing what I suggested? Taking it day by day and not catastrophizing?"

"Mostly." He nods and dips his head a little as he steps closer. "I've been working out, following my regular training routine, eating right, studying some old games to see where I can improve, and studying other teams."

"And emotionally, what are you doing to fight off the negativity?" I ask gently because this is me doing exactly what he seems to hate, my job. On him.

"I've been hanging with my cousins," he says. "Hard to be in a bad mood with them around. Oh, and I've been sending inappropriate drunken voice messages to this hot woman I know. That's been fun."

Our eyes lock. His mouth turns upward a little at the edges, sheepishly. I have to look away, a small smile of my own growing on my face. "Yeah... about that... I wanted to clear something up there."

"No need to explain yourself," he says quickly and steps back, putting more space than I'd like between us. "I overheard you talking to Tenley in your bedroom before I left with Callie that day. You changed your mind about what we were about to do. You have every right. I don't need an explanation."

"You overheard me trying to convince myself, out loud, that something so incredibly out-of-character was wrong. Even though I wanted it so bad I was literally shaking."

"It?"

I glance down the hall. Now there are two nurses at the station but both seem so distracted by the donuts they aren't watching us. I turn my gaze back to him. "You. I wanted *you* so bad I was shaking. And I panicked so I lied to your cousin because I didn't want to admit the truth to her or myself."

He takes a step closer again. Damn, he's gorgeous. His strong, stubbled jaw relaxes a little, and his eyes hold a cocky gleam that is damn hot. "So you can psycho-analyze yourself too, huh?"

I shrug. "That wasn't exactly hard to unravel. I mean, no offense Conner, but your self-esteem isn't very good if you think there is a woman on the planet that would have turned you down in that situation. And FYI, that has nothing to do with what league you play in."

My heart is hammering in my chest and I can't quite catch my breath. I'm also keenly aware that both the nurses and now an orderly are chomping away on donuts at the end of the hall and have finally noticed us. They're leaning on the nurse's station, staring at us.

Conner doesn't seem to notice though. He stares at only me, his gaze heavy, and it makes my heart beat even harder. "I brought these waffles over as an excuse to see you so I could figure out a way to apologize for that message. I was..."

"Blunt. Direct. Crude." I swallow and lock eyes with him.

He blinks and then he gives me this smile that almost makes my legs forget to support my body. I want to collapse from the desire that is suddenly pumping through me. "And you liked it?"

"Loved it."

"When do you get off work?"

"Right now."

"Maybe I can follow you home and give you that thing I mentioned in the message?"

The fuck of your life.

His words from that message, all rough and slurred and full of confidence, fill my brain. He steps closer, his hand reaches up, and he gently holds my hip.

"Are you... is this because people are watching?" I whisper as he leans even closer and now I can feel his breath on my cheek.

"All I see is you, princess," he replies, his breath dancing across my cheek as he moves his lips there, kissing me lightly before whispering, "So?"

I can't believe I'm saying this but I am. "Let's go."

He pulls me into his side with an arm around my shoulders that feels both possessive and casual at the same time. We walk like that right past the nurses station and down the hall, past the main reception desk where we are met with wide eyes from the guy working there, who clearly recognizes Conner.

Once we walk through the automated doors and the cool morning slaps me in the face, I wait. For the wake-up call. For the cold light of day to force some sense into my brain. But it doesn't make me change my mind. I keep walking right to my car and after I slide in and put the food on the seat in front of me, I let him lean in, kiss me gently on the lips, and when he says, "I'll follow you there" I don't say no.

Chapter 14

Conner

The drive to the barn apartment is quick and easy because literally, no one is up at this hour on Christmas Day. Probably a good thing because Mac won't have time to talk herself out of this. Random hook-ups aren't in her wheelhouse. They aren't exactly my area of expertise but I've had a few. They can serve a purpose in certain situations, and I know both Mac and I are in those situations. I am in desperate need of a positive distraction from the impending doom and she needs to get her groove back after a bad breakup.

This isn't as off-base or insane as I know she's thinking it is.

When we get to the barn, I park beside her car and jump out so I can hold her door open. She looks... well, a little panicked. So as soon as she gets out of the car and I swing her door closed, I press her up against it and cover her mouth with mine. The kiss is short but deep, and she melts into it, almost dropping the container with the waffles.

I take it from her. "Let's get these, and you, inside."

She nods, and one minute later she's peeling off her coat as I put the waffles and syrup down on the kitchen island. Our eyes connect and a ripple of heat shimmies down my spine. "You should really eat these while they're warm. They're better this way."

She shakes her head. "That's what microwaves are for. Besides, I'm not hungry. For food."

And that's that. This is happening. It's a Christmas miracle. Thank you, Santa. She walks toward me and I walk toward her and then we're making out like horny teenagers in front of the sad little string of blinking Christmas lights in her living room window.

Our lips are urgent, and our tongues are ravenous. Her hands are working frantically, unzipping my jacket and pushing it off my shoulders. It falls to the ground. I reach around her, palming her ass in both my hands without a lick of hesitation. I pull her against me, and she doesn't resist. She leans into it, wrapping her arms around my neck, slipping her fingers into my hair, and tugging on the messy ends.

My cock is stiff as a board, wedged between our bodies, and I push my hips into her, squeezing her ass at the same time. It's full and lush and feels like heaven under my palms. She mews and I swear to god my dick grows. She is very quickly making me absolutely wild with want. Jesus, it's crazy.

"You feel so fucking good," I whisper into her mouth before kissing her one more time, my tongue sliding over hers, my teeth dragging across her bottom lip before I pull back again. "I need to feel more of you, princess."

"I'm not a princess," she murmurs, her voice breathy as my hands slide from her ass to grab hold of the edge of her scrub top. "Don't treat me like one."

"Right then." I step back and in one hard, fast motion I yank the top up.

She lifts her arms without hesitation and I pull it right over her head. She's left in nothing but a simple black sports bra from the waist up. Her ponytail holder has slipped with the tug of the shirt over her head, half her curls tumbling out, so I reach out grab it, and tug it out, dropping it on the floor with her shirt. Then I wrap an arm around her waist, reveling in the feel of the bare skin of her back against my forearm, and I tug her to me again. My lips pull her earlobe into my mouth and I suck and she mews again and my dick dances in my pants.

I kiss her roughly because she seems to like it. Shit. Mac is emotionally mature and direct and decisive, and it's even more intimidating than the fearless, cocky confidence she sauntered around with when she was a kid. I feel a flutter of inadequacy that I've become much too familiar with lately, at least professionally, and I'm not about to let it infiltrate this too.

So I brush my knuckles against her cheek and her thick, dark eyelashes flutter like a hummingbird. my hand reaches up to move back another wayward curl. "You should probably kiss me again, so we can get to that sex part."

I smile at her words. She smiles back and adds, "

"A-game, Garrison. Bring it."

Challenge accepted. And boy does she ever. I kiss her like I own her, hard, strong, without restraint, and she responds in kind.

I pull back from the kiss, after giving her bottom lip a little nip and look at her while our foreheads rest against each other, and run a hand over her messy curls. "Being back here, with all this career drama playing out in front of every person I know and love hasn't been easy. It's just plain sucked," I whisper and then kiss her quickly for courage so I can continue with this obscenely vulnerable confession. "Running into you has been the only highlight. In fact, it makes it all bearable. And now, this is the only place I want to be. Here, getting naked and tasting every fucking inch of you."

She lets out a noise that's a cross between a sigh and a moan and then she's kissing me, long and hard, as I walk us into her bedroom. Even though we're alone in the apartment, I close the bedroom door, because the last logical brain cell I have that hasn't been splintered by lust knows that about forty members of my overbearing, nosy family know how to get into this apartment, I close the door. And then press her back into it, using it to help me hold her up so I can move my hands, not that I don't love grabbing her ass because, Lord, it is one fine ass. But I need to touch more of her, all of her. She's wearing far too many clothes. We both are.

As my mouth moves to her throat I press my hips into the center of her to keep us against the door. Mac moves her hands from my hair to the back of my shirt and as she fists it, she yanks it up. I lift my arms and let her pull it over my head and then immediately bury my face in her neck again. I inhale deeply as I suck the skin there. She smells like peaches and I instantly decide it's my new favorite fruit.

"Conner..." I pull back to see those light eyes of hers sweeping across my exposed chest as her hands slide up my shoulders. "You're... unreal. Like how does one person look like this without Photoshop?"

I smile, because who the hell wouldn't. "Hockey, babe."

"Praise Lord Stanley," Mac whispers as her hands glide over my pecs greedily.

"Actually Lord Stanley didn't invent hockey. He just donated the trophy. The sport was invented in the United Kingdom of all places and..." She's staring at me with the deadliest STFU expression. "And I am going to shut up and get you naked before I ruin the mood entirely. Please feel free to go back to ogling me like a lion eyes raw meat."

"Thank you, I will," Mac replies and kisses me quick, but hard.

My fingers trace their way up her rib cage, finding their way to the black mesh edging of her sports bra. She makes these incredible fluttery moans as I explore, fingertips skirting the edge of the fabric and thumb pads sliding over the swells of her breasts, rubbing her pebbled nipples through the thin fabric. Finally, I have to put her down so I can explore even more. I wrap my arms around her back and feel her legs hook even tighter around my bare waist.

As eager as I am, I don't throw her down on the bed. I lay her down gently and hover above her, slowly lowering myself onto her. I'm savoring every second of this that I can because I don't know how we got here or if we'll ever get here again.

Chapter 15

Mac

We learn in school that self-analyzing is not a good idea. It's hard to see yourself objectively and you don't usually have the ability to review the motives behind your own behavior. I have a mentor, Doctor Madeline Fleury, who I check in with every week about work and my personal life, but not this week because of Christmas. All psych interns do this, to review cases but also to make sure our own mental health is on track. Madeline, as she insists I call her, has been really great helping me navigate my breakup with Beckett. I don't know what she'd say about what I'm about to do. Is it reckless? Is it a bad idea? Is it the start of something? Is it foolish? All of the above? All I know is I've had a really rough year and I just want to have sex with a hot boy. So that's what I'm going to do.

Fooling around with a hot, nice man built like he was meant for sex is a gift. I won't turn it down. Conner pulls back again, and the heated look in his eyes cools a little. "Mac, princess, tell me you want it, loud and clear. If you meant a word of that you said to Ten—"

I wrap my arms around his thick neck and pull his lips back

to mine. I want to be wild and free, even if the potential consequences scare the shit out of me. "I want you to give me the fuck of my life. You promised, now deliver."

Conner grins, wild and bold as he rolls off the bed, and stands beside it, reaching for the front of his joggers. Reality slaps me in the face. I'm in way over my head. Conner probably has more sexual conquests than hockey trophies. And he has *a lot* of hockey trophies. I'm not exactly a naive virgin but I haven't had a real one-night stand. Beckett was supposed to be my college fling and we ended up with each other for years. So will I be able to impress Mr. Sexy Skates here?

"Mac... you look like you're changing your mind..." he whispers, leaning forward and pressing his mouth to the sensitive curve of skin above my clavicle. "You can. I get it."

"No. I just..." I let out a sheepish giggle. "I mean, has anyone ever turned you down?"

"Honestly? No. But there's a first time for everything," Conner replies. "And it's okay. My ego can take another hit."

"My only thought right now is should I take off my pants or should you," I reply boldly, and he grins down at me.

"I'll take off mine while you take off yours," he suggests. "Teamwork makes the dream work."

I giggle at him as I reach for the waistband on my scrubs. He drops his joggers in one quick motion and if he was wearing underwear, it went down to his ankles with them. I can't help but stare at his erection because, I mean, it's *right there*. And last time I saw it, I was too panicked and embarrassed to take a good look. Now... well damn, how can I not?

"This is not an even playing field," he murmurs and palms his cock. "I'm naked and you've still got on your sports bra and underwear."

"Then maybe you should do something about that," I tell him.

He's back on the bed before I can blink. His hands slip under my bra, and the rough patches on the pads of his fingers from his hockey gloves send a deep quiver down my spine as they graze my nipples before he pushes the whole bra up and off my body. I exhale a moan and he kisses it away before moving his mouth to my breasts. He sucks and licks and nips at my right and then my left until the pulse between my legs pounds like a snare drum in a marching band.

I've heard that a woman can come from breast play but I never believed it until now. But I don't want to come this way, I want to come *with* him, not without him, so I reach for those panties he forgot to take off. I push at them as best I can, with an urgency I can't be bothered to hide. Without taking his lips off my skin, he helps, and the next thing I know he's using his feet to push my underwear down my legs and off my ankles.

"Oh god. Oh fuck. Please stop!" I pant and wiggle. He nips my left nipple one last, quick time and immediately sits up in the space between my legs.

He puts his hands up like I'm holding a gun, but his smile is anything but fearful or worried. "Sorry. Were you going to come?"

"Yes. How did you know?"

He puts his arms down and shrugs. "It's been known to happen."

"You talented bastard," I hiss back, like I'm offended by his arrogance when in fact I'm even more turned on by it. Because it's not arrogance, it's confidence.

"If you'd like to come another way, I'm happy to oblige," he offers, his eyes slipping down my naked body. He's looking right at me, the bare space between my legs, and I am flushing from head to toe now.

Conner may be fine being naked, in broad daylight, on full display, and letting me drink him in like he's a free margarita at an all-inclusive resort. But I'm a little less comfortable and confident with him doing it to me. And he's definitely doing just that. Those hazel eyes linger and stare.

"Mac?" he prompts, but now he's palming his erection again and I'm transfixed. "Tongue? Fingers? Cock? You got a toy you want me to pleasure you with? Whatever you want, I'm game."

How does one respond to a perfect man offering any and all sexual favors? I can't seem to find the right words, so instead I lean forward, grip his neck, and when our lips connect again I push my tongue into his mouth. The way he responds gives me a jolt of much-needed confidence. It's not that I'm shy or even unsure. I don't have sexual hang-ups. But I just can't shake the feeling that we're playing with fire. Not that it's going to stop me. I'm perfectly willing... eager even, to get burned.

Conner isn't a patient man, apparently, because while I'm gaining confidence from the kiss, he moves his hand between my legs and dips two fingers into me, sliding right in thanks to the fact that I'm so turned on. I can feel his response—a smile—against my lips.

He gives a husky command as his fingers move and my knees quiver. "Touch me too."

I let a hand slip from his shoulder and find his cock. It's warm, thick, and hard. I give it a firm, slow tug. His breath rushes from him in a heavy, happy exhale. I want to smile at bringing him pleasure, but his thumb is doing the perfect dance over my clit and I'm once again on the brink. "I think I want you to do more."

"You think?" Conner repeats, and I rub his cock, which earns me a deep, satisfied grumble. "I need you to *know*."

"Oh fuck..." I pant and push my hips forward. His fingers move in the perfect rhythm just like his thumb. "I know. I *know* I want more."

"Spell it out for me Mac. In glorious, graphic detail."

He's still. Everything has stilled. My eyes flutter open and I tip my head back just a little so his handsome face is in focus. "I want you to fuck me, Conner. As hard and as long as you can."

With his free hand he gently grabs my chin, tilts my head, and claims my mouth again. There's a new energy in his kiss. It's almost feral and it confirms he wants me as badly as I want him. Again, this is all unfathomable, really. I mean hell, we haven't seen each other in years, and I never ever thought this was how I would be spending the early hours of ...

"Please for the love of God tell me you have condoms."

Condoms? Right. Of course. We need those. And... I don't have them.

"Ah... nope." I sigh and just like that, the mood pops like a balloon hitting a pin cushion. I squeeze my eyes shut and try not to look at him because what grown single woman, let alone a medical professional who knows all the risks, doesn't have condoms? "I swore off sex when Beckett and I broke up, and men as a whole, so I just didn't think I would ever need to have any in the house."

His shoulders sag. Then his hand is gone, leaving me feeling exposed and a tinge embarrassed. I open my eyes. He looks like his goldfish just died. "You've got to have some, right? I mean, you're a single, professional hockey player. You probably keep the condom industry alive. You... are *single*, right?"

Oh shit, I never even asked if he had a girlfriend. My bad. I mean I'm not an idiot. I know *some* of these professional athletes play fast and loose with the definition of 'committed relationship' and it isn't always the ones you'd think. But Conner gets this cute little line between his eyebrows as I wait for confirmation. "I wouldn't be trying to fuck you if I wasn't single, Mac. I was raised right. Also, I was coming home to admit defeat to my family and suffer through the holidays as a failure. I didn't think a condom was required for that. I didn't plan ahead and I just assumed you'd have them."

I'm suddenly filled with defiance. Like level ten 'We're not gonna take it' mode. I blink and bite my lip as I try to talk myself out of it, but then I look down. He's still as hard as a rock. "You know for a guy who has it all, looks, sex appeal, talent, charm, intelligence, you sure as hell give up easily. You need more fight in you, Con. For your career and this.

Chapter 16

Conner

Before I have a second to figure out what the hell she's talking about, Mac's palms hit my shoulders with a little smack and I'm tipping over. My back hits the mattress with a little bounce, my head at the foot of the bed, and then she's climbing over me. I just see her hair, wild curls bouncing everywhere, and then she's dropping lower. And... holy hockey sticks.

Mac's hand is around the base of my shaft again, but now her lips are on my tip. White hot heat shimmies down my spine. She circles her tongue around the head gently, like she's tentatively tasting ice cream for the first time in her life. And then, the flat of her tongue swirls across me again, harder. Like ice cream is her new favorite thing. I exhale on the back of a moan and reach for her, my hands landing in her hair. "Mac... fuck me."

She's in full swing now, her hand sliding up and down my shaft as her head bobs in a perfect rhythm and I can't keep my thoughts straight. All I can do is drown in the sensations of her full lips around my cock and her hot, wet mouth sucking and licking every inch of me. *Every* inch.

I'm going to come and it's going to be embarrassingly fast if she doesn't stop the magic with that mouth. "Oh God... Mac... Wait..."

She pulls back, my cock slipping from her lips with a wet pop. She's smiling just a little bit, and her light eyes glint with something mischievous. "Are you changing your mind, or just trying not to come."

"Latter," I pant out.

"M'kay. Not stopping." And then she's swirling her tongue around my length again. I give up and give in to the delicious heat, friction, and pressure of this relentless, very goal-oriented, and incredibly gorgeous woman. It's not even three minutes later I have to warn her the end is nigh. But she doesn't move, she lets me come in her mouth, greedily sucking every last drop from me.

I lay there, fighting for breath and the ability to feel my limbs again. I would honestly just pass out I'm so spent but... it's my turn. Or her turn, I guess. I'm betting I'm just as eager to taste her as she is to find release. And now I have a goal. She's going to break apart on my tongue in less than three minutes. I can't be the only quick shooter here.

"Come here," I demand, trying to sound like I'm in control.

The mattress shifts and then she's straddling my waist and leaning forward. Her hair wild around her face. She's still smiling that sexy confident smile. I push myself up on my elbows and kiss her. I keep kissing her and lift off my arms, grabbing her ass and pulling her whole body forward. I break the kiss to lay back on the mattress and pull her up as I slide down.

"Conner you don't have to—"

"I want to," I correct. Her bare pussy is hovering inches from my mouth and she's looking down at me with wide eyes. Her skin starts to flush around her cheeks. She's exposed to me in every intimate way possible and it's hitting her hard that we're doing things to each other no one would believe considering we barely know each other anymore.

I push that thought from my head, close my eyes, and press my mouth to her perfect pussy. She's wet and sweet and with just the first pass of my tongue over her folds her thighs quiver. When my tongue slides up again, I make sure to press the flat of it over her clit before pausing and giving it all the extra attention it deserves. She starts to mewl, all breathy and shaky, and then her hips buck just a little, rolling and grinding. She's desperate for release. I open my eyes and see her hands on her breasts, her nipples pinched in between her fingers. It's the hottest thing I've ever seen.

I grab her ass as she pushes her wet, eager center at me again and I guide her across my tongue, steering her by the grip I've got on that firm round ass. "Con...ner... I... yes!"

Mackenzie Larue, my childhood crush, is coming on my face. And it's fucking heaven. I feel good and valuable and happy for the first time in a long time. So I promise myself, right there as my tongue laps up every last drop of her desire, that somehow, some way, I'm not going to let this thing I've started with Mac end. Not that I have any idea how to keep this going, or if she even wants to.

But right now she's dropped onto my chest, her left cheek against my pec as she struggles to catch her breath. She's moved her legs so they're straight out, resting together between mine and when I wrap my arms around her she doesn't flinch or tense. Her heart is still hammering wildly against my own, which is galloping like a wild colt.

I don't know what to say or do next. I fight against the reality of this situation because it's filled with questions and uncertainty. I'm so sick of those feelings. So I am almost grateful when my phone starts buzzing from the pocket of my pants on the floor. "I gotta get that in case it's Callie and she starts a search party."

Mac huffs out a tiny laugh and rolls off me so I can sit up and dig for the phone. As I pull it out of the pants pocket, I feel the mattress shift behind me. Mac crawls off the bed gracefully and crosses the room, all tanned smooth skin, taut nipples, and round, perfect ass. My mouth salivates. I will bite one of those lush cheeks one day, I promise myself.

She catches me staring as she reaches for her robe on the back of the closed door. She looks back because I'm just as naked and on display, and my limp dick is finding its second wind between my spread legs. "Damn, Mac, I might have to smash the glass at the Silver Bay pharmacy. Condom emergency."

She laughs and turns away. "Answer that phone, prince."

"Whatever you say, princess." I see the name Mayhem across the top of my screen. I take a breath and hit the green button. "I'm on my way."

"Theo and Tate said you left before them," Mayhem tells me. "How are you not here?"

The whole family was meeting at Uncle Jordy and Aunt Jessie's house as they were hosting Christmas Day this year, which is rotated every year from house to house. "I stopped to give some dick."

Mac's face makes the risky joke totally worth it. She looks like she might drop dead and her mouth falls open so wide and so quickly I'm surprised she doesn't bruise her chin on the floorboards. I clear my throat to cover my laugh and keep talking to Mayhem before she can analyze what I just said. "Dick's Donuts. He opened this morning, so I dropped in to grab some donuts and leave them at the hospital. Spreading cheer and all that."

"Oh," she sounds genuinely floored. Meanwhile, Mac just

picked up her scrub bottoms, balled them up, and hurled them at my head. She clocks me dead-center in the side of my head.

I cover the phone with my hand and whisper "You really do have a hell of an arm. Almost as amazing as your ass."

"Con!" she hisses.

"Hello?" Mayhem says through the other side of the phone. "What did you say? Are you talking to me? Who are you talking to? Why is the phone all muffled?"

"Ease up with the interrogation, Tenley two-point-oh," I tell her, smiling at Mac's face as she turns red, opens the bedroom door, and unfortunately disappears from view. "I'll be home in five minutes. Have my Bailey's latte waiting."

"I'm not your barista, Co—"

I hit end on the call and pull on my clothes as fast as possible. I run my hands through my hair and glance at myself in the round mirror above Mac's dresser. I look more relaxed than I have in... probably months. The creases in my forehead are gone. I feel lighter too.

I head out of the bedroom and find her pulling the food I brought her out of the microwave. She places it on the island and pulls a fork out of a drawer. I drop my elbows on the counter on the other side and watch her as she slowly cuts a piece. "You put the syrup on the waffles before heating it up. Pro move."

"Yep. Also, I pour a little syrup on the plate before the waffle or pancake, and it absorbs it from the bottom ensuring every bite always has syrup," she explains and raises the fork to her lips. A little dollop of syrup tries to escape and hits her bottom lip as she presses her lips around the fork. She chews and her eyes light up and she makes a mewing sound again. Not quite as sexy as the one my mouth teased out of her, but close. She swallows, fork immediately going for another piece. "These are insane. Best waffles I've ever eaten."

"Gram's family recipe," I say proudly. "The cousins used to always have a big sleepover Christmas Eve at their place and she would make it for us in the morning while we waited for our parents to come back over so we could open presents. Now the boy cousins still spend the night, usually because we're too trashed to stumble home, and she always has them ready for us when we wake up."

Mac listens as she devours another bite with a pleased smile. "Thanks for sharing them."

"Thanks for... letting me eat... something else," I reply still feeling obscenely bold. "Only thing I've had on Christmas morning that beats the waffles."

"You are..." She shakes her head, staring at her plate with her cheeks on fire.

She never finishes that sentence so I do. "Late for Christmas Day activities. I have to go."

"Sure. And I need to finish this and sleep the day away," she replies and lifts another bite but she doesn't put it in her mouth. It hangs there on the fork between us as I reach over and use the pad of my thumb to wipe that dollop of syrup off her bottom lip. As my thumb glides across her lip she sucks it into her mouth, licking it clean and forcing my other hand to adjust my erection.

And then, as I slowly pull my thumb from between her lips she turns the fork around and offers me a piece of the waffle. Seriously, this woman just keeps getting more perfect. I open my mouth and she places it inside, and I pull the warm, puffy deliciousness off the fork. I chew and slowly lean my body across the island. As I swallow I cup the back of her head, fingers tangling in her curls, and press our lips together. Our mouths open and our tongues, both sticky with syrup, dance.

I can't. If I don't leave now, I never will and the family will make this into a big deal. To be frank, I think it is a big deal, this thing blooming between us, but it's too soon to tell. And if I'm going to be disappointed, I want to do it without an audience. It's bad enough my family has to watch my career humiliation unfold, they don't get a front seat to my personal life. So I break the kiss and slide slowly back away from her and off the island.

She rights herself too and we both square our shoulders on either side of the island. "I'll text you."

She nods as I walk backward toward the door. I turn to grab my jacket off the living room floor. She watches my every move as I shove my feet into my boots and shrug into my jacket. "Merry Christmas, princess."

"Merry Christmas to you, but I'm no princess," she argues back softly.

"Yeah, you're right." I open her front door. "You're a fucking queen. And I will worship you again anytime. Just say the word."

And then I step through her front door and close it behind me. Because I'm not brave enough to see her reaction to that offer.

Chapter 17

Conner

I wake up on December twenty-seventh because my phone starts blowing up with phone calls and text alerts and message pings at seven in the morning. Guess the Barons didn't waste one second announcing I was waived. I send Mac a quick text.

> D Day. Turning off my phone for my own mental health. Be in touch later.

Then I turn my phone off. If Clark has news, he can call my family's home line because we still have one of those and he's one of the few people who know the number.

I get out of bed and throw on sweats and socks and make my way through the quiet house. I can only assume, since the sun is barely up, that everyone is still asleep. But when I head down-stairs and make my way to the kitchen I figure out how wrong I was. Callie and Aunt Jessie are at the coffee machine, making one latte after the other, like veteran Starbucks baristas. My dad is sitting at the island holding a coffee and staring intently at his phone. Theo, Grady, and Tate are spread out on the sofas in the family room, glued to the sports channel on the seventy-five-inch television. Tenley, Shelby, Mae, and Liv are sitting on the vibrant throw rug, gathered around a laptop they've propped up on an ottoman.

"TSN says that there's been interest by Vegas and Los Angeles," Liv announces.

"I can call my coach and ask," Tate replies.

"He won't tell you anything," Uncle Luc reminds him from where he's sitting at the kitchen table with Uncle J and Aunt Rose. "Legally, they can't."

"They didn't even tell me when they were negotiating to get Jordan traded to play with me and Luc," my dad pipes in, eyes still glued to his phone. He takes a sip of his black coffee. "Twitter says he's going to the farm team for sure."

"Twitter is full of fat old men who can't qualify for a beer league. Their opinions mean less than nothing," Aunt Rose announces, which almost makes me smile because she is never salty. She's always honey, never vinegar. "I will never cheer for the Barons again. If they retire your jersey, Luc, I'm not going to the ceremony."

"*T'enquiette, Fleur,*" Uncle Luc says and gives her a smile. "We need to present a calm front for Con."

"A little too late for that." Every person, in both rooms, swivels their heads to see me standing in the doorway from the hall.

"Morning honey!" Callie walks over and hugs me. I don't hug her back. She hugs me harder and then she kisses my cheek. "Hug me back or I'll never let go. You know how this works."

I sigh and wrap my arms around her to give her a quick squeeze. It does actually help a little but I still untangle myself from her as soon as I can. Aunt Jessie is right behind her but I sidestep her as she extends her arms. "I don't want a bunch of sympathy hugs Aunt J. No offense."

She gives me a sad smile. "Fine. I'll save it and turn it into a congratulatory hug for when you get picked up by a team way better than those asshole Barons."

"The team owners are still solid people," Uncle Jordan argues. "It's the coaching staff that needs to be gutted. And that GM. I knew when they hired Chance Echolls to be their general manager it would all be downhill and it has been."

"Not all Echolls are assholes," Tate says and his green eyes are sheepish. "Mallory is awesome."

"Yeah well they should have made her GM," Liv replies. "But they didn't so fuck the Barons and the Echolls and the hockey sticks they rode in on."

"Besides," Mayhem adds. "You only like Mallory because you were banging her best friend for two summers."

"Mallory is best friends with Diana?" Callie asks. "Are you going to be bed buddies with her again this summer? I'm not sure I like her."

"Can we not talk about my son's sex life?" Uncle Jordan asks.

"Sex lives are a healthy part of life, Big Bird," Callie retorts. She's been calling Uncle Jordan that since they were teens apparently. He always gets a sour look on his face when she uses it. "They're all in their twenties. I'm more worried when they don't have a sex life... *Livvy.*"

"Mom! God!" Liv blurts out and every exposed inch of her skin turns bright red.

Uncle Jordan turns to Uncle Luc. "Can you look up what Sports Net is saying about Conner so Callie will stop talking sex?"

"They say a source has both the Vancouver Comets and the Portland Riptide interested," Luc says as he stares at his phone.

This is exactly what I did not want. My entire family sitting here, waiting for something to happen to my career. Because what if nothing happens? What if Twitter is right and

I'm on a farm team in twenty-four hours when the waivers end?

"Take a seat, Con," Theo advises, sitting up and stretching out his long limbs, which were all over one of the couches, to give me space.

"Can I get you a latte, kiddo?" Callie asks. "I have that Speculous syrup you love."

"I'm gonna head to the gym," I tell her as I shake my head. "Maybe later."

My dad shoots me a concerned glance, finally pulling his eyes off his phone. "Shouldn't you stay here, in case Clark calls with news."

"He can tell you," I reply. "You know where I'll be."

Grady stands up. He's in sweats too, but his are labeled with the Seattle Winterhawks logo. I have already shoved all my Barons clothing into a garbage bag which is tucked into the corner of my closet. "I'll go with. I need to train."

"No, you don't," I reply flatly. "You're injured. Don't placate me."

"I can still lift some weights. And I just don't want to sit around here listening to everyone natter on," Grady admits. "They're giving me a headache."

"Thanks," Tate says.

"Ouch!" Callie adds.

"Douche," Theo mutters.

"Who needs a black sheep of the family when you have a redheaded one," Tenley snarks. Her gaze turns to me. "Might as well let him come with you. Mac is at work so if you're lying and want a booty call to get your mind off of this, you're out of luck."

"I know she's at work," I reply and now all my aunts are staring at me with intensely curious stares. "Because we're *friends*."

"With benefits?" Callie asks, her eyes hopeful. I swear she's the only 'mom' on the planet that supports bed buddies.

"Going to the gym," I repeat. "If Clark calls, come find me. In the meantime, continue to annoy your virgin daughter and leave my sex life, or lack of one, alone."

"Conner! Fuck you!" Liv yells at me while I leave but it's hard to hear her over the laughter of everyone else in the family. At least my generation. The uncles definitely do not want to discuss Liv's virginity.

I love my sister and don't judge her for her celibacy, but I needed a diversion to get the hell out of this house without another word about my career. Grady follows and I don't object when he grabs his coat and shoes and gets in my car.

We drive in comfortable silence to the barn gym. It's absolutely miserable outside today. The sky is a stark depressing gray and the snow, which had been white and fluffy, is now hard with ice and tinged a grubby gray on the sides of the road. It's as bleak outside as it is in my soul at the moment.

The gym is a comfortable temperature even though it's cold outside because Jordan and Jessie installed heated flooring. I shrug out of my coat and walk right over to the treadmill. Grady makes his way to the padded mats in the corner and does some stretching. I probably should have too but I'm too agitated.

"Music?" he asks.

"Whatever you want."

He nods and gives me a lopsided smile. "You might regret that."

A second later, after punching a few buttons on his phone and connecting to the Bluetooth sound system, the speakers in every corner of the room start blasting pop music. Taylor Swift, Lola Jaymes, Lexi Jade, Olivia Rodrigo, Lady Gaga. Grady is a basic teenage girl when it comes to his musical palette and has been our whole lives. Theo and Tate teased him mercilessly when we were kids and he listened to the Jonas Brothers and Shawn Mendes non-stop. I actually don't mind his music though.

After twenty minutes of running hard, I slow the machine and use my shirt to wipe the sweat from my face. Grady has moved from stretching to the bench press, his face almost as red as his hair as he pushes a mind-blowing amount of weight. His bicep muscles bulge with the effort.

I get off the treadmill and walk over to the hanging leg lift to do ab work. Grady puts down the weights and starts singing along with some song about being scorned by a lover as he gets off the leg press and walks over to the fridge in the corner of the room. He grabs two Gatorades and walks over to me and places one by me. As he walks back to the mats he cracks his drink, chugs half of it, and picks up the free weights. I do forty crunches before I notice he's just standing there like a statue, a ten-pound barbell in one hand and his phone in the other.

"Trying to find a new sugary pop dance tune to inflict on me?" I ask, a small smile tugging at my mouth. Grady is good company and the endorphins from the workout are starting to hit my brain, thankfully.

"No... I... Nope." He drops his phone on the mat and reaches for the second weight.

"What?"

"Nothing." He starts doing reps, but I stop doing mine. I stare at him as he does slow steady bicep curls facing the mirror.

I drop to the ground and walk over to his phone because I didn't bring mine. He realizes what I'm doing too late, and I have his phone in my hand and have the password punched in before he can put down the weights and stop me. Lucky for me his password has been 9292 since he got a phone. ninety-two has been his jersey number since he was five.

"Hey!" Grady barks as he scrambles to put down the

weights without dropping them and I stride over to the other side of the room.

I immediately check his search history. My name is the first thing that pops up so I hit it and... the headline on the first article is like a gut-punch.

Conner Garrison. This apple fell far from the hockey tree.

It's from a popular sports blog and I scan it before Grady can reach me. Conner Garrison's dad already had a Cup by his age. So did his uncle. Coach Landry says he wasn't a positive influence in the locker room. *'A Captain has to lead, not coast on the fact that his dad was a leader.'*

"That fucking asshole," I hiss.

"He'll be fined by the league," Grady says as he reaches for his phone, but I block him by turning my back. I want to keep torturing myself. "You can't bad mouth a player you're trying to sell."

My eyes slip to the next paragraph and I read out loud. "GM Chance Echolls says that Garrison might not live up to the hype around his family name but he's a solid third or fourth-liner that still has something to offer a team, just not the Barons."

Third or fourth line? That's... harsh. I've never been on a second line let alone a third or fourth one.

"Every player on a team counts, Conner. You *know* that," Grady says, his tone matter-of-fact. "And before you argue remember you're talking to the *back-up* goalie."

My eyes meet his and I feel like garbage. "I don't care what fucking line I'm on. Honestly. It's just... Grady, no one is paying *my* salary for a fourth liner."

Now his expression softens. "Lucky for you, this is just a coach and general manager hurling blame grenades to try and keep the world from realizing they're the problem."

"Is it working?" I ask feebly.

"Not for everyone," Grady says. "There are teams out there who will spot the bullshit. Anyone who knows Uncle Devin and Uncle Jordan and Uncle Luc will call them directly for the scoop on you, and trust their opinion."

I sit on the bench press and run a hand through my damp hair. "I don't want them to bail me out of this. That's just a different form of failure."

"Dude, in the end, as long as you're still in the league, you shouldn't care," Grady says, his hands on his hips as he stares down at me. "I mean hell, we're privileged as fuck. Even me, and my dad never even made the league. But in the end, even if our family name, or family members, open the door for us, we've always proven we deserved to step through it. You have *always* proved it Con, and you will again."

I sigh. "I hate every fucking second of this day."

"I know. I'm sorry."

His phone buzzes in my hand with some kind of alert so I glance at the screen. There's an icon of a yellow face... no, a mask. It kind of looks like a crudely drawn hockey mask, maybe? I turn the screen to him. "What, is this like a goalie chat group or something?"

His face drains of color and he rips the phone out of my hand. "It's nothing."

"Seriously, are you talking about this with other goalies in the league?" I ask, wondering if this is a new level of humiliation. I mean, are Tate and Theo texting with their teammates about their poor, loser cousin? Oh god. I can't face them again today. Maybe ever.

"No, you idiot," Grady snaps as he shoves his phone into the pocket of his sweats. "It's not a chat group. It's not hockey-related. I actually have my own life outside of this sport, and this family. You should try it sometime."

"I have a date with Mac Larue for New Year's," I tell him.

His brown eyes widen. "So Tenley isn't talking out of her ass? You and Mac are a thing?"

"We're a... mutual distraction," I say because the explanation feels right. Well, close to right anyway. "She's trying to get over her shitty breakup and I need something to focus on other than this. So I'm pretending to be her boyfriend for this party her ex and his girlfriend invited her to."

"Huh." Grady shrugs. "Well, not as interesting as I'd hoped, but it's cool. Mac's great. I like her and I'm sure Beckett is annoyed with the idea of his ex with a Garrison."

"Yeah." I nod. "All of that is true."

He grins. "So let's get back to working on your abs. Wouldn't want Beckett to look like he's in better shape than you."

Chapter 18

Mac

I feel a burst of panic when I look up from my phone and see Dr. Fleury watching from the doorway. I quickly shove it into the pocket of my lab coat and sit straighter in the soft round chair in front of her desk. She walks in, closing the door behind her, and makes her way to the desk. She's got her trusty tablet with her and her reading glasses low on her narrow nose.

She sits down and props the tablet up on an empty coffee cup on her desk. It's a Christmas-themed one that has a gingerbread house molded into the ceramic and a gingerbread man as a handle. She has also changed the decorative pillows on the small loveseat by the window to ones with embroidered pine trees on them. She does that, theme decorates every season. It's her quirk. Dr. Fleury is a very no-nonsense person in just about every other way except decor.

"Has he been picked up yet?" she asks as she positions herself in her chair.

"Not yet, but the internet is buzzing with rumors of interested..." I stop talking. How does she know I was looking up Conner?

Madeline smiles. "So, for once, the hospital rumor mill is right. You're dating Conner Garrison?"

"You heard that? My god this place is horrible." I can feel my cheeks heating and I can't look her in her big brown eyes.

"I'm a born and raised Silver Bay girl, Mac," Madeline reminds me. "The Garrisons are our royal family. We've been waiting for our Prince to find his Kate Middleton."

"I'm more of a Meghan Markle," I reply and then shake my head. "Actually, I take that back. I'm more of a nothing. I am not dating Conner. We're friends."

"Oh." Madeline blinks and her expression says she thinks I'm lying, to myself or to her, I'm not sure. And maybe I am, so I avert my eyes again. She drops the subject and taps her tablet. "Okay let's go through your cases."

We spend the next forty minutes talking about the patients I've been consulting on. When we're done with work we start the part of the mentorship that involves my mental health. Madeline, who is probably in her late fifties, but looks about ten years younger, pulls off her reading glasses and leans back in her leather desk chair. "You've been working more shifts than necessary again."

"Not again, still," I admit sheepishly. She's warned me before, sternly, about burnout. "I wanted people to be able to spend the holidays with their loved ones. I, no matter what Silver Bay General whispers, don't have any loved ones in town so I pulled a few doubles. It should settle down now."

Madeline nods slowly and her brown eyes bore into me as she assesses everything about me from my demeanor to my body language to the way I still can't hold her gaze. "So, you're nearing the end of your residency here. Have you given more thought to your next steps?"

"I wish I could stay a month in Hawaii and then maybe summer in the Hamptons before I decide what top-notch, already-established private practice I'll be joining," I quip and Madeline smiles at me. "But sadly, I am still deciding if I should go work with my mom at her charity or start my own practice in New York or... elsewhere."

She tents her fingers in front of her and nods. "The else-where part still Portland?"

I nod. "Yeah. I really like Maine... despite everything."

Madeline laughs. "Oh you mean Dr. Echolls?

I give her a small nod. I don't know why I'm embarrassed. Madeline was the first person I told when Beckett cheated on me. I didn't even tell Tenley, not the details, I just asked her if I could move into the empty apartment. Madeline knows every single gory detail and worse, she knows how it made me feel.

"Maine has a very under-served homeless community so I could definitely be of value," I say. "I've been to Portland a lot and I like it. It's got New York's charm without the same population and... hustle."

"Well, I didn't want to have to sell you on it, and thankfully it looks like I won't need to," Madeline says, smiling as she leans forward and digs around on her desk for a thumb drive. She hands it to me and I take it and wait for more information. "I have a friend. Colleague. We went to school together. His name is Norman Bradley and he is opening a place in Portland based on the model of your mother's charity. It will have youth services, but be open to all homeless trying to get back on their feet, especially those with addiction issues looking for help."

"What? Seriously?" I can't help but let my mouth fall open because this feels too good to be true. "He's credible? Legit?"

"Very much so." Madeline nods firmly and her smile gets softer. "I know your history. I know why you have a need to stand on your own two feet, but everyone needs help finding their first job. Norman is like you, from the system, so he under-stands it on the same level as you and your mom and dad. He's looking for a couple psychiatrists to add to his team. That thumb drive has the presentation he gave me when he was trying to woo me to work for him. I am very happy staying here in Silver Bay but I told him about you and we both agree you'd be a perfect fit. It's got a step-by-step plan for how the charity will run. They've already bought the building and gotten grants from the state. A month or two after you graduate is when the place is projected to be up and running. Gives you time for that Hawaiian vacation."

I laugh and press the thumb drive between my fingers, half expecting it to evaporate because, well, it's too good to be true. My history has me drowning in pessimism on any given day. I work diligently to avoid it, but when I get shocked or surprised it's my default factory setting. Madeline knows this too. She's the one who advised me on the tips and tricks and mantras and brain training I use to avoid being a negative Nelly. "Check out the presentation. If you're interested, give him a call. His number is in there. Also, consult your parents. He has had meetings with your mom when he was in the developmental phase so she knows him."

"Okay. Yeah. I'll do all of that." I nod stand up and walk to the door.

"Mac?" Madeline calls and I glance over my shoulder at her as I reach for the door. "If you go on that Hawaiian vacation with Conner Garrison, can you get him to sign something for my son? He's a huge fan."

"Oh my God!" I laugh and Madeline joins in.

"His name is Dudley," she calls as I leave her office. "Thought I'd just throw it out there!"

I'm still laughing and shaking my head as I head back to the psychiatric ward, the thumb drive next to my phone in the pocket of my lab coat. Once I'm off the elevator and have checked with the nurses on the status of my patients, I head to my office and call my mom.

"Hey baby!" she says as she picks up. "I'm in a meeting with your auntie Len. Say hi."

"Hi Auntie Len," I call out to the woman who has been my mom's best friend her entire life. She's not her actual sister, but in our family blood ties mean little. Aunts, uncles, parents, and grandparents earn their titles from more than just blood bonds. "How are Uncle Mike, Essie, and Ethan?"

"We're all good over here!" Len calls back. "How's Conner Garrison? Rough day for him."

What? "Umm... yeah. I guess. I don't know how he is but I'm sure not good."

"Mac, honey, can you tell me why I had to find out you're dating him from a WAGs gossip site?" Mom asks. "Well, Aunt Len found out that way and told me."

"It was an Insta account," Len clarifies. "They sometimes mention Ethan on there. And they had the cutest throwback picture to Chooch in his rookie season the other day."

Len also married a hockey player, like my mom. She married goalie Mike Choochinsky, who everyone calls Chooch, including her, which always makes me laugh. But I'm not in a laughing mood right now. "It's on the internet?! Jesus. It's not even accurate."

"You're not dating him?" My mom sounds disappointed. "He's such a lovely boy."

"No. I'm not... really." I swallow and frown. "I mean we're going on a date, to the hospital New Year's party. And we..."

I am not about to tell my mom and Aunt Len about our foray into bed buddyhood. I shake my head. "It's not a thing. We are not a thing. God, that Heather has a big mouth. I can't wait for my residency to be done so I can leave Silver Bay, which is why I'm calling. Mom, do you know of a doctor named Norman Bradley?"

Mom's voice gets high with excitement. "Yes! We had several conversations about a year ago. He came and volunteered at the charity for a month too. Smart and kind. Is he starting his foundation?"

"He is, and I might potentially be able to work with him," I say and thankfully that gets my mom and my aunt off the topic of Conner and me and our impending date and fake relationship.

I feel more and more hopeful as my mom details all she knows about Dr. Bradley and his ideas for this Portland Foundation. I have to get off the phone to do rounds with the doctor on duty before Aunt Len can grill me about Conner again, thankfully.

After rounds, I make my way down the hall toward the break room and that's when I glance at my phone to check on whether Conner has been picked up by a new hockey team. He hasn't. The rumors are swirling now that he will, in fact, be sent to the minors and my heart clenches in sympathy. I know this is his biggest nightmare.

"Mac?"

I drop my phone into my lab coat pocket and turn to see who called my name. Callie Garrison is standing in the hall by the sign that points to the oncology wing. She's in an elegant black winter coat and what looks like a cranberry-colored home-made scarf and hat. Her cheeks are pink and I can tell she's just come in from the cold outside. Callie is a breathtaking woman. I've thought that from the moment I met her when I was a kid. She's not just beautiful with her big brown eyes and thick, glossy brown hair, wide mouth, and flawless skin, she's fierce, independent, and unashamed of who she is. I've never been intimated by her, but I've always been in awe of her.

"Hi! How are you?" I ask and start to walk toward her. "Is everything alright?"

It's more than a little weird she's in the hospital today. She nods and waves a gloved-covered hand in front of her face. "Oh yeah. Have a follow-up with Dr. Perry. I had cortisone shots in my back a few months ago for sciatica. I blame Liv and Mae. They were big babies and my body has never been the same."

I smile and nod. "The Orthopedic department is in the blue wing."

She nods. "But you know, I'm happy I ran into you. I was going to ask you a favor."

"Oh?" I can feel my eyebrows pinch. "Sure. You know I'd do anything for a Garrison."

Somehow that sounds incredibly suggestive, even though I don't mean it that way. Strange how putting Conner's dick in my mouth has altered my perception. Callie squints at me. "Are you okay? You look... flushed."

"I'm fine." I wave a hand in front of my face. "I've just been running around all day. Lots of... work. Working hard."

"Well, I promise not to keep you but I just... I heard you and Conner have become reacquainted in the short time he's been back home," Callie says and the look on her face is purposely diplomatic. I know instantly that she's heard all the gossip too. Great. Ugh. Kill me now. "I'm not going to poke around in your private business, or Conner's, although I will say I hope the rumors are true. But I also want to say, even if they aren't, and you two are just acquaintances, I'm asking as a concerned stepmom who loves him like my own, can you keep an eye on him?"

"What? Yeah. I mean... how?"

"Conner is so much like his dad," Callie confesses. "Prideful, stubborn, and also incredibly hard on himself. He isn't used to failure. It's kryptonite to his DNA and I just don't want him to spiral more than he already is. Whether he's picked up by a team tonight or not, he's still going to take it hard. See the whole thing as a reflection that he isn't good enough. Devin did that with his divorce and let me tell you, it was not pretty. He made all the wrong choices. Can you just..."

She pauses, her eyes dropping to the scuffed-speckled flooring and then back up to me. "I know you can't treat him, because of ethics and whatever, but can you monitor the situation? And just let me know if I need to intervene or get him someone like you. There are sports psychologists. I do not want him to lose himself like his dad almost did."

I find myself nodding, even though it somehow feels a bit wrong. I remind myself she's not asking me to treat Conner, which I would never do. I was too close even before we saw each other naked. But I can, as his friend, keep an eye on him. She hugs me and I swear my ribs almost crack. Callie is a hell of a hugger. "Thank you, Mac. And don't be a stranger, okay? Please come by the house and hang out with Liv or Mayhem or even just me. You and I have a lot in common. I love your dad and mom and promised I would look out for you and I intend to."

"I'm good Callie, I promise," I tell her. "But I might swing by when I'm not working. I've let my friendships kind of fall apart. It's been easier to throw myself into work than face people after being cheated on."

"Well, at least you realize what you're doing and work isn't that bad of a vice," Callie says. "Devin threw himself into booze, puck bunnies, and self-loathing, which is what I'm worried about with Conner. Although he did go to the gym with Grady this morning so that was a productive choice."

I nod because it is a smart choice. I should text him and check on him. Callie hugs me again, just as hard as the first time but briefer. And then she trots off down the hall. When she's gone from sight, I pull my phone out of my pocket and pull up

Conner's number. We've messaged a few times since our Christmas morning sexcapade. In his last message, he said his phone would be off, but I texted him anyway. In case he decides to turn it back on.

> I finish work at 6pm. Home all night if you need a place to hide out.

I hit send and start walking. I make it three steps before the phone buzzes with a response.

> Thanks. See you tonight. After I buy condoms.

Oh my god... well, I'm not about to stop him. I simply text him back a thumbs up. And, because I'm feeling as crazy as this whole thing with him, I add an eggplant emoji.

Chapter 19

Mac

I take a shower at the hospital in the changing rooms before I leave, in case Conner is already there when I get home. But he's not. When I park, my apartment is in darkness. There are lights aglow at the main house. Almost every single room is lit up and I can see the hideous Christmas tree Tenley put up in the window. It's from the eighties or something and it's fake in a way that is purposefully and painfully obvious even from here, a hundred yards away. The entire tree, needles, branches, and all is Pepto-Bismol pink. She thrifted all the ornaments, looking specifically for the ugliest ones she could find. At least that's what Tate says when he complains about it every year.

There are also a few cars parked in front of Tate and Tenley's house but it's too dark to see if one of them might be Conner's. Maybe he's over there hanging with his cousins until I get home. Or maybe he's changed his mind and isn't coming. Maybe something happened with the waiver situation and he no longer needs me as a distraction. That thought brings a wave of both good and bad feelings. Of course, I want him picked up, but I don't want him to not need this. Us. Because I do. I mean, we've come this far, we should have actual sex once to finish this crazy, unplanned journey we've been taking.

I get out of my car, which started to make a strange grinding sound on the way home tonight. I'll have to deal with it sooner rather than later, but not right this minute, I think as I open the door. That's when I hear it. The crunch of boots on the snow behind me. I jump and spin, the keys lodged in between my glove-covered fingers like a bunch of jagged little knives.

There's a dark shadow a foot away and it jumps at my sudden movement. "Whoa! It's me! Conner. Please don't brain me again."

"Con! Don't sneak up on a woman in the dark!" I hiss out in relief. "And I wasn't going to throw my keys at you this time."

"Good."

"I was going to stab you with them instead," I explain. "Because I couldn't throw them. I need them to open the door and call the cops."

"Oh. Well, that's... disturbingly well thought out," Conner remarks and finally moves close enough that I can almost make out his features.

"I'm a woman," I remind him. "We think about these things every day because we have to. Also, I may have had to do it more than most. So it's instinct."

"Well, that's not a fun fact at all," Conner tells me and now he's right in front of me, so close I can smell his aftershave. It's warm and spicy and already so familiar and soothing. The scent makes my insides feel like I'm waking up from hibernation again. I guess that's what Conner does to me. Wakes up parts of me that stay dormant with everyone else. He tips his head up, and my eyes are in line with his Adam's apple thanks to our height difference. With the moonlight and the closeness, I can get a nice view of his thick, muscular neck and the way his smooth skin bulges at his artery a little. I want to kiss him there and feel his pulse under my lips. See if it starts racing at my touch, but I refrain. "You don't have a porch light."

"I don't have a porch," I reply. "It's literally just a door on the side of a barn. Where did you come from? I don't see your car."

"I walked."

"From your parents' place?" I question, shocked. "That would take like..."

"One hour and four minutes," he replies, and I see his broad shoulders lift and fall in a shrug. "I needed the exercise and the time alone and the fresh air."

"The air is *freezing*."

"You need a light out here. It's far too dark without one," Conner mutters, ignoring my weather forecast, and then tips his head down. I can feel his eyes on me more than I can see them because of the darkness.

"I appreciate this whole concerned fake boyfriend routine," I tell him, hoping he sees the smile on my face. "But I've been managing just fine here."

"I'm sure you have," he agrees and I feel his hands rub the sides of my arms through my thick coat. "You're even stronger than you are beautiful, and you're absolutely gorgeous. But I still want a light out here. I'm gonna tell Uncle J."

Well, I can't argue with him because now I'm all flustered by that compliment. He doesn't act like it's meant to flatter me, that he just called me strong and beautiful, so that makes it even more confusing. And addicting. I haven't had a boyfriend bomb me with compliments the way he does. "Any news yet on the hockey front?"

"Nope," he says simply and rubs my arms again. "Can we go inside? I'm freezing my nuts off here and I was hoping I would need them later."

I laugh and turn away to open the door.

We climb the stairs to the apartment and as soon as I open the door at the top, and we're in my front hall peeling out of our winter wear, he pulls a package out of his puffy coat and hands it to me. It's a brown box about the size of a shoe box. He smiles as he loops his scarf over the hook where he hung his jacket. "Merry belated Christmas."

"I... you can't give me a gift," I stutter, holding the box out in front of me like it's some kind of lethal weapon I'm terrified of. My eyes fly from it to his face. He looks amused. "I didn't get you anything."

"First of all, gifts don't have to be reciprocal," Conner tells me as he toes out of his boots and places them on the waterproof mat by the door. "Second of all, it's not so much a gift as a replacement for something I accidentally stole."

I walk to the kitchen, grab a knife, and carefully tear into the packaging. Inside is the bubble bath he used. The same pricey French brand. It's also got a bottle of body oil, cream, and a small soap all in the same scent. I blink at the contents in awe because I know how much just the bubble bath costs. The sets like this, with shipping, are a hundred bucks or more.

"You... I can't... it's too much."

"It's not," he argues. "It's also a really selfish gift because I love the smell of this junk and I may be hoping to take another bubble bath with it... and you."

"Well, then." I smile and place the box on the counter. "Thank you for being a selfish, presumptuous ass."

He grins so big it's contagious and I start to grin too. He steps into me again like he did outside, but with the lights on I can see every hard line and sloping curve of his gorgeous, sculpted face. I can see the heated look in his hazel eyes too. His hand reaches up and he brushes his knuckles against the edge of my jaw before his fingers thread into my hair at the back of my neck. They're chilled and a shiver runs down my spine. "Do you want to take a bubble bath right now? To warm up?"

"That depends," I say quietly. "Do you have any other boxes with you?"

He looks confused but only for a second and then he smiles. "Actually I do. In my coat pocket. A box of condoms, ribbed for your pleasure."

"You don't need help giving me pleasure," I inform him. "But I appreciate the thoughtfulness."

He grins at the compliment before crushing his mouth to mine in a toe-curling kiss that has my heart thundering by the time he pulls away. He slips his hand around to cup my cheek and his thumb presses against my lips. "You sure about this? And you're doing it because you want to, not because you feel bad for the about-to-be ex-professional hockey player?"

He seriously thinks I would pity-fuck him? For real? My expression must reflect my shock and distaste at that idea because his normally cheeky expression grows somber. "I am not some puck bunny, Conner. I don't care if you're the star center or you drive the Zamboni."

"Huh..." His face grows quizzical and then that cheeky smile of his returns. "You just gave me a career plan. I can drive the Zamboni at the rink here when I don't get picked up. I'll apply in the morning."

I know he's joking so I wrap my arms tightly around his neck and answer him as flippantly as possible. "Cool. How about you thank me for the career advice with an orgasm?"

He doesn't say another word, and neither do I because we're locked together in a series of scorching kisses as we make our way to the bedroom. He makes a pit stop to pull the condoms out of his jacket pocket and then drops the box on the night table while we tug each other's clothes off.

We end up on the bed, under the duvet, Conner's big, hard

body covering mine, hard edges pressing into me in all the right places. His length leaking against my abdomen. He doesn't rush, though. He keeps kissing me long and slow, his hands moving languidly over my body, playing with my nipples, tickling my stomach, gripping my hips before moving further down and center.

He smirks against my lips. "You are more than ready, princess."

"So don't keep me waiting," I whisper back and swallow down the urge to reprimand him about that stupid nickname he's adopted. It irks me in a way that I enjoy if that makes any sense. Oh, I'll keep telling him to stop using it, but I'll smile inwardly when he ignores me. Not sure what that's about. I don't usually play pointless flirting games like that. He kisses me again, his tongue sliding into my mouth as two of his fingers slide into me and his thumb circles my clit.

"I'm gonna draw this out," he replies. "But don't worry. You're gonna like it."

And then I feel his body slide down a little and his mouth is on my breasts. Conner licks and sucks and kisses his way across my body and I let him because it feels incredible. Not just the sensations of his wet mouth teasing my nipples or his fingers pushing and curling inside me, but the non-physical feeling is incredible... the feeling of being savored and worshipped. I haven't felt like this with a man before. Not to this extent.

So when his big body slides even lower, pulling the duvet with him, leaving me exposed, and his hands hit my thighs and push them wider so he can settle between them, I tip my head back into the pillows, and all my inhibitions are evicted from my brain with the gentle pass of his tongue over my pussy. Conner Garrison has an incredibly talented mouth. In minutes I'm twisting the sheet in my hands and my back is arching off the mattress while I pant. I come apart on his tongue as he grips my thighs to hold me still.

Moments later, as I lie there boneless, I hear the tear of the condom wrapper and my eyes flutter open to see him kneeling between my legs rolling it over his thick shaft. When he's done he leans over me, his hair hanging in his eyes as he stares down at me with heat blazing in his hazel eyes and positions himself at my entrance. "You want more?"

I manage a smile and reach up and push his hair back. "Bring your A-game, Garrison."

He chuckles and then pushes into me. I reach up and cup the back of his neck, but he isn't going to let me pull him down. Instead, he says, "Hold on," and then pulls me up. The next thing I know, without ever breaking our connection, he's back on his heels, and I'm straddling his lap, his cock firmly wedged deep inside me.

"Oh god..."

"Tell me about it." He kisses my neck, sucking hard for a second. "You're still spasming from that orgasm."

"Sorry not sorry," I whisper. "My legs aren't going to work either."

"Wrap them around my waist," he commands and I do. Then he wraps an arm around my back, holding me tight, using his other hand as a prop behind him.

He lifts me a little, letting me drop back down on his dick. And then he does it again, and again, and we're in this perfect rhythm suddenly and I feel another orgasm building for release. It's there but it's just out of reach and I arch my back and he tips his head back and curses. Conner is close. He's within touching distance of his release and then, I catch the sight of us in the full-length mirror on the back of the closed door, which faces the side of the bed. Every muscle in Conner's naked body is flexed, his head tipped back, his back curved, his bicep bulging as it lifts me up, then down, over and over. My tits bounce, my skin is flushed, my hair is as wild as the look in his eye when I catch it in the mirror. He's watching us too, and he's loving it as much as I am. And that's when I come for a second time, harder than the first.

I moan out his name and maybe even black out for a moment because the next thing I know I'm on my back, Conner's body pressing me into the mattress as he cusses against my ear as he comes. After a few minutes, he reaches down, careful to hold the condom as he pulls out of me and pulls himself to his feet a little unsteadily. He huffs out a shaky breath as he pulls off the condom, ties it, and drops it into my wicker wastebasket next to the night table. I watch him with heavy eyes, the feeling finally returning to my limbs after that last orgasm.

"I'm going to the bathroom to run us a bath with your fancy bubbles," he tells me. "Do not fall asleep."

I nod. It's all I can manage. I refuse to let my brain overanalyze what just happened. What we're doing here, beyond the physical. I just want to enjoy it. It's been a very long time since a man has made me feel this desirable and valued and I don't want to steal my own joy away by analyzing this. So I don't. And when Conner walks back into the bedroom, unabashedly naked, and holds out his hand to pull me up off the bed, I let him.

We both climb into the tub and I settle between his massive thighs, my back against his chest, and we soak in the luxuriously scented water, play with the bubbles, and then we wrap up in towels. We crawl back under the thick duvet on my bed, still naked, and I use his bicep as my pillow as we spoon and sleepily discuss maybe ordering food, but we both fall asleep before we can make a decision.

When I wake I don't know if I've been out for minutes or

hours. The room is pitch black and the other side of the bed is cold. I sit up. The door to my bedroom is cracked, and I know we'd closed it when we came in from the bath. "Conner?"

There's no response. My heart starts to slip, but I refuse to let it sink. He wouldn't just bolt in the dark of the night without a word. This isn't some dine-n-dash thing. We're.... friends. Fake boyfriend and girlfriend, which is more than friends, right? There should be a level of respect in that. I think.

He's probably just in the bathroom and can't hear me. I call his name again and pull back the duvet. I turn on the bedside light. My scrubs from the night before are lying on the floor, but his clothes are no longer tangled up with them. I grab my robe off the chair in the corner and put it on. I had no problem walking naked through the apartment with him earlier, but now, it doesn't feel right. I step out into the hall as I cinch the belt on the robe. Everything is dark and still. I flip on the light and that's when I see the piece of paper. It's speared through the key hook where I hang my keys.

I walk over to it. It's from the notepad I keep by the fridge for grocery lists and such. He's got pretty standard male chicken scratch writing but I can read it easily.

Mac

Agent called at 2am. I was picked up. Holy shit! But I have to fly to Colorado to join my new team ASAP. I'll be back for the NYE party! Thanks for... everything.

Talk soon. Con

He just avoided his biggest fear, was given a pardon in the eleventh hour, and he didn't bother to wake me up to celebrate it? And he's going to play in *Colorado?*

I'm happy for him, technically, but yet my heart is still sinking, and I'm letting it now. I don't know what I thought would happen after I indulged in this little physical fantasy with Conner, but I think I was holding out hope we'd maybe turn this into something regular. That's not a possibility now. Because people who want to turn their casual sex into something more don't bolt in the middle of the night with nothing more than a note. And how the hell would we pursue this with one of us living in Colorado? Long distance is tough when a relationship has a foundation of more than a quick lay and a barely rekindled friendship.

Girls like you don't get the fairytale ending with the local town hero. The neglected and abused little girl I once was comes alive once again to whisper that negativity to me as I crawl back into bed. But I refuse to listen to that old ghost of who I once was.

It was fun, Mac, I tell myself as I pad my way back to the bedroom. *But that's all it was. He doesn't owe you more. He didn't promise more. It's all good.*

Only it doesn't feel good anymore. My post-hook-up haze has a sting of rejection attached to it now.

Chapter 20

Conner

So far so good. I mean, I've been with the Portland Riptide for all of seven hours, and it's been more than a bit of a blur, but I'm feeling pretty fucking good. I dodged a bullet. I survived the league's guillotine.

When my phone buzzed on Mac's nightstand in the middle of the night, and I saw Clark's name, my heart seized in my chest. I swear it didn't start beating again until I crept into the hallway outside the bedroom and he blurted out, "Portland Riptide picked you up. Official. It's done."

In a whisper, I asked him to repeat it twice because my phone was buzzing in the background with a slew of calls and text messages from my family at the same time. "This is great, Con. It's an expansion team, filled with cast-offs from other clubs and veterans with chips on their shoulders. They're eager. Bad News Bears vibes."

"I don't know what Bad News Bears are, but if I'm still in the NHL I don't care who I'm playing for, honestly," I whispered.

Clark told me to get to Boston Logan by six in the morning because the Riptide had me booked on an eight o'clock out to

Colorado to meet the team for their road trip. I snuck back into the bedroom and looked down at a sleeping Mac. My entire body vibrated with the need to tell her this news. To share it with her first even as my family was still blowing up my phone so intensely I had to leave it in the hall so it wouldn't disturb her.

Mac was sleeping on her stomach, her curls splayed out behind her head which was twisted to the side of the bed I'd been sleeping on. Her tanned skin exposed from her mid-torso up. She had a small grouping of dark round freckles on her back between her shoulder blades. They looked like a little arc, like a rainbow. She was sleeping so peacefully that I couldn't wake her. She wasn't my girlfriend after all and she'd already dealt with so much of my drama.

She worked so hard that sleep was precious, so I made the split decision not to wake her. I gathered my stuff, wrote her a quick note, and texted my dad to come pick me up. He was awake, of course, and had texted me four times since I got the call from Clark. He must have been glued to the sports news all night, waiting for word on my career. Fuck, I love that man.

Dad picked me up while I scrolled through all the well wishes from family and some of the Barons guys I was close to. And then there was a small flood of interview requests from the really pushy media outlets that always somehow seemed to find and use player's personal email. I ignored those and texted the family in the group chat and some of my former teammates. Callie had packed my stuff and given it to Dad so we could drive straight to Boston.

Dad was upbeat the whole trip, and it was really nice to get that time with him. An hour and a half later while I was pulling my bag from the back seat, he pulled me into a hug on the curb beside the American Airlines gate. "I'm happy for you Con," he whispered, his words ruffling the hair by my ears. "But know that I don't give a shit what you do for a living. You're the best damn kid I could have ever hoped for and I will always be proud of you."

Shit, if that didn't make my vision blur. I squeezed him, hard, and stepped away, turning to wipe my eyes and hoping he didn't see. I haven't cried in front of him, or anyone, in a decade, and for some reason I really want to keep it that way. "Thanks, Dad."

Do I believe him? Maybe. I am just really glad I have the option of doubting his words because I'm still a professional hockey player. He isn't saying this to the first Garrison to fail. I hug him again but keep it brief.

"And when you get back I'll drive your car over to Portland," he tells me as I clap him on the back. "And you can explain to me why I was picking you up at Alex Larue's daughter's apartment in the middle of the night with your shirt on inside out and backwards and your hair sticking up all over the place."

Oh. My eyes fly down to my shirt and I see the tag, which is supposed to be tucked into the back of my Henley, sticking up by my chin. I run a hand through my hair and grab my duffle bag. "I'm gonna run to the bathroom before security. Bye, Dad."

I entered the airport, leaving the sound of his chuckles behind.

The flight was seamless and I was exhausted so I passed right out, praising my new team for booking me a business class seat that turned into a bed, and had to be woken by the flight attendant for landing.

I had meant to call Mac from the airport in Colorado, or on the way to the hotel where the team was staying, but one of the assistant coaches picked me up at the airport, and he talked non-stop about the team and what I needed to know about it. Then at the hotel Coach showed up as soon as I got to my room and introduced himself and made small talk. I could tell he was sizing me up. Kicking the tires on his purchase so I had to give him my full attention and try to impress him. He didn't seem impressed when he left. And then the captain showed up at my room to say hello and sat with me on the team bus to practice.

I sort of knew Abbott Barlowe, the Riptide Captain. He was older than me, but I played against him before and also saw him in the minors a lot when we were kids because he was also a Mainer. He's tough and has an incredible percentage of face-off wins. He was also openly gay. He came out after he won the Cup with his former team. He'd just been traded to Portland. They hadn't even started their first season yet and rumors around the league were that management, coaching, and media relations were all not happy. He was diverting attention from the newly formed team to his personal life. I, personally, rolled my eyes when I heard that. Abbott wasn't diverting anything. He was living his life, just like any straight player on the team did, and the media was the one making it a big deal.

"So, are you happy about being on the *home* team?" Abbott asks me as we sit in the front seats of the luxury coach taking the Riptide to the arena. "That mattered to me, but I get it doesn't always matter to others."

I lean back in my seat but try not to get too relaxed. I'm exhausted and I don't need to get even more drowsy and be sluggish for practice. "Honestly, I haven't had a second to let that aspect sink in. I told my agent I was just happy to still be in the league, you know? But now that you ask... yeah. It matters a lot that I'm playing for Maine. It's like a gift actually."

It hits me hard. I'm playing for my home state. The first Garrison to do it, because they haven't had a team before. And I'll only be two hours from my hometown. From that gorgeous woman I left sleeping in the converted barn. This thing with Mac might have real potential now. I really like that idea.

"It's a lot," Abbott says, his blue eyes filled with sympathy.

"The whole rollercoaster that goes with waivers and trades. But you dodged the minors bullet. I didn't but I didn't have your family name."

I stiffen a little at that. Abbott catches it and looks immediately sheepish. He scratches the back of his blond head. "That was a dick thing to say. I didn't mean it to be. I think you're talented in your own right, Conner. I do and I'm pumped to work with you. You've been a bitch to play against all these years, and I mean that as a compliment. But I just... I mean people see the name... and it gives you credit even before they see you skate. I haven't had that. I bet it's a blessing and a curse."

"I'm a nepo-baby for sure," I tell him without hesitation and without malice because it's a truth that would be ridiculous to deny. "That's why I've worked extra hard my entire life to prove that I should be picked even without that name on the back of my jersey."

Abbott nods. I stare out the window, snowy buildings blur by before I focus back on Abbott. "I don't know what went wrong in the last couple of years in Brooklyn but I'm determined to make sure it doesn't continue here. I'll earn my keep."

"Dude, you don't have to sell me." Abbott smiles. "Also, I wanted to talk to you about living arrangements."

"Team can put you up in a rental apartment," Abbott says. "But I always offer mid-season transfers a room at my place. I have a house on the beach, twenty minutes from the arena. The town is like something out of a Hallmark movie in all the best and worst ways, but I dig it. The locals love hockey players. My partner's family owns the best lobster shack in the state so there's always good food around the house. He brings home leftovers and his mother stuffs our fridge with stuff. Anyway, you decide what you want. No offense taken either way."

He gets up as the bus slows to a stop in front of the Colorado arena and we start to filter out.

Abbott, like me, had a few rough patches in his career before being traded to the Riptide. He actually did get dropped into the minors for a while and suffered through some injuries. He was also in the Player's Assistance Program for alcohol. I wouldn't need a place to squat for long. Maybe a month while I found my own apartment or house. Half that time I'd be on the road at away games anyway. Abbott's history was similar enough to mine, career-wise, that maybe he'd be able to understand my struggles lately. Hell, maybe he could explain to me why I was having them. Or at least give me tips on how to get my shit back together here.

So after we're suited up in practice gear and are waddling to the ice on our skates I grab his shoulder with my gloved hand. "I'd like to take you up on the offer."

He blinks and smiles. "Really? Great! I'll let Deck know."

"That's your partner's name?" I ask.

He nods. Slowly. Like he thinks I'm just figuring out his partner is a man, and he's waiting for me to what? Have an issue. I don't. "Cool. Are you sure he won't mind?"

His smile turns soft with relief. "Nah. Declan is from this giant family of really invasive, over-sharing siblings. You could literally eat food off his dinner plate or raid his closet and it wouldn't be anything new."

I laugh. "Sounds exactly like growing up a Garrison."

Abbott laughs too. "My condolences then."

My first practice with the team goes okay. I'm not a disaster but I am a wee bit sluggish with the jet lag and exhaustion. But I think I hold my own. After practice Coach pulls me aside. "You'll probably float around, play a little tonight on every line, so don't take it personal if you're on fourth or third or whatever at some point. Gotta put you everywhere and see what works. I'm not giving you anything you don't earn. And son, you're really going to have to try harder than you think."

Oh. Okay...

By the time we get back to the hotel and I'm in my room, I have to field a bunch of texts from my family. Every single damn one of them has sent me separate text messages asking how it's going, telling me how happy they are for me, and asking me a million questions. I open up the dreaded family chat and send one message to all of them at once.

> The team seems good. Barlowe is letting me crash with him until I get my own place.
> Looking forward to proving myself in the game tomorrow. Need sleep so can you all STFU, please?

I feel a little like a shithead for that so I add another message.

> Thanks, everyone. Best family ever. Sorry if I've sucked. I appreciate you all.

I plug my phone in on the nightstand, peel out of my clothes, and crawl into bed. My phone is blowing up because of course none of them listened to the STFU part.

> MAMA C: We love you Con! You got this!

> DAD: You'll kick ass tomorrow. Proud of U, kid.

> GRAMPS: I can't believe we have a Garrison playing in Maine. Love it.

> TATE: Harlow owes me forty bucks. She totally bet on Con going to the minors.

> HARLOW: FU Tater Tot! Liar. I only bet ten bucks!

> TENLEY: Living with the Captain? Abbott
> Barlowe? He's hot.

> GRADY: You're not his type.

> MAYHEM: See you when you're back in Maine.
> Can't wait to go to a home game!

I actually smile at that and respond to Mayhem.

> Can you bring Mac? If she's not working.

There's a moment of silence, which is a lot for this gaggle of unrelenting chatterboxes. I know there are other family chat groups I'm not a part of, like one for just the female cousins and one for all our parents. I wonder if they're all off on those now, gossiping about me and Mac. I decide to add another text even though I really just want to sleep.

> Forget it. I'll ask her myself.

> Tenley: Look at you, big boy!

Her snarky praise, along with three clapping hands emojis, is a bit much, even for her sarcastic ass. I send her a middle finger emoji, and then silence my phone and put it face down on the night table so I can finally grab some shut-eye.

Chapter 21

Mac

I shouldn't have come anyway. It's pure stupidity on my part. I can't believe that I'm wasting a night off, alone, at a party I didn't want to come to in the first place. I sip my wine but it's like acid on my tongue. I give up on the small plate of charcuterie I have in my hand too and place it on one of the empty tables in the corner of the room by the fireplace, which is roaring and making my back sweat.

"Can we move?" Shelby asks, her blue eyes looking pained. "I'm too hot on this side of the room. Maybe we can lurk by the windows."

"Or we could go stand in our own apartments," I suggest with eager eyes. "How about I go stand in my bathroom, while I draw a bubble bath and you go stand in your living room, watching the rest of that series you told me you had started marathoning."

Shelby smiles. "I understand why that seems like a good option to you, but let's give it at least until midnight. It's only twenty minutes away. Then we can sneak out."

"Fine. Whatever." She takes my hand and pulls me over by the bay window that overlooks the ninth tee. "It was nice of you to come with me. As much as I hate being here I would have been in the seventh layer of hell without you."

"As opposed to the fourth layer with me?" Shelby questions and grins. "Don't thank me, when Con called and told me he was trapped by a cyclone bomb I couldn't say no. He literally threatened my life if I didn't help. But don't worry, I would have never left you hanging."

I take another sip of wine at the mention of my fake boyfriend. Conner had planned to be here, as he promised, and had texted me, the day after leaving me that note in the middle of the night. His team had a game in Minnesota on the thirtieth, but he told me he would be flying back to Maine that night, right after the game. His texts were brief and almost business-like, but they still took the sting off the way he'd disappeared in the middle of the night.

And then the doorbell rang as I was getting ready for this party and I just assumed it would be him. Between my shift at work and getting ready, I had been too busy to reach out. And I didn't want to appear too desperate. But it was Shelby on the other side of my front door, not Conner. She was wearing a sparkly red dress, heels, and a sympathetic smile. "Conner sent me."

And that's how I learned what a cyclone bomb was and that I should have probably looked at the weather in the Midwest. I tried to cancel and just stay home but Shelby insisted we go. Conner texted me and told me I had to do it, and that wherever he was, he would FaceTime me at midnight so TP could see how happy we were whether he was actually there or not.

I wanted to tell him not to bother, that this was getting ridiculous. We should just let the charade go, but Shelby was dressed up and well, it kind of felt like I had to play this out. But I'd spent the last two hours unhappy about it.

"Oh my gosh, why are you two hiding over here?"

And I was about to get unhappier. I look over to see Heather coming up to us with the biggest fake smile I've ever seen. Tenley's Christmas tree looks more authentic. She stops dead in front of both of us. "You guys should be on the dance floor, like everyone else. The DJ is killer!"

Why does she have more enthusiasm than a cheerleader at a pep rally? Shelby sips her wine. "We're good."

I love the casual coolness Shelby always has. Nothing ever seems to get under her skin. I wish that was me. Heather turns to be, her brown eyes inquisitive. "Where's Conner?"

"Stuck in a blizzard in Minnesota," I tell her and her face drops into a frown as exaggerated as her smile was.

"Aw! That sucks," she says in a way that is too upbeat and perky to get me to believe she thinks it actually sucks.

"Babe! There you are," Beckett's voice hits my eardrums and I have to bite back a groan. He sidles up to Heather and nods at Shelby but I get nothing more than the stare. He turns back to Heather, reaching for her hand right in front of me. It doesn't hurt to see like it would have months ago, but it's still awkward. "I need you upfront with me, I have to make an announcement."

"I was just consoling Mackenzie here. Her date bailed," Heather tells Beckett.

"Conner is stuck in Minnesota. The airport is closed because of the weather," Shelby pipes up for me. "He's Face-Timing her at midnight though. Doesn't want to let her start the year without him."

Beckett's expression dims and he looks back over at me. Still, he says nothing. I feel the animosity in his glare though. He's loving being the victim in this. I hate that I made that up. I wanted to hurt him by making him think that I cheated on him first, but I didn't realize it would let him off the hook for feeling bad for what he did to me. "I can't believe anyone picked him up."

"He's a great player," I say even though I haven't actually watched one of his games, ever. But my dad used to sing Conner's praises all the time.

"I heard the owner of the Riptide just wants to collect all the hometown players like trophies," Heather tells us. "So it really doesn't matter if he's good anymore."

"Riptide? What do the Portland Riptide have to do with Conner?"

Shelby's face confirms I've fucked up. She leans in. "Con was picked up by Portland. He plays for the Riptide now."

"I thought... he said Colorado..." I stutter.

Beckett gives me the most condescending smile. "Your boyfriend plays for the Riptide, Mackenzie. Are you telling me you don't even know that? He didn't tell you that?"

"I... I must have misunderstood," I stutter. God, why am I so bad at lying?

Beckett has the balls to shake his head and make a tsk-tsk sound. "Poor Conner. Another reason to feel sorry for him."

I open my mouth to tell him something. Like maybe just to go fuck himself, but before I can say a thing he and Heather have sauntered off. Shelby leans close to me, her eyes wide and a look of utter confusion on her face. "You didn't know Con played for the for the Riptide? Really? How?"

"He said he was going to Colorado!"

"On a road trip," Shelby clarifies. "And Minnesota is the second leg of the road trip. I thought you guys have been texting? Talking?"

Why did tonight have to become such a nightmare? I sigh and put my wine glass down, giving up on this night entirely. "He never clarified. And I didn't google it or anything. I mean, I guess I should have."

"The local paper had his face on the cover, and he was on the front page of the Portland Herald's sports section," Shelby explains and rubs my shoulder, giving a squeeze of support, but there's no way to fix how stupid I looked in front of Beckett now.

"I didn't even know Silver Bay had a paper," I confess. "I mean who even reads papers anymore? I can't believe I had to screw that up in front of Beckett of all people."

"Ah, fuck him," Shelby says consolingly. "His opinion doesn't matter."

"We've got five minutes to go until midnight, everyone!" Heather's voice comes over the speakers. She's standing by the DJ's set-up and someone has given her a microphone. "Find your special someone!"

"We should just go," I say.

"But Con said he was going to call you," Shelby replies.

"I'll text him that I left. It's fine." I pause. "I mean, I can stay if you really want to..."

She grins. "Hell no, I've got the newest season of *Bridgerton* waiting for me on Netflix and my favorite fuzzy pajamas." She hooks her arm through mine. "Let's get the hell out of here."

We weave our way around tables, and past that stupid fireplace that's making the whole place too warm, and around the massive Christmas tree in the corner. We're seconds from freedom, moments from leaving this whole humiliating night behind when... Heather screams.

Okay, it's more of a squeal. It's piercing, and shrill, and draws the eyes of every single person in the room, including Shelby and me. There, in front of the DJ, is Heather with her hands in front of her open mouth, staring down at Becket who is on one knee in front of her. "I want to start the new year with a fiancée. What do you say, Heather?"

"Oh fuck no," I hiss and charge out the doors.

I basically rip my coat off the hanger in the coat room and am halfway to the front door before Shelby catches me. "Are you okay? Jesus, that was... well, I mean it has to have sucked. Even if you're over him."

"Yeah. It sucked," I confirm as we step out of the golf club and into the frigid night. "Especially because I found that ring in his sock drawer and thought it might be for me at first until I also found a package of condoms."

"Oh my God, Mac." Shelby hugs me.

"It's okay," I promise her but I squeeze her back. "I mean it was one of the worst possible moments of my life at the time, but now... I honestly don't think I give a fuck. At least it doesn't break my heart or anything. I don't love Beckett anymore. And I doubt he ever really loved me, so I dodged a bullet."

Shelby squeezes my shoulder as she breaks the hug. "You wanna come over and watch *Bridgerton* with me? We can make popcorn and you can borrow some sweats and we can just forget this ever happened?"

"No. I just wanna go home, take a bath, and sleep," I admit, and she nods.

Shelby looks like she might be a little bit worried about me. Like maybe I'm faking this indifference I'm feeling, but I don't think I am. I'm kind of numb emotionally right now. As I was saying all the wrong things in front of my ex and then watching him propose to the woman he cheated on me with, it kind of felt like I was watching it on a really bad television drama or something. I just watched it all unfold and thought, somewhere in the back of my brain, *yep this seems about right.*

As Shelby waves goodbye and walks an aisle over from me to get in her car, a memory I've long tried to forget, and thought I'd succeeded, pops back into my head.

My very cruel fifth-grade teacher the second day I was at a school in Queens, where I had been enrolled after being placed with yet another foster family, said, *'You, Mackenzie have always been and will always be a have not, not a have. And the sooner you accept that the better off you'll be.'*

I don't remember why she said it to me. I just remember it was in front of the entire class. All these new kids who already didn't look at me, in my ratty clothes with my bad haircut and secondhand no-name sneakers, with kind eyes.

A shiver runs down my spine, cold and painful, and settles in the center of my rib cage as I force myself to finish walking to my car and get in the driver's side. Inside there is a roar of cheers and yelling and I feel my phone buzz, the light from the screen shining through the thin fabric of the small satin purse. I dig it out and see Conner's name. It's a video call, just as promised.

I accept it, but I really don't want to face him right now. "Hey, princess. Happy New Year I miss you so mu... Are you there? I can barely see you. Why is it so dark? And quiet?"

"I'm in my car in the parking lot," I mutter. "You can cut the act."

He's at the airport, I think. I can tell by the stark lighting and what looks like concrete walls and a gate sign behind him. His hazel eyes lock with mine and he narrows them trying to make out my features in the dim light. "So... it's going well then?"

He grins, it's pure sarcasm and I laugh. I laugh so hard I swear I start to tear up. He is chuckling too, but not nearly as hard as me. "I told them you played for Colorado."

"What? Who? Why?" he questions, still smiling.

"Beckett and Heather, his *fiancée*," I explain, wiping gently at my eyes to make sure my makeup isn't sliding down my face. Not that it matters much. I'm just going to wash it off the second I get home, but if Conner can see a glimpse of me in this dark parking lot, I at least want it to be a nice sight. "You wrote on the note you left me that you had to go to Colorado and I thought it was because they picked you up. I never Googled it or anything and so..."

"And you don't know the schedule, or follow the league so you had no idea," Conner finishes for me. "Shit. I should have been more clear. I was rushing and excited. Sorry."

"I should have figured it out. Anyway, I'm pretty sure our fake relationship looks fake to *everyone* now." I sigh. "Or at the very least loose and non-committal. I mean, a serious girlfriend would know what team you were picked up by."

"Wait... I'm sorry, but did you say fiancée?" When I nod Conner balks. "Since when?"

"He proposed right before midnight," I croak out.

"In *front* of you?" He sounds truly horrified and for some reason it makes my humiliation feel deeper.

"It's fine. Honestly." I shake my head. "I have to go. I just want to get home."

"Damn, Mac, I wish I was there. I really do." He swears under his breath. "They say they may be able to get our flight off the ground in the next hour. The flight is almost five hours, but we don't play tomorrow so if you want I can get back to Silver Bay somehow and come see you."

I shake my head. "You're sweet to offer but the gig is up with the fake relationship thing. Thank you for... well... all the shenanigans. For all the stuff we faked and the stuff we didn't."

"It was my pleasure," he replies but his voice is weird. So is his expression. He looks uncomfortable like he has something to say that he shouldn't. "So... that's it?"

"Well, I... yeah. I guess so." I want to tell him that this doesn't have to be it, that I don't want it to be, but I'm... numb. I can't put myself out there with him right now, seconds after making an ass of myself in front of my ex and watching him propose to someone else. Maybe in the light of day when this night is over. "I should get going. I need to drive home. Night Conner. Safe travels."

"Thanks. Goodnight, princess."

"I told you, I'm no princess."

"Whatever you say, princess."

"Argh. Night." I hang up but I'm smiling, which is amazing because I definitely didn't think I'd be capable of that tonight.

I tuck my phone back into my bag and place it on the seat beside me. The windows of the car have fogged up from me sitting here blabbering so I wipe at the windshield and punch the start button.

Nothing happens.

I punch it again.

The only thing that changes is the smile on my face. It disintegrates.

Chapter 22

Mac

I really don't want to be a bitch but I also don't want to stand here all night either. It's a simple question but the waitress had to get the head waiter who had to find the manager. And now I'm standing outside the ballroom they rented for this stupid staff party listening to everyone toast my ex and the woman he had an affair with while they celebrate their engagement.

I text Shelby and ask if she can swing back and pick me up. I don't think I'll be able to get a cab anytime soon. Silver Bay doesn't have any of them, and on a night like New Year's, they'd be hard to wrangle.

"I probably have to ask my manager," the manager tells me. "They're not on tonight so it means calling them at home."

"I thought *you* were the manager," I question, trying not to sound as annoyed as I am. I just want to make sure it's okay to leave my car in the parking lot overnight. I don't need it impounded.

"I'm the *assistant* manager," she informs me like I'm an idiot for not knowing that. "I report to the general manager."

"Okay, you do that and I'm going to use the restroom." I

point to the women's restroom door sandwiched between the two event rooms. Without waiting for an answer I head across the hall and push open the door.

And my heart sinks.

"Oh my God, can you believe how lucky Heather is," someone is saying in a sing-song voice. "I think it's so amazing the way Beckett and Heather found each other again. High school sweethearts who found their way back to each other. It's perfect!"

I turn to walk out of the small room but both the person who talking, a blonde who I think is a pediatric nurse like Heather, and the person she is talking to have turned their attention to me. It would be weird to walk in, do nothing, and walk back out, right?

"Sorry, Mackenzie, we're hogging the mirror but the stall is free if you're here to tinkle," the other one says and I think her name is Cindy. She's a resident like me but in cardiology like Beckett.

I nod and slip past them into the stall. I pray to the universe and any and all deities that the two of them have vacated by the time I get out of here. I would also sell my soul for them to be quiet. But apparently, the devil isn't interested in my offer because they keep talking.

"I feel like I'd rather be with Beckett's brother Emmett, but I'm happy for Heather," Cindy says.

Emmett Echolls is the youngest of the three siblings. He was drafted last summer and plays for... I forget. I was at the party to celebrate it though because I was still with Beckett. Their dad acted like Emmett had won the Nobel Peace Prize. I had never heard him praise Beckett, who was about to become a doctor, like that.

"That's because you're a puck bunny," the blonde laughs at her own dig.

"I grew up in this town, it's like a non-negotiable," Cindy laughs too, unoffended. "And why wouldn't you want a hot, athletic man who makes buckets of money? I mean sure, they cheat a little sometimes, but that can happen in any profession."

The stall is cramped and it smells like chemical cleaner and it's giving me a headache. My bladder is drained and I've stood up but I'm just standing here because if I flush I have to go out there and stand next to them. Ugh.

"O.M.G.!" Cindy squeals out the abbreviation. "Mackenzie! Wait a minute. Heather said you're dating a hockey player. A freaking *Garrison!*"

She emphasizes it like you would a type of shoe. Not just heels but *Jimmy Choos!* Dear God, kill me now. I stifle a sigh by flushing the toilet and unlocking the door. When I get outside I jostle between the two of them to get to the sink and give them the vaguest non-answer I can think of. "That's the word on the street."

The blonde whose name I still do not know is glaring a little. Enough that I notice. Cindy though, in her own professed puck bunny-esque fashion just wants to hear about Conner. "How did you land yourself Conner Garrison. He's probably the hottest of all."

"I..." Oh boy. I don't want to lie. The whole charade is over anyway.

The door to the bathroom swings open and of course, it's Heather. How could it be anyone else in the universe at this point? She stops abruptly, the door clipping her shoulder as it swings shut behind her and she winces. "I thought you left."

"I did. I just... I'm going now." I quickly run my soapy hands under the water which is like ice but I don't care.

"Cindy was just grilling her about Conner." The blonde rolls her eyes.

Heather folds her arms over her chest and purses her lips

like she smells something vile. I pull my soaking hands from the water and give them a shake before wiping them on my coat because I am definitely not standing here another minute to use the hand dryer.

"I've known Conner since we were kids." The door swings open again and Shelby bumps into Heather. Great. It's a freaking convention in here. But at least I have a way home now. "But we aren't dating."

"Oh honey, I'm sorry," Cindy says immediately and she sincerely means it. Her big brown eyes are genuinely sympathetic. "Those Garrison boys are notoriously easy to lay but hard to hold down. My friend Diana has been on-and-off and off-and-on with Tate Garrison for two years now."

I have no idea who Diana is but I'm not about to ask. "We were never dating. It was... a joke. We're just friends."

"Come on, Mac." Shelby waves me over, a gentle smile on her lips.

"Wait..." The blonde looks confused. "I thought you cheated on Beckett with him?"

"That's what she said," Heather pipes up. She's channeling some major Regina George vibes right now. "You lied? About dating Conner? What kind of person does that?"

"Well, Heather, I'll tell you," Shelby says as I reach her and she holds open the door for me to get the hell out of here. "The type of person who is not nearly as bad a human being as the one who fucked someone else's boyfriend for over a year. Happy fucking new year!"

Shelby spins and hooks my arm and marches me the hell out of the golf club. And I let her. My car might get towed for leaving it in the parking lot overnight without permission, but I'd rather deal with that than stay here a minute longer.

Don't cry. Don't cry. Don't cry.

We're halfway home before either of us speaks. Shelby is

the first to break the heavy silence. "You didn't have to confess about Con, you know. You could have told them you were madly in love. He would have kept up the lie with you. Con's always up for a good prank, especially if it'll burn an Echolls."

I sniff. I've managed to keep the tears at bay but I'm emotionally exhausted. "The whole thing had kind of backfired anyway. People were whispering that I was the cheater. I want that title to land solely on Beckett. And besides, Conner has a lot to deal with right now. I don't need to add fake girlfriend to his list."

"I don't know... I think he enjoyed the distraction," Shelby says thoughtfully as she turns up the road that leads to my apartment. "I think he liked you."

"Ha!" It bubbles out of me before I can stop it.

Shelby snaps her head to stare at me, red hair glinting copper in the moonlight spilling through the windshield. "Why are you laughing at that?"

"Because we're not... I'm not his type," I croak and the tears are stinging the back of my eyes again. Fuck.

"Why? Because you're a little bit older than him?" Shelby questions. "He doesn't care. No one would care. He's the oldest twenty-five-year-old I know. Always been an old soul that one and a bit of a curmudgeon sometimes."

I think of the flashes of Grumpy Con I've seen in our brief but intense time together. Shelby keeps talking as she pulls to a stop in front of the barn. "And you guys have busy lives separately, but you're both dedicated to the things that you want, which means you'd be dedicated to a real relationship if you decided to go for one."

"A relationship?" I say the word like it's something scandalous and unimaginable. Because it really is, at least to me. "No. Seriously. Not with us. No. But thanks for what you said back there. I should have said it myself but... I just..."

She reaches across the seat and wraps her arm over my shoulders, giving me a makeshift hug. "Always Mac. Sometimes you need someone to have your back, and I've got yours. Conner does too."

I smile because it's all I can muster and climb out of the car. I wave goodbye. Conner may always be there to fool around with or be a fake boyfriend but that's all. This will never be more. My fifth-grade teacher's condescending tone rings in my head.

'You, Mackenzie have always been and will always be a have not, not a have. And the sooner you accept that the better off you'll be.'

Chapter 23

Conner

The last month since New Year's Eve has been... not great. I'm absorbing new information, like how the team dynamic works, and where I fit in that, both on the ice and off. How the coach runs hot and cold. Well, mostly cold. He is not happy with all the local attention I'm getting for 'coming home'. He's not a Mainer and he doesn't get the extreme pride the state has in local players, and my family in particular. Also although he isn't as openly hostile to me as Landry was, he's not big on positive reinforcement. I'm already struggling with my performance and a wounded ego and he's not helping. Every time I miss a pass or screw up one of the new plays I'm still learning, he makes comments like "This shouldn't be so hard, Garrison" or "Earn that paycheck kid."

I've been pulling my weight, mostly, during games. No goal so far but five assists. Has he mentioned it? Nope. But I'm not special. He's bitchy with all the players. Abbott gets it harder than anyone, making it clear he resents the fact Abbott gets so much attention because he's a fan favorite. "It's a team sport, and good players never forgets that.' And he glares at Abbott when he says that. Abbott doesn't let the coach's horrible coaching style affect him and he's trying really hard to boost morale in the locker room but everyone is kind of like a kicked puppy. I swear that's why the team is hot and cold, winning a game seven to four but then turning around and losing the next one three nothing.

I've been a giant chicken and told my family not to come to my home games yet. I just wasn't in the headspace to add their expectations onto my mental load. I called Uncle Luc and confided this in him. He bounced around to a couple teams when he was playing so I thought maybe he would get this feeling I was having. He said he did understand and he would make sure the family didn't come until I said I was okay with it.

We played last night and won, but only after a shoot-out, which means the other team got points too. It's a dirty win, not a clean one. Not one we celebrate even if we're relieved by it, which I was. The last thing I needed was the media murmuring about how the Barons always lost when I was on the team, and now the Riptide were too. Because the Barons had won three of the last five games they'd played. Luckily they also played last night and lost, badly. Nine to nothing. So that quelled any rumblings the media might have been looking to start.

Being back in Maine has been an adjustment I wasn't expecting. After all, it's my home state. But it's so weird that this is actually home again, full-time. And I've never lived in Portland so it's not familiar but it's fucking amazing. I have always loved being a Mainer and to play for the first professional team they've ever had? It's a fucking *gift*.

I'm... well not happy exactly because the stress is still too heavy for a word like that, but I'm on the road to happy. At least career-wise. On a personal level, something hasn't been sitting right since my last conversation with Mac. Since our good-bye. I've been thinking about her a lot and trying to figure out an excuse to reach out again.

Last night, after the game, I hitched a ride home with Abbott and Declan, because I was still crashing in their guest room, and I laid on the bed brainstorming the perfect message to slide back into her texts with. But I fell asleep with my phone on my chest debating what to say. And then, because it hadn't been charging all night, I had four percent battery when I woke up and had to leave it charging at home when I went to practice. Abbott and I carpooled because my car was still in Silver Bay. So while Abbott does some PR thing with the team's media coordinator, I'm wandering the streets of the Old Port, getting a feel for whether I want to live in the area. It's a really nice area, and I could easily afford to buy a place here, even if I didn't sell the loft in Brooklyn right away. But I'm also oddly drawn to the small town Abbott lives in. It has Silver Bay vibes but with an ocean. But I wasn't Abbott. I wasn't settled down. If I picked a house in Ocean Pines, would it just make me more aware I was perpetually single? Something that didn't bother me before, but I'd been thinking about a lot since my brief sexcapade with Mac.

I stop for a latte at the Loose Moose, a local beanery, and spend a good half hour strolling around the area. I even noted some for sale signs on condo buildings. The streets in this part of town are lined with trendy stores, local brewhouses, and upscale seafood joints. It's a vibe—a good one—but I don't know if it's *my* vibe. I stop to look in the window of a hippie store called Mexicali Blues. I'm looking at the vibrant cotton clothing in the window. There's a pretty top with bell sleeves that reminds me of Mac because it's got a bright orange and pink pattern to it that reminds me of the shower cap she wore that first day after I'd slept over.

I'm in the process of promising myself to put texting her at the top of my To Do list when I get back to Abbott's when I turn the corner and see a guy sitting on the brick sidewalk. He's wearing a tattered coat, has a torn sleeping bag over his legs, and a mangy-looking mutt curled up beside him. He sees me and tucks in his legs so I can pass, but I don't. I look down at the cup, a paper one from the same coffee shop I just got my latte. It's got about forty cents in it. He doesn't ask me for money though.

The dog blinks up at me with the saddest damn eyes I've ever seen, human or animal. I also note I can see the dog's ribs. The man notices me eyeing the dog and grabs hold of its stained purple collar, gently but possessively. "I feed him. And I don't let him freeze."

"Yeah, okay," I say with a small nod. "Want some help doing that?"

"If you can spare some change, yeah. It would help thanks," the guy says, loosening his hold on the lab mix who drops his head on his owner's thigh.

I pull my wallet out of my back pocket. I wish I carried more cash. I only have a twenty. I bend over and stuff it in his cup. "You gonna be here a while?"

"Why?" the guy asks and immediately takes the twenty, pulls it out of his cup, and stuffs it in the pocket of his dirty coat. Our eyes meet for the first time, and I realize this man is probably only about my age. He just looks older because of the dirt and the creases on his brow.

"I wanted to go get more cash for you," I tell him. He nods hesitantly like he can't believe me. I give him a smile. "Look, I swear I'm being honest here. Do you need anything else?"

"A sandwich or something would be cool," he admits. "Even with money, I get kicked out of places a lot before I can even pay for anything."

Shit. I nod. "Be right back."

I have no idea where I'm going but I head down a nearby side street with a bunch of colorful awnings. I find a deli and head inside and order a bowl of clam chowder and a bowl of chicken corn chowder and two sandwiches, one roast beef and one stuffed with grilled veggies and goat cheese. As I'm waiting for the order I wander over to the plate glass window and spot an ATM sign sticking off a building kitty-corner to here. It's across from a pet store, which is fantastic luck.

"I'll be back for the order in five minutes," I tell the woman behind the counter who is making my first sandwich. "Is that cool?"

"No problem," she mutters, not even looking up.

I head outside, pull a hundred out of the cash machine, and then dodge a pick-up truck as I cross the street and head into the pet store. It's bougie and overpriced, but whatever. I have the money to blow. I grab a couple tins of dog food, knowing more than that will make it a bitch for him to carry, and three bags of organic treats. I also grab a coat I think will fit the dog.

When I get back to the deli I march right over to where I can see my order waiting in a big paper bag on the counter. I'm so focused on getting it and getting back to the dude, I turn and bump into another customer waiting for her order. I smell her before I can focus on her. She smells like decadent, expensive French bubble bath.

"Mac," I say the name before my eyes fully focus on her pretty face.

She's staring at me, her blue eyes wide and the pink in her cheeks from the cold outdoors glowing. Or maybe it's a blush from the shock of coming face-to-face with me unexpectedly. "Con... ner?" She says my name in two different chunks like she's sure she's imagining me and is reluctant to voice it.

"Yeah. Hey! I've been meaning to text you." I know the second I say it that it sounds like a line. A terrible, classless line right out of the Man Whore textbook. "I mean, no. I mean, not like that."

She raises one of her eyebrows and the flicker of a smile that

I thought I saw dance on her perfect mouth is definitely not there now. "How are you?"

"Good. You?" I ask.

"Fine. Good." Her eyes move from mine to the door and back to me.

I notice she's wearing makeup. Just some mascara and maybe something on her face that makes her skin kind of dewy, a bit shimmery, and smooth. I can barely see the beauty mark she has on her left temple but not in a bad way. She looks natural but, like, glossy. Like a good TikTok filter.

"What are you doing here?" we ask each other at the exact same time.

"The arena is just a few blocks away." I point as if I'm giving her directions. "I just finished practice and was checking out the area for potential housing."

"How is it going with the new team?" she asks and then grows sheepish. "I haven't had a chance to watch a game but I've Googled scores and you guys seem to be doing okay."

"Yeah, but obviously we want better than okay," I reply, and she nods in understanding. I'm sure her dad was the same way. Ultimately all any hockey player wants is their name on that famous silver Cup and an 'okay' season isn't going to get them there. "And look at you Googling! If only you'd picked up that trick before telling Trash Panda you thought I played for Colorado."

She laughs. The sound warms my insides. "Bonus points for calling him one of my many TP nicknames. But never forget, you could have woken me up that night and explained yourself, in detail, instead of ghosting me like a bad puck bunny."

Was that a burn or a rib? Feels like a bit of both.

"I've never been with a bad puck bunny," I start and she cuts me off before I can finish the sentence.

"Right, of course. I'm sure they all bring their A-game for

Conner Garrison. The crown prince of hockey," Mac says, and okay, so that definitely feels like a burn. "Do they curtsey before or after orgasms? I didn't do either. Will I be banned to the dungeon?'

"With that attitude, yeah," I quip back because I'm stung. Her whole attitude is like a bunch of bees swarming my ego, stinging it relentlessly. "And I was going to say I've never been with a bad puck bunny because I've never *been* with a puck bunny. Look, maybe not waking you up was the wrong move, but I didn't mean it to be. And I really have been meaning to call you. I don't even have my cell phone on me right now. I swear you've been on my mind."

She stares at me, but thankfully I can see her expression start to soften. Her eyes move from my face to the door. The lady behind the counter calls out her order. A hazelnut hot chocolate. I step aside, holding my giant bag of food so she can grab the cup, which I notice is a real one, not a takeaway cup. When she turns back to me she pauses for a lengthy exhale and then she blinks slowly and locks eyes with me again. "Look, I'm sorry for being so... bitey. I'm actually... I have a lot going on today and I really don't have time to unpack us."

"Unpack us?" I repeat.

She nods. "What we did. What we do next. All of that. Look, if it was just a one-night stand... two-night stand, or whatever, that's fine. I am a big girl and I don't expect much from life. And definitely not from men."

Ouch. It's hard not to take that personally, but I try not to. I think of the food in my hand and the guy it's for and remember, Mac was that guy. When she was twelve. A baby. I have no idea the types of trauma she endured back then, but I'm sure it all left some scars. She has a right to feel however she is feeling. I just have to make it clear what I'm feeling. So... I will. As soon as I figure that out. "I never said it was a two-night stand.

Honestly, I don't know what it was, but I know I want to find out. Which is why I was going to call you. I was going to ask you out on a date. Much more charismatically than blurting it out in a deli."

"Out? On a date?"

Her confusion is actually cute. "Yeah. A real one. Maybe even with wooing."

"Wooing," she repeats back to me as her eyes move from mine to the door again, and it reminds me that I have to get this food to the dude. Why is she here again? Did she say?

"I think we both have somewhere to be right now so I'll let you go," I tell her. "But I'll call you. Okay?"

"O... Kay," There she is, so stunned she's splitting up words again.

I lean in, using my free hand to touch her upper arm so she doesn't bolt on me, and I lightly press my lips to her cheek. "I'll text you tonight. I promise. In fact, as the crown prince of hockey, I swear on my family jewels."

Her mouth, painted a soft deep coral color I note, splits in a smile. I turn away from her, which doesn't feel natural but has to be done. I head out the door, thanking a guy coming in who is holding it open for me, and force myself not to look back at her. I find the guy and his dog right where I left them. He looks genuinely shocked I came back.

I spend the next ten minutes giving him the food and the dog food and the jacket for his dog. He tells me his name is Josh and the dog is, unironically, named Lucky. Finally, I hand him a hundred bucks and ask him if there's anything else I can do. "Are you kidding me? You're fucking Santa Claus dude," he tells me, giving me a smile with teeth that need a good brushing. "This is more than anyone has done for me all year. I can rent a room for a couple days with this money in this boarding house I know. It's not great but it's warm and dry and takes dogs and has hot water for a shower."

Jesus, all the things he's listing as a treat, are things that have been in my life, without even thinking about it, my entire existence. I nod and jerk my thumb back toward the arena. "I just started work over that way and am in the area a lot now... so like maybe I'll see you again."

"I hope so. And thanks. Really, like thanks."

I pat Lucky's head and nod then turn to walk away, which feels kind of shitty despite his kind words. Because there's got to be more I can do. I make it to the corner and shift my weight from foot to foot anxiously as I wait for the light to change. I shoot a look over my shoulder to find Josh opening a tin of the dog food and dumping it into a metal bowl he must have pulled out of his old backpack.

But then I see something else further down the street, which slopes up. Walking side-by-side is Mac and a man I've never seen before. She's smiling up at him, looking beautiful and happy, and he's talking animatedly. He's older than me. Older than her. He's holding a takeaway cup with the logo of the deli we were just in.

Was she waiting there for him? For a date with him? It looks like a date. He pulls out a key and turns to the building and I realize he's opening a door to... his apartment? That's the first leap my brain takes and it causes me to feel like I've thrown myself onto jagged glass. Which is... not great. In fact, it sucks.

I watch him hold the door open for her and she disappears inside. Someone bustles by me into the crosswalk because the light has changed and is currently about to change again, so I wrench my eyes from the sight of Mac and her mystery dude and walk away.

Because what the fuck else can I do?

Chapter 24

Conner

The food is incredible. Declan came home from work with takeaway containers of lobster bisque and the best lobster rolls I've ever eaten, and as a Mainer, I've had my fair share. I don't know if I should be eating lobster rolls and bisque during the season. I normally wouldn't, but fuck it, it's been a day.

Abbott is eating them too so I don't feel too much like I'm breaking the rules or anything. Staying with them has been interesting. His life is so different from mine. I know he's got a few years on me, but still. I feel like he's a decade ahead of me when I observe this family life he has.

The two are like a typical married couple, even though they aren't officially married. They bicker over silly things, finish each other's sentences, and shoot each other smiles only they seem to get the meaning of. Right now they're debating the menu details of Abbott's sister's spring wedding. Declan has been put in charge of catering it through his family's restaurant. They make me homesick, honestly, because they remind me of what life is like in Silver Bay with all the Garrisons and Richards... and Mac.

"So, Con, when is your family finally going to come to a game?" Abbott asks me as he finishes his bisque. "The marketing department is itching to do some reels with your dad or uncles and you."

"Ah... I've kind of been asking them to stay away," I admit. "I wanted time to settle in first. I don't know if the coach is really vibing with me yet. And I know when my family comes to games, the media attention can be distracting for me, the fans, the coaches. The Barons used to hate it. I mean, the marketing department loved it, but Coach hated the way it pulled focus off the team and onto me when my dad and uncles were visiting. He actually asked that I not participate in the father-son weekend trip last year."

Abbott and Declan are both staring at me in shock now. I just give them a bit of a shrug. "Wow. He sounds like a piece of work."

"I hope you participated anyway," Declan tells me.

"I didn't," I confess. "I honestly jumped through hoops for that team and that management and no matter what I did it just never worked."

"I feel that way with our coach sometimes," Abbott confesses and then he immediately looks guilty. "I can't say he's as bad as what you've described with Landry. Not at all. But it makes sense you're not feeling like you're vibing with him. I still don't and it's been almost two years. The guy is brutally old-school in a lot of ways. He doesn't understand why players have become brands, or why they all have to have social media accounts of their own and let the fans into their lives. And he especially has issues with the way the owners stick their fingers in the management side of the team."

I think about the rumors I've seen buzzing on sports sites and that some of the hockey trolls have been bold enough to put on my own seldomly used Instagram. I finish my soup and reach for the pitcher of water in the center of the table, topping up everyone's glass before refilling my own. "About that. I did the obligatory 'thanks Barons for a great run. Looking forward to my future with the Riptide" post on my usually neglected Insta and a few people made the usual mean girl type comments."

"Gotta love the internet," Declan growls and rolls his eyes.

"The main dig I keep getting is that the owners are the ones who pressured management to pick me up," I explain, and my eyes lock on Abbott's face, looking for some sort of sign that shows me if this rumor is true or not. "They just want local boys."

I don't have to wait long for a sign. And it's not a facial tick or the way he averts his eyes or any usual sign of bluffing, because Abbott doesn't bluff. "Yeah, it's probably true."

"Oh." Not what I was hoping for.

"Coach told me, flat-out when they scooped me up that they were forced to pick me by the owner because I was the home-town hero." Abbott pauses to sip from his water. "Maxwell didn't even want to make me captain, even after Briggs retired, but owners pushed him on it. Hometown angle is important to them. They're local nerds who accidentally made a few hundred million on a chip that improves MRI imaging and could retire at forty and install a hockey franchise in their home state for shits and giggles. We are, quite literally, their Barbie Dolls and the Riptide is their Barbie Dream House."

"So it doesn't irk you?"

Abbott shakes his head, and his wheat-colored hair flops over his forehead. "Every now and then it tries to bug me. When I'm having a weak moment but I don't let it," Abbott says, his blue eyes flashing with exhaustion for a minute but then he shrugs. "I know I'm working my ass off. I know I'm trying to earn every opportunity. I know I'm not in control of other people's motivation or their opinions."

"I get pissed when they say he only got chosen as captain because he's gay," Declan adds and his angular jaw tightens. "First everyone said it would cost him his career, now those same trolls are screaming it *gave* him his career."

Abbott squeezes his hand momentarily. "It's a win-win situation."

"You mean lose-lose," I correct him because that's what I think he means when someone can't win no matter what they do.

Abbott grins. "Nah. I only win. They don't have to give me credit for it, but I'll do it anyway."

I smile at his cocky attitude. It gives me a small jolt of confidence. I hope I can transfer that over to the ice.

"So any thoughts so far on where you might live?" Declan asks as he starts to clear the dishes.

"I'm still debating either around this area or the Old Port," I tell him and take the plates from him and bring them over to their dishwasher.

"Two very different vibes between here and the Old Port," Abbott muses as he walks over to the coffee bar. I've realized he loves an after-dinner espresso. "I love the quieter life out here, and the ocean, but if you're single, the busy nightlife and restaurants of the Port are what you need. I never asked if you had a girlfriend."

"Or boyfriend," Declan adds.

I smile. "I'm single. Mostly."

Now they're both staring at me with eyebrows raised so I swallow hard and try to explain. "I think I like this woman, an old family friend I recently got reacquainted with but she may have started dating someone else. I'm not sure."

"Thank God my sister isn't here to hear this," Abbott says with a wry smile. "She was a private investigator. She'd take it upon herself to get to the bottom of not only this woman's dating status but also her criminal history and credit score."

Declan chuckles. "You don't need a P.I., just ask her. Do you know how much time Abbott and I wasted second-guessing each other or misinterpreting things that caused us to almost break up. Trust me, Conner, tell this woman you're interested."

I close the dishwasher door and decide I should take Declan's advice and I might as well do it now before I talk myself out of it. "I have to make a call.."

"Smart man," Declan replies.

I slip out into the hall and jog up the stairs to my room where my phone is still attached to the charger on the bedside table. I flop back on the king-sized mattress covered in a royal blue striped duvet. I don't know which one of these guys has the decorating sense, but this whole house is on point. The perfect mix of masculine and beachy. If I do end up with a place in Ocean Pines, or nearby Old Orchard Beach, which I've also been looking at, then I will have to ask them for decorating tips. Another thing I never gave a second thought to in Brooklyn.

I hit Mac's number before I can let the negative thoughts get too loud.

"Hey," she says, and I note immediately that something is off in her tone. She sounds flustered. Frazzled.

"Hey, do you have a minute?" I ask more tentatively than I'd expected to sound. There's a lot of noise coming through her phone, rumbling and zipping, like traffic. "Where are you?"

"About forty minutes from Portland. On the side of the turnpike."

I sit up and my heart slips down into my gut. "What? Why? Are you okay?"

"Fine. My stupid car though... I think it's finally bit it, once and for all," she tells me.

"Get away from the shoulder, even if you have to go stand in the snow, do it," I command as I get off the bed and head toward the door. "When the road's slippery, cars can and have plowed into people on the shoulder."

"I'm being careful," Mac says, and she sounds a little annoyed at getting instructions. "And I called a tow truck. They'll be here in... like anywhere from twenty minutes to one hour from now. They couldn't give me a better window."

"I'm on my way," I tell her as I open my bedroom door and head down the stairs.

"Conner, no. I can handle this," she argues.

"I know you can, but you're going to have to get back to Silver Bay. The tow truck driver isn't taking you that far," I remind her as my feet hit the hardwood in the front entry and I open the closet to get my coat. "How did you intend to get home?"

"I was going to call a friend."

"Well, hi friend," I say with a smile. "I'll see you soon. Drop me a pin please."

"Conner."

"Pin, princess. I'm not taking no for an answer," I warn. She sighs but it's an admission of defeat and I feel great. "See you soon."

I hang up and head back into the kitchen. Declan and Abbott are both by the coffee station now, fussing with fancy caffeinated beverages. I clear my throat. "Hey so, remember when, Declan, you mentioned I could borrow your car if I needed to?"

"Yeah. You need it tonight? Now?"

"If it isn't too much trouble," I reply. "That woman I was telling you about is stuck on the turnpike with a broken-down car."

"Keys are on the credenza in the hall," Declan says without blinking.

"You got a repair shop to tow it to?" Abbott asks and when I just shrug he adds, "I'll text you a place. Reliable and fair prices."

"Thanks."

"Go be her hero, Garrison," Declan declares and waves me off. "And take as much time as you need. Abbott can drive me to work tomorrow."

I thank him and grab the keys to his truck off the table in the hall before leaving. I'm not trying to be a hero, but I have been feeling pretty useless since the waivers incident, except when I'm with Mac. Being with her, and helping her, is the one thing I seem to be able to get right.

I reach her in decent time. The tow truck must have just gotten there because he's still hooking the car up when I pull to a stop behind them. I put on my four ways and hop out. Mac is standing just like she promised, off the shoulder, away from traffic. She actually flashes me a grateful smile when she sees me. I walk right over and wrap her in a hug.

She kind of melts into me, which I love. I kiss the top of her head. "Got you, princess."

"I'm no princess," she tells me for the millionth time. "I'm definitely Cinderella and my stupid carriage has turned into a pumpkin."

"Lucky for you, I don't drive produce," I quip and lead her to Declan's truck. "Go warm up and I'll make sure the tow guy is good to go."

"I want to argue with you, but I'm too cold," she replies, then pulls something out of her pocket and hands it to me. "Give him my credit card so he can charge the tow, please."

I nod. As she gets in the passenger seat, I go over to the burly guy who has finally finished hooking up the car. I stare at it. Why the hell is Mac driving this hunk of junk anyway. It's about ten years old and has rust patches on it all over the place.

"It's gonna be forty-five for the tow back to town," the driver grumbles at me.

"Can you tow it to Ocean Pines?" I ask and pull up my phone showing him the address of the repair shop Declan sent me.

The guy furrows his brow as he reads the address but nods. "Yeah, sure, but that's gonna be an extra twenty because of distance. I'll need a credit card to run."

"Fine," I reach into my wallet and hand him my Black Amex. He takes it and trots back to the cab of his truck. When I put my hands in my pockets so my fingers don't freeze off while I wait for him, I feel Mac's credit card and realize I completely forgot she gave it to me. I was just so focused on getting this sorted.

The guy gives me a nod from the cab of his truck and hands me back my credit card as his engine roars to life. I thank him and head to my own car. Yeah, I fucked up the credit card thing, but I'm not about to spend another ten minutes out here in the cold. It's not like I can't afford to tow her. And besides, I like being her knight in shining armor.

I hop back into the truck and give her a smile. "Now let's get you back to your castle, princess."

"You and that damn nickname..." she mutters but she's smiling.

And when I put the truck into drive, I am too.

Chapter 25

Mac

"Do you have to work in the morning?" Conner asks as he relaxes into the driver's seat, ready for the almost two-hour drive.

"Noon to midnight," I tell him.

"You can use my car," he offers. "It's still at my parents. They were going to bring it the day after tomorrow when they all come to a game, but you can just keep using it until yours is fixed. I don't need it."

"I appreciate that, but..." I swallow down the no, even though it's painful to do it. Fact is, I will need a car, at least for a couple days while I figure out how to get the money together to buy a new one. I'm sure this one is toast. "Okay. Thanks. I won't need it long. I can deliver it to Portland myself as soon as I get a new car or figure out another solution."

"Our family is friends with a lot of the local car dealers," Conner tells me as I rub my bare hands together. Even with my gloves on I froze waiting for the tow truck. I still can't quite feel my fingertips. I hold them up in front of the heat blowing out of the vents in the dash. "Everyone is trying to get us into their cars, they think it's like free advertising, so we get great deals. I can hook you up with someone and get you a great discount by association."

"I appreciate that." I try not to frown or sound ungrateful. "But I'm not going to be able to afford a brand new car unless the discount is like eighty-five percent. And certainly not a fancy Garrison-style car. Your whole family is in Range Rovers and BMWs and Mercedes."

"And your dad drives a ten-year-old Kia Soul, like you?" Conner questions. My dad drives a Jag. When I don't reply he smirks like he won something. "Can you explain to me why he lets *you* do it? Drive an old car on its last legs?"

"Because I refuse to let him or my mom pay my way in life," I confess and turn my gaze off his face, which isn't easy because damn, I swear he gets more handsome every time I see him. But I hate the look of amused confusion people give me when they hear this. "I have also paid for my own education. All of it. Well, the parts I didn't get scholarships for."

"Huh. Interesting," is all Conner says and I sneak a peek at him. It's very dark in the cab of the fancy pick-up truck he must have borrowed from a teammate or something, so I can't read his expression.

"You think I'm ridiculous," I announce because it's the usual person's response.

"No. I think you're more stubborn than I realized," Conner replies. "And that you might feel like Alex and Brie have given you enough already. Because you've been keeping a running mental tab on the emotional and physical support they gave you when you were a kid and you feel like it's already a loan you can't pay back and so once you hit eighteen you refused to accept more. Or else you just don't feel worthy of the love at all. I'm trying to figure out which it is."

Whoa. I'm actually winded. If the airbag in front of me had suddenly deployed and punched me in the face, I would feel less attacked. I take a deep breath and hold it, count to ten, and empty my lungs entirely before inhaling slowly. "I think you should let the shrinks do the shrinking, Con, and stick to hockey."

"I thought we didn't like the word shrink?"

"We don't," I confirm and now I'm glaring at him. My cold fingers are curled into fists in my lap. I hate what he just said. I hate that we're stuck in this car and I can't escape them, or him. I hate that there's a truth to his words that I can't shrug off. And I knew that, because Madeline has given me a similar analysis, as has every psychologist I've ever seen, and I saw one every two weeks of my life after moving in with Brie and Alex. Because they're both big advocates for mental health. So why does this feel so... yuck? I don't know and my defensive brain won't let me find out. I sit silently stewing for about twenty minutes and then I come out swinging like Michael B. Jordan in *Creed*.

I turn in my seat so I'm sort of facing him. "You find a place to live yet?"

"No. I was looking today when I ran into you though."

"Yeah I saw about five for sale signs on some mighty nice-looking buildings," I note. "And I also know there's a healthy rental market. Lots of availability."

"I am narrowing down the area I want," Conner mutters. "I'm thinking I might rent an Airbnb in the Old Port to test it out. And then rent one in the coastal town I'm in and see how that feels."

"Well by then the season will be over and you'll be back in Silver Bay," I say and he lifts his shoulders like he's shrugging. "How convenient."

"How is it convenient?"

"Because you'll have avoided committing," I point out, my psychiatrist brain in overdrive. "Less mess to clean up when you get traded or waived or whatever at the end of this season if you haven't invested in property, right?"

Finally, he's pulling off the turnpike at the exit that will take us to Silver Bay. He steals a glance at me, and we happen to be passing a street light so his face is illuminated. He looks angry, jaw clenched, eyes narrowed. "You think I'm going to get dumped again?"

"No, but you do," I reply flatly. "You haven't scored yet. You had a rough night in the last game with the penalty and a missed pass on a key play. You're worried and still stung by the fact the waivers happened at all. You haven't shaken it off. You need to, by the way, if you're ever going to get out of your own way and get your mojo back."

"Mojo?" I can hear the sneer in his voice. "Is that a clinical term Doctor Larue? You paid the big bucks and drove around in a piece of shit to learn the term mojo?"

Oh, fuck him and his pompous attitude. "No. I pulled that term out of the hockey daughter's dictionary. You guys are always talking about mojo and vibes and lucky socks or jocks or whatever. Because god forbid any of you believe in yourself."

"You don't know what you're talking about," he growls. "I know my talent doesn't come from luck."

"You have no idea where it actually comes from," I shoot back, unable to shut up because I'm on some kind of horrible roll. I'm lobbing out truth grenades recklessly, which isn't at all professional or kind. But then again he's not my patient. He's a man I've seen naked and have a *serious* crush on. There I said it. "You tell anyone who will listen you don't want to coast on that last name because it doesn't matter and yet you're terrified of not living up to it. And because one stupid coach tried to make it seem like you didn't live up to it, you've let it suck your ego dry. Honestly, Conner, you need to forget where you came from when you're on that ice. If you wanna shake off the struggles you're having on the ice, play like there's no name on the back of your jersey."

The farmhouse is in sight now. The barn looms like a dark ink spot on the massive, snowy canvas. Conner accelerates a little and I'd bet money it's because he can't wait to be rid of me. I've been harsh and my psycho-analysis of him was entirely uncalled for. I bite my lip as he turns up the long driveway and try to figure out how to backtrack. I don't think I can.

"Word of advice, don't go into sports psychiatry," he tells me, his voice low and hard. "You don't have the bedside manner for it."

"Ha. Ha. Don't worry. I intend to work with at-risk families and youth," I tell him even though I doubt he gives a crap about me after I just stripped him down like that.

"

"You know how you could have helped yourself?" Conner asks and before I can figure out an answer he continues. "By taking the help, Mac. The money and resources that your parents have to offer you. Stop acting like you didn't earn it. They're your parents, and their love doesn't have to be earned."

"I know how parents work, Conner, thanks," I snap and unbuckle my seatbelt. "I don't pay my own way because I don't think I've earned their support. I do it because—"

"Because you are still trying to prove to people that you can take care of yourself," he interjects and then leans over the console between us, bridging the gap. His face is swimming in front of mine. "Instead of accepting the fact that you *deserve* to be cared for."

Boom. Conner just launched a nuclear-level truth bomb.

"Thanks for the lift," I croak and leap from the car like it's on fire.

I march my way around the side of the bar, which is illuminated by a brand new bunch of motion-activated, solar-powered lights that Jordan installed two days ago. I'm sure thanks to Conner.

I'm sure I would be able to see the path to the door and everything around it as clear as day if my eyes weren't swimming in unshed tears. Conner just stripped me bare, and I hate him for it. I'm blindly shoving the key at the door, where the lock should be but somehow I keep missing it, when a pair of hands land on my shoulders. They're big and warm and I hate them.

"Go home Conner," I hiss.

His hand wraps around mine and he guides the key into the lock. I shake him off and turn it myself. But when I open the door he steps inside with me. "Conner, go home."

"I am home, princess," he whispers, and I know he's dipping his head to be close to mine because his breath dances across my cheek. "Being in this stupid little apartment with you is the only place I've felt like myself in months."

"You can't just attack me like that and expect to, what? Stay?" I ask as he reaches up and pulls off the knitted hat that was on my head.

"Everything I said was the truth and you know it." His voice is a whisper but it's firm. His palms land on either side of my face. They're warm against my chilled cheeks. "And that's why it makes you angry. Same reason why everything you said to me makes me want to rage."

"So let's just leave each other alone," I mutter, but my body isn't listening to a word I say. My hands are traveling up the front of his jacket, seeking out his zipper with the full intention of lowering it. "Maybe we need a time out from each other."

"Maybe we've given ourselves enough time outs from our truths," he replies. And then his lips graze mine. The kiss is soft and tentative. He's waiting for me to double down on my words and push him away. But I don't. I can't, even if every fiber of my being knows it's the easy way out.

He tries to break the kiss but I lean into it and open my mouth. As my hands pull the zipper on his coat down, and then shove it off his shoulders, his tongue barges into my mouth, claiming me. And everything just comes to life. Roaring, screaming, technicolor 5g life. Every nerve ending, every artery, every thump of my heart, every flutter of my eyelashes, everything is burning and aching and screaming for him.

"Princess, you're crying," he gasps as his thumbs hit the wetness on my cheeks. "I'm so—"

I kiss him, hard, because I refuse to let that word leave his mouth. I don't want him to be sorry. Something has changed inside me. A switch has flipped and it's awful and amazing at the same time. If he apologizes and gets all remorseful and gentle, the awful will overtake the amazing. And I want amazing. I can't handle anything else right now.

So my tongue pushes into his mouth, taking over and forcing the word back down his throat. No sorry. No regret. No sympathy. I reach down and push my fingertips into the waistband of his joggers. Without a moment's hesitation, I start sliding them down his narrow hips and over that apple ass of his. Damn. He's not wearing underwear.

His cock, hard and already leaking, bobs between us. He ignores it as he begins unwrapping me, all the layers of winter wear I'm cocooned in. Like an eager kid at Christmas pulling wrapping paper off a present he tears away the scarf, the jacket, my cardigan.

I'm jerking him, slow and steady, as we make out and he finally stills his busy hands when they land on the front of my jeans. "If we don't get upstairs soon, I am going to fuck you right here in the entry, pressed up against that wall."

"Sounds like a plan," I murmur before my thumb glides over the wetness at his tip and he shudders.

And then the ground is gone from beneath my feet. Just gone. My boots are dangling half a foot off the ground as the wall is suddenly pressed into my back. His mouth is still fused with mine, but we aren't really kissing, we're just breathing each other's breaths. He lowers me gently, allowing my feet to touch the floor long enough that he can unzip my jeans and tug them down my thighs. Thank god they aren't skinny jeans. They're loose and so they slip right to my ankles without much more help than gravity. My underwear happily goes along for the ride.

He doesn't waste a second before plunging two fingers into me. The moan I let out is stifled by his tongue in my mouth as he kisses me again. I kiss him back, arching my back as I ride his fingers and pump his cock with one hand and tug on his hair with the other.

"Last warning, Mac," he pants into my mouth. "Let's get upstairs or I am fucking you against this wall."

"Wall."

"Condom?"

"IUD," I tell him and then whimper as his thumb rubs my clit and sparks coarse through my veins like fireflies. "Had STD testing after Beckett. Clean. I didn't tell you the first time because—"

"Because you didn't have to. We thought we were a random hook-up," Conner interrupts, his mouth against my ear, his hand still working magic down below. "So there's been no one but me since Beckett?"

"No one but you," I confirm. It should be pretty clear, from the glimpse into my life he's had over the last few weeks, that I do nothing but eat, work, sleep, repeat.

I should ask about him, I tell myself, as I fight the urge to come all over his fingers, which is getting stronger and stronger every second. I don't know who or what he's been doing. But before I can ask he tells me. "Had my new team physical last week. They always do a panel. Clean, and you've been the only girl in a couple months," he replies. "But princess, if I'm fucking you bare, then I'm not going back to condoms. I won't be able to. So you're mine and only mine until this ends."

"I agree to your terms and conditions," I promise him and he smiles against my mouth. I can't see it but it feels cocky and it's such a turn-on I whimper. "Signed, princess."

"Holy fuck," he slaps my hand off his dick.

He's panting now, like a feral animal, and he starts moving as erratically as a caged one. His hands are everywhere, yanking and tugging and moving me. He manages to get one of my legs free from my jeans, cupping my ass, and lifts me further up the wall, pushing his hips under me, and then, he's slipping into me. Not his fingers, but his cock, hard and fast, over and over.

There wasn't even a moment of burn from the abruptness because I'm so wet for him. I wrap my arms around his neck as my legs circle his hips and he grunts and bites my neck and whispers perfectly obscene things into my ear. "You're so goddamn perfect. You feel like you were built for me. God I can't stop looking at you... at me coated in you..."

My eyes flutter open and I realize his forehead is on my shoulder, his face looking down, eyes narrowed in the small space between us where he can see his cock slide in and out of me. When he finally lifts his head, the look in his eyes is... awe, desire, lust, and something else... something that may begin with the same letter as lust but is so much more scary.

The back of my head taps the wall with a thump as I beg, "Touch my clit."

"Gotta hold you up baby," he reminds me why his hands are occupied. But then he smooshes me harder into the wall, his whole body flat against mine and he changes the angle of his hips as he pushes up into me and... ohmyfuckinggod. There's friction against my clit and the tip of his cock is punching a button inside of me that instantly launches me into orbit.

"Conner, oh my god, Conner," I chant over and over as I come harder than I have in my life.

He swears over and over. "Mac, you're so tight I can't... oh fuck... Jesus Christ... I'm coming."

We must look insane, half our clothes on, half of them off as we cling to each other fiercely and make obscene sounds and swear into the abyss. I feel him lower me back to the ground, my feet land on the tile, and I realize for the first time I have one boot on and one-off. He slowly tugs up his joggers but I don't reach for my own pants, dangling off my one boot-clad leg. I just watch him and revel in the fact that he seems as shaky as I feel. His orgasm wrecked him as much as mine did me. I wonder if the emotions swirling around his head and heart are as wild as mine are too.

He looks down at me, pressing our foreheads together for a second before he swoops me up like I'm a bride on her wedding day. I want to argue but honestly, my legs are still so shaky I might collapse if I try and climb the stairs myself.

He carries me up. "I'm spending the night."

"Good."

I feel like there's more to say, but neither of us says it. We just get inside my apartment, peel off what's left of our clothes, and crawl into bed together.

Chapter 26

Conner

I feel hungover when I wake up. My head is achy, my muscles are tight and sore at the same time. And I'm ravenous. Not just for food. I roll over and find her curvy body warm and naked beside me. Yeah, this is heaven.

My lips press into the crook of her neck and she sighs and stretches and then curls over onto her side, giving me her back. I don't think it's a cock block though because she pushes the swell of her ass into my morning hard-on. "Morning princess."

"You have got to stop with that," she murmurs. "Mac. Say it with me M-A-C."

"Mac. Mackenzie. Mackenzie Gabrielle Larue." I kiss her neck between her nickname, her full first name, and after I say her entire name, I kiss her gently on the mouth because she's turned to look at me over his shoulder.

"How do you know my full name?"

"Because you picked your new middle name when they were doing the paperwork for your adoption," I say, moving to kiss her shoulder as my hand slides over her hip, fingertips dancing over her belly button. "I remember my mom saying how sweet it was that you picked your mom's name as a middle name. And then I asked if I could pick a new middle name and they said no."

She laughs quietly. "What would you have picked?"

"Iron-Man," I confess and her giggles get louder. I bite her shoulder. "I was eight. Cut me some slack."

She giggles harder and I slip a hand between her legs and that shuts her up. Well, actually it doesn't. The giggles turn to breathy pants and I like that much better.

We have morning sex, and it's the best morning sex of my life. We're both slow and lazy and yeah, sliding into her without a barrier will never get old. It's my new favorite thing. That and the way we both seem to be bare in other ways too.

I pin her wrists above her head on the bed and pump into her slowly, making every stroke count. When she comes I lift her left leg over my shoulder to get deeper and let the tight pulse of her pussy draw my own orgasm out of me. I come with a shudder and collapse onto her, moving only once my cock has slipped out of her on its own.

"I have to get back to Portland," I begrudgingly admit. "It's an off day but I have a media thing to do. Twenty questions with the Instagram team."

"You should thrilled." She smiles.

"I hate this part of the job," I admit. "I didn't used to because I used to be hot shit. But since the waiver thing..."

Her big blue eyes lock with mine. "You're still hot shit, Con. I meant what I said. You need to play like there is no name on your jersey. Like you have nothing to prove."

It's easy to say, but not easy to do. I don't tell her that though. I get out of bed and walk to her bathroom. I turn on the shower and wait for the water to warm. I'm going to have to head straight into the arena for this interview. No time to head back to Abbott and Declan's first so I have to shower here. She walks into the small room as I climb into the tub. I hesitate before pulling the curtain closed. "Care to join?"

She unties her robe.

We shower in silence that I wouldn't exactly call comfortable. Her bringing up that conversation we had last night bursts the carnal bubble we've been in. That was some heavy shit. For both of us. I remember the feel of her tears under my thumbs. She's in front of me, the spray of warm water rinsing the soap off her body, and I encircle her in a hug from behind. I kiss her shoulder.

"Are we okay?"

"Yeah. I mean, I need to see my therapist, but I'm not mad about it." She takes a deep breath and exhales slowly. "I think we both needed to hear what was said."

"Yeah." She slips out of my arms and out of the shower. I turn off the water and she hands me a towel. "So this twenty questions thing with the social media team... they're gonna ask me a whole bunch of stupid stuff like my favorite pre-game meal and my favorite movie. But they might ask me if I'm single or taken."

"Oh yeah," she nods firmly like, of course, they would and it's no big deal, but I'm waiting for her to meet my eye in the mirror and she doesn't. "The puck bunnies need to know."

I might as well just shoot my shot. "I want to tell them I'm taken."

And now her eyes finally lift to find mine in the mirror. She looks... well it's hard to describe but she definitely doesn't look horrified or annoyed so that's a good start. I fidget with the knot in the towel at my waist. "But I saw you the other day in Portland. After I saw you in the deli. And you were going into an apartment building with a guy I don't know."

She blinks, her face blank, and then it lights up. "You saw me with Norman?"

"I don't know who he is."

"He's a doctor. Psychiatrist. He's starting a non-profit in Portland," she explains and turns to face me. Her face is lit up with excitement as she explains. "There's a focus on youth, but really anyone homeless will be welcome. He needs psychiatrists on staff and he wants me to come work for him when I've graduated. It wasn't an apartment building you saw us go into. Well, it was, but it's being renovated into a non-profit shelter."

"Oh," I cock my head as all of this new info settles in my brain. "Shit. You're going to be working in Portland?"

"Yeah. If I take the job and well, I want to take the job," she admits.

"That's fantastic!" I pull her into a hug. "Congrats Mac. I'm really happy for you."

"Me too." She hugs me back, squeezing me hard as she adds, "Because soon I'll be living in the same town as my boyfriend."

I pull back a little. She's looking down, avoiding eye contact because she is shy. This strong, brilliant, invincible woman has gotten shy over me? I put my hand under her chin and lift it until she has no choice but to look at me. "He's one lucky bastard."

It takes everything in me not to seal the official decision to be together with another earth-shattering orgasm but I really do have to get back to Portland. And she has work in a couple of hours. So we both get dressed and I give her a toe-curling kiss at the front door. It's long and would have gone on longer but Tenley starts whistling from the farmhouse porch.

I flip her the bird as I walk to my car. She cackles of course. Mac disappears back into her apartment and I drive away, knowing full well Tenley is going to clomp on over there in her snow boots and demand gossip from Mac. I smile at the thought even though it's also annoying.

I make it back to Portland with time to spare so I text Declan and let him know all is well with his truck. He isn't worried in the least and just texts me back a thumbs-up emoji and lets me know that he and Abbott will be out tonight and I'm on my own for dinner.

> Hey also wanted to ask if you could recommend a good realtor in your area?

I didn't really think about it, but now that I'm back in Portland it makes sense. I want to live away from the arena but near the beach. I like it there, and also Mac will probably have an apartment close to her work. If I'm by the beach it will be like a getaway every time she stays over, which I hope is a lot. I'm smiling to myself at the idea. Declan sends a name and a phone number a minute later, and after thanking him, I pull up the only family group chat I like. It's just for the male cousins and it's got a picture of Tate, Theo, Grady, and me as pre-teens in snowsuits and skates holding sticks and wearing helmets out on the frozen Silver Bay lake. The name of the group changes occasionally. It's currently called The Boyz, but when it started, as teenagers, we egotistically named it Hockey Gods. When Tenley saw that, she stole Tate's phone and changed it to Small Dick Energy. That lasted longer than we would have liked because she somehow locked us out of the admin part. When we got control back it became The Boyz.

I type out a message as I enter the arena and make my way to the social media offices.

> Hey. So don't be smartasses but do any of you see a sports psychologist?

There's a fairly long pause. Long enough that I can greet the social media team and make small talk. Then, as we walk down the hall to the elevator, my phone literally blows up.

> TATE: Nah but I've thought about it.

> THEO: Hell no. Can't improve on perfection.

> GRADY: Doctor Mario Wayne. Located in San Fran but does Zoom sessions.

He follows that up with a text with the guy's phone number and website. Pennie, our head of marketing, is waiting for me in the room she booked for this recorded questions session. She gives me a friendly smile and taps the chair she wants me to sit in.

> Thx. Gotta go. Doing an Insta interview thing for the new team.

Of course, they don't shut up. That just floods the chat with snarky comments.

> TATE: Oh yay! What's Conner Garrison's astrological sign?

> GRADY: What's his favorite position? That's what they really wanna know. Off-ice more than on.

A bunch of laugh emojis get posted.

> THEO: What's it like being related to the next hockey king Theo Richard?

A bunch of eye roll emojis, including one from me.

> TATE: Can't wait to find out all your secrets, cuz!

"Ready, Con?" Pennie asks.

"As I'll ever be," I reply and punch out a quick response to Tate's last comment.

> Here's a secret. I'm officially Mac Larue's boyfriend. Later boyz.

I turn off my phone so it doesn't buzz a hole in my pocket.

Chapter 27

Mac

"The only time I find this adorable is when it's on a girl under the age of ten and the name above the jersey number is Daddy," I grumble through the closed bathroom door.

"We can put Daddy on it if that's what gets you and Con off," Tenley suggests.

"Oh my God, if you didn't come out of my body I would swear you were Callie's spawn," Jessie proclaims as she shrugs into her coat and gets ready to leave my apartment.

"Don't let the woman fool you, Mac, she has her dirty secrets," Tenley tells me as I smooth my hands over the front of the jersey. "Ask her why there's a piece of countertop in the farmhouse kitchen from the seventies that she and Dad won't let anyone touch no matter how many renos we do."

Jessie Garrison smiles. It's a smile that says everything and absolutely nothing at the same time. A smile so intense I have to fight the urge to blush and Tenley pretends to gag. Or maybe it's not pretend. Jessie composes herself and smiles at me. "You look great Mac. You girls have fun and give Con my best. Drive safe."

She opens the door and leaves. Tenley stares at me, rubbing her chin in thought. "We're close. I'm gonna lend you my leather leggings and that should do it.

She grabs my coat off the bench and throws it at me. "Let's go to my place real quick. You can change there and then we're off to see your man play!"

My man. I smile as I lock up and let her drag me over to the farmhouse. She's right. The world knows now. Conner didn't call me by name but of course, they did ask him if he was single in that question thing they did for the Riptide's social media, and with a confident smile he said, "Nope. I'm happy to report I'm off the market."

I change into Tenley's leather leggings, which I have to admit do wondrous things to highlight the shape of my ass and legs. And it looks really cute with Conner's jersey, which Jessie had already ordered off the NHL website to add to their grandparents' basement, which displays every pro jersey any Garrison or Richard has ever played in. Tenley told her I needed to wear it to the game first and Jessie agreed.

I hope this isn't overkill. I don't know how Conner's going to react. I've worn a man's hockey jersey before but it was my dad's. I used to roll my eyes at the girlfriends of players who would saunter through the VIP areas at games branded in everything they could find with their man's name on it. But... I'm smiling as I look at myself in it. God, I'm a cliché.

The journey is fun but I'm glad I'm driving so I can keep my eye on the road and not the knowing smirks and side eye being thrown my way. In my car are Tenley, Harlow, and Mae who came back from Boston College for the game. Liv had to go back to UCLA, Tenley would be there too but she's taking a semester off. The other male cousins are back on their teams, except Theo who is riding in the other car with Devin and Callie. The rest of his aunts, uncles, and grandparents have decided to attend a different game, so they don't overwhelm Conner.

We get there and I'm buzzing with nervous energy. I'm extra careful parking the Range Rover. I'm still not used to this SUV. It's bigger than any car I've owned and a literal dream with all its bells and whistles. I could get used to it if I let myself. And I'm beginning to wonder if I should let myself. My mom keeps offering to replace my car. She says I can call it an early graduation gift and for the first time in my life, I told her "maybe" instead of a flat-out no.

Because Conner's words are still bouncing around my head. My parents help me because they love me, unconditionally, and their affection and help are not a loan I have to pay back. I'm worthy of it. Stupid hockey player and his scathing voice of truth.

"Why are you smiling to yourself?" Mae asks. "Are you thinking about my brother? Oh my god, you two are like something out of a romance novel."

"She should know, she reads enough of them." Harlow rolls her eyes but loops her arm through Mae's to soften the judgment.

We're given the ultimate VIP treatment. I've been to games as the family of a player but this is above and beyond because the iconic Devin Garrison is coming to see his boy play. We're whisked into the media suite where Devin gives an interview with the NHL Network, and then we're shuffled through a meet-n-greet with some of the management.

Everyone looks at Devin like he's a bigger celebrity than Tom Cruise. He is a King in this sport, for sure. Callie glides along beside him with grace and an effortless smile. I take notes. I don't know how to be the partner of hockey royalty, but she does. Devin keeps her within touching distance the whole time. When he's not holding her hand, he's got a hand on her back.

He always makes sure she's included in a conversation. These two have a bond like my parents. Something about that feels comforting. Conner has a good example to follow, just like me.

I know that doesn't guarantee anything. Just like you're not doomed to failing relationships if you don't have a good example to follow. My dad grew up with no love and acceptance to aspire to and he's the perfect husband and father. Because he did the work and he will be the first to tell people that.

The owners are the next group of people we meet. Two portly, middle-aged men who dress like they're on a permanent Hawaiian vacation. Even now in the dead of winter in New England, they're both in shorts and polo shirts. They're nice and welcoming, fanboying all over Devin because they grew up watching him play. They invite us to sit in their private booth with them.

Devin makes a point to introduce us all. "And this is Con's girlfriend, Mac Larue."

I shake both their hands, trying not to feel imposter syndrome like I shouldn't be here and that title shouldn't be said out loud. It's going to take a while, I realize, for me to settle into this role. It came out of nowhere after all.

"Very nice to meet you," the taller of the two owners, whose names have slid in and out of my mind the minute they were said, says. "That last name is familiar."

"Yeah my dad used to play hockey," I say.

"Your dad?" The shorter owner blinks. Repeatedly. "He's not Alex Larue, is he?"

"He is," I confirm and the shock isn't new. I'm a half-black, American woman only seventeen years younger than Alex, a white French Canadian. It's a total disconnect if you don't know the backstory. "I'm adopted. As is my sister Cassia."

"Oh. Wow. So like Alex... your dad is Alex. Larue. Wow."

The other owner is chuckling and shaking his head. "Good

player he was. And excellent coach since then too. Didn't he coach Conner?"

I nod and smile.

"Yeah he was an assistant coach with the Barons when they drafted Con," Devin confirms. "He's a good friend of mine. Former teammate. Mac was already like family so we are thrilled."

I smile but feel weirdly self-conscious. The owners exchange a look and a grin. Why is this weird?

Luckily the national anthems are about to be sung so we can stop talking. They play Canada first since we're playing the Quebec Nationals tonight, and then the Star-Spangled Banner. I sing both because I learned the Canadian one for my dad and mom who were both born there.

The game starts and it's rough. Physically rough. The Nationals are a team that doesn't shy away from body checks. They have more brute force than refined skill. The Riptide struggle except for a few players who can handle the aggression without losing their finesse. Conner is one of those few. And he scores twice tonight, once in the first and once in the third. That and a goal by Abbott Barlow gave the Riptide three, but unfortunately, the Nationals scored four, including one intercepted off a pass from Conner. It's a tough loss, but it wasn't anything to be ashamed of, which is what Devin tells a reporter who corners him as we make our way to the friends and family lounge.

Callie stays next to me as we weave our way through the bowels of the arena. She reaches over and gives my hand a squeeze.

"I'm happy for you and Con," she says gently, which is rare for Callie. She's usually a bull in a China shop. "When I asked you to keep an eye on him... I'm sorry if that was weird. Or created tension."

"Thank you but I never really gave your request a second

thought," I say with a small, sheepish smile. "I was already looking out for him for my own selfish reasons."

She grins. It lights up her whole face and for a brief flickering moment she looks as young as I am. "I was hoping you'd say that."

We enter the room, which is filled with wives, children, girlfriends, the usual. I am slightly used to this from going to my dad's games years ago. Tenley drags me and Harlow to the candy table, which is laid out like a five-star buffet of sugar. Tenley grabs a plate and piles it high. Harlow gives her a hard stare. "It's for everyone."

Theo reaches in to grab a Twizzler and Harlow smacks his hand away. "You aren't going to be drafted top ten if you've got a candy belly."

He grumbles and stalks off. Tenley laughs. "Kid could eat a truck full of McDonald's and not gain an inch."

"Yeah, I know but how often do you get to say that to a dude," Harlow asks with a devious grin.

"Con!" Devin and Callie call out his name in unison and I smile as I watch them hug him.

He smiles but he looks a little uncomfortable, like the attention is bothering him, which isn't a Conner I've ever seen before. Then his eyes land on me and slide up and down my outfit and his grin explodes like a firework. He untangles himself from his parents and marches right over to me, ruffling Theo's hair as he passes like he's a kid.

"Hi, princess."

I give him a wry smile. "Good game, prince."

He wraps me in a hug and lifts me off my feet. Tenley makes an "aww" sound but Harlow tugs her away, giving us a moment alone. Well, as much as we can be alone.

"You okay?" I ask because he's got the faintest crease on his forehead.

"Long story, but that pass they intercepted is gonna haunt me. Coach is pissed about it." He sighs and then his eyes find mine with a glimmer of hope in them. "Can I kiss you? That will help."

I lean in and we kiss softly. It's PG but Theo still groans like he walked in on his parents naked. I laugh and pull away. Conner wraps an arm around me, tipping his head to whisper into my neck. "You still good to stay over? I rented us a room at the cutest oceanfront motel near the town where I'm staying."

"Yeah. Ten and Harlow are going to get a ride home with your parents," I explain. "I have a change of clothes and my toothbrush in a knapsack in the car."

He grins and nuzzles my neck, setting my skin on fire. "You won't need a change of clothes. I'm not letting you take that jersey off. But everything else can go."

And now everything else is on fire too, not just my cheeks.

Chapter 28

Conner

Four Weeks Later...

She grips my forearms and I know she's close. I open my eyes as my tongue circles her clit and her fingers press harder into my skin. I have a lot of new favorite things these days—my new house by the beach, my new car, and my therapy sessions with my sports psychiatrist to name just a few. But the top of that list is definitely watching Mac come.

I've learned over the time we've been together that Mac is a very composed woman. She's rational, thoughtful, and self-sufficient. But all that flies out the window when she's naked and on the edge of an orgasm. That's when my princess is irrational and needy and unable to form a coherent thought. She just begs and moans and both curses and praises my existence at the same time.

"Please... oh... damn you Conner... so good... oh my god..."

Exhibit A, right there. I smile before sucking her clit in between my lips and sliding a second finger between her slick folds. That's it. She falls.

"I'm... coming. Oh God. Fuck, Con. Oh God, yes."

Exhibit B.

Her grip on my arms loosens and her hands slowly find their

way to her face, which she covers as she struggles to take a long, deep breath. I kiss my way up her body, until I'm on top of her, my lips at her temple, my cock rigid and leaking between her legs, and my phone ringing on the night table.

Both of us shift our gaze toward it. Normally I would silence it, or turn it off, or throw it out the goddamn window before I'd interrupt our naked alone time. We don't get nearly as much of it as I would like. Mac's in her last couple of months in her residency, and she doesn't get many back-to-back days off to drive to Portland. And between the Riptides' game schedule, practices, and PR obligations, I can't just pop up to Silver Bay often either. We haven't seen each other as much as we'd like. We both know it's temporary, but it still makes moments like this precious. So I'd normally never think about answering the phone.

I lean toward it.

"Seriously?"

"I know. My dick wants to murder me too," I tell her and then sigh when I see the name. "But there's shit going down with the team and it's Abbott calling. I just need to check in."

She lets out the tiniest, cutest protest groan as I reach for my phone. "Hey."

I move off of her and roll onto my back on the pillow beside her. She curls into my side and kisses my neck, her right palm flat against my chest. "I know Mac is visiting you. I hate to do this but we have to head to the arena. Emergency team meeting."

"What? Really? Now?"

"Yeah buddy, I'm sorry. I'm already on the way there," Abbott explains. "Left a baby shower for one of Deck's brothers and his wife."

"Is this asshole seriously fucking with our day off? It's our only full day off in the last eight," I grumble and I have half a mind to just say no. I can't do it. Not today Satan, and by Satan I mean Coach Maxwell.

"That's just it, Con, it's not Maxwell calling us in," Abbott explains. "It's not even the GM. It was the owners."

"Oh." That is definitely not normal. "Do you think...?"

I don't dare to finish that sentence because I'm worried that even saying it out loud will be getting my hopes up. But... I mean it's got to be hard for the owners not to feel the mounting dissatisfaction the team has for Maxwell.

"Yeah. I think he's been axed. But only one way to find out," Abbott replies. "See you there?"

"Yeah. I'll be there," I promise and end the call.

I turn to Mac. She looks perfect with the wild curls and cheeks still pink from her orgasm. Her blue eyes are glassy but bright. She doesn't look mad, just disappointed which is totally fair. I feel the same. "I have to go to the arena. Emergency team meeting."

"Oh. Fuck. That's big. I don't remember my dad ever having one of those," Mac says as I get off the bed. I'm still hard. Mostly. God, what I wouldn't do for even five minutes to have a quickie with her.

"You still have to head back today?" I ask stupidly because she's scheduled on the night shift and there's no reason that would have changed.

"Yes. It sucks and I hate it but yeah. I don't have a choice." Mac folds her arms over her chest, which is barely covered by the sheets.

"Well, at least we made up." I wink at her.

"Don't think that orgasm was me surrendering to your dumb idea," she counters, frowning. "And just because I'm gonna drive your car home doesn't mean I'm accepting it. You can't gift someone a car Conner."

"A *used* car," I argue because the facts in this are... well they're irrelevant. They don't make the gesture any less flamboyantly generous, but I don't give a fuck. "I have a new car, Mac. I don't need two and you don't have a car and have been borrowing mine anyway. So like just consider it a permanent borrow."

"That's not a thing. Permanently borrowing something is stealing."

"I promise not to press charges." I bite back a smile as I shove my neglected cock into underwear and then pants. "Okay. Fine. We can talk about it on Thursday. You're still planning on coming?"

"Yep. But you won't be coming again, not in the good way, if you don't agree take your damn fancy car back," she says, trying and failing to keep a smile off her face at the threat. "And let me pay you back for that tow you paid for, even though you had my credit card."

I laugh as I tug the sweater over my head and then lean over her on the bed to give her a searing kiss. "Princess we both know that's an empty threat. You can't live without my mouth on your pussy."

She gasps at my dirty words and feigns shock. I kiss her hard, my tongue stealing a moment to remind her how talented it is. I know she can taste herself on me.

"You're not fighting fair," she says, breathless as I pull away.

"Because you love it when I'm dirty," I reply.

I make my way through the modest bungalow collecting the things I need as I go. My wallet off the kitchen counter, my keys on the hook by the front door, my coat from the closet. The house is a tiny two-bedroom. I could afford bigger, but I also don't need bigger at the moment. Plus this place reminded me of the barn apartment in Silver Bay, which holds some pretty great memories so I had to scoop it up. And it's one house off the beach. At night, when it's still, you can hear the ocean rumble from the bedroom window.

Mac loves it too, which I knew she would.

"Drive safe, princess," I call out as I leave.

There's not a lot of traffic on a Sunday afternoon as I drive to the arena. The weather is clear and dry, just like the roads, so I'm pulling into the staff parking garage in record time. I park and walk towards the entrance with my security pass around my neck. I shoot Abbott a quick text.

Here. Where to?

Locker room.

There's a weird feeling as I walk through the halls on a day I'm not meant to be here. The place is mostly empty since the office and backend staff don't work Sundays unless we've got a game. The locker room is half full when I get there. Players are sitting by their stalls, murmuring amongst themselves, keeping it quiet like students in a library. I catch Abbott's eye as I walk over to sit down and he gives me a silent nod of recognition.

"I'm going to keep this brief boys," one of the owners, Chris Caldwell, says as he moves swiftly into the room.

Dave Langston, the other owner, is right behind him. He claps his hands once to get our full attention. Walking along behind them are three men, all former hockey players. I can tell by their builds and the scars on some of their faces. And one I know for sure is a former player because it's Alex Larue. Mac's dad.

Our eyes meet and he flashes me a lightning-quick smile.

"We've relieved Coach Maxwell and his team of their duties," Caldwell announces.

Good, is my very first thought but then... oh. Fuck.

"Some of you may know Alex Larue, Mike Choochinsky, or Sebastian Deveau. They're all former players. All Cup winners. And they are now your new coaching team," Langston tells us.

The room is peppered with applause. I join in but I can barely feel my hands as they come together. I stare at Alex as he walks a little in front of the other coaches.

Mac's dad.

Is my coach.

I think professionally this is leaps and bounds better than Coach Maxwell but... personally. It might be a bit of a shit show.

"I know transitions like this are never smooth, and to do it with playoffs looming is bold, but I truly believe..." Alex keeps talking. His words are motivational and the room seems to responding positively. I can't hear anything with the buzzing in my brain, but when everyone claps, I clap.

Did Mac know this was coming? She would have given me a heads-up, right? This is kind of a big deal. I don't even know if her dad knows about us. He must... right?

And as Choochinsky says a few words, starting with the suggestion we all just call him Chooch, I notice Pennie for the first time. Our head of marketing and PR is standing in the corner filming us all on her phone. Because social media rests for no one. All fans want nowadays is the behind-the-scenes scoops, like this.

Finally, all three coaches have said something and Alex steps up again. "Thanks for interrupting your day off, boys. I'll talk to each of you one-on-one in the coming week, but for now, dismissed and I'll see you tomorrow for morning skate."

Everyone stands, and Abbott walks right over to me. "Well now that our wildest dream has come true, how you feeling?"

I swallow. My throat is dryer than the Sahara. "I... guess good."

"Well, I think this is a better fit. I mean, it can't be worse," Abbott replies and leaves me to walk over and shake the new coaches' hands.

I run my hands through my hair, pull my phone out of my pocket, and text Mac.

Hey. Did you know?

There are bubbles as she reads it and is writing a response.

Know what?

She doesn't know.

When was the last time you talked to your dad?

I stare at the screen waiting for a response.

He actually texted me right after you left. Said he wanted to come to Silver Bay tonight and take me to dinner. I told him I couldn't, because work. Why?

She doesn't know. Ah, fuck. Do I tell her? I doubt ruining the surprise my new coach is keeping from his daughter is a smart way to start the relationship.

Nothing. Talk later. Stop texting and driving.

I'm not. Your car has voice text, remember?

YOUR car.

Keep saying that and I swear, you will never see me naked again.

"Con!"

I spin like a bomb just went off at the sound of his voice. My phone is flat in my hand, screen up, threat of revoked nudity privileges from his *daughter* on my screen. I yank my hand back and try to shove the phone in my pocket but it falls to the floor, landing screen down with a deadly-sounding crack. Alex and I stare at it between our feet.

"Shit," he huffs out in his French Canadian accent which has gotten a little softer through the years of living in the United States.

We both bend to pick it up and almost crack skulls. Yeah, this couldn't get more hellish. Oh wait, it can. He reaches the phone first and turns it over. My eyes snap shut, and I send up an urgent prayer for the sweet release of death. I don't know what Alex knows about my relationship with Mac but I do know that even if he knows it's serious, he does *not* need to read about it.

"*Tabernac*," he hisses the French swear and gives me a sympathetic smile. "Your screen is toast."

I look down. Ugly cracks run every which way on the glass, like the ice after a game before the Zamboni cleans it up. Mac's text message is still up but not really visible because half the screen is dark.

"Easy fix." I shrug and manage to take it from him and shove it in my pocket without incident. "I was due for an upgrade anyway."

I'll buy forty-seven new iPhones at full price before I let him see that message. I smile and extend my hand to Alex who laughs at it and pulls me into a hug. "I've known you since you were eight, Con. No need to be so formal when I'm not behind your bench. You're practically family."

So... yeah. Does he mean that in more than one way or...

I clap his back and try to keep the smile on my face from

seeming awkward. He squeezes my shoulder when the hug breaks. "How you been? I know the situation in Brooklyn was rough. I'm glad you landed on your feet here."

"Yeah. I mean, I feel like this could be a great fit," I tell him honestly. "But it hasn't been as smooth as I hoped. This change. We all needed it."

Alex nods. "I treat my team like I treat my kids. I have high expectations, but I'm fair."

I nod. "Well you raised an amazing kid with Mac so I have even more hope for the Riptide now."

Alex beams like a lighthouse in a storm. "She's incredible, my Mac. I'm glad you two have rekindled your friendship. She's moving to Portland, as I'm sure you know, when she graduates and I like the idea that she already has friends. And of course me. She needs more than work in her life, you know?"

"Yeah." He doesn't know? Like, at all? He thinks we're friends? Why do these revelations feel like gut punches to my ego? Maybe Mac doesn't share everything with her family like I kind of have to. Maybe her relatives aren't so overbearing. But I mean, you'd think it would come up.

He's staring at me. His smile is still there but it's tighter. Less friendly, which I've never seen from Alex who is renowned throughout the league when he played with my dad and uncles to be an easy-going joker off the ice. On the ice, he was a tough-as-nails enforcer. He never met a punch he couldn't take.

"You wanna hear something crazy? When I signed my contract just a few hours ago, Chris asked me if it was going to be awkward coaching my daughter's boyfriend." Alex laughs like that statement is a joke. His hand hits my shoulder again, but his grip is tighter. Not aggressive but definitely not casual. "I told him that was insanity because Mac just went through a really bad breakup and she wouldn't throw herself into something else right now when she's got so much pressure on herself to finish school. Also, she knows not to date a hockey player. I mean, come on..."

"Beckett wasn't a hockey player and he hurt her. Badly." I really should just shut up. "And I mean, every hockey player I grew up with is a happily married man so they aren't all heartbreakers and home wreckers."

Alex lifts his eyebrow, one that is scared from stitches, and gives him alley-cat vibes. I open my mouth to say something but what? If she didn't tell him about me, I have to think it was for a reason.

"Mr. Larue!" Pennie calls out and he turns. "Can we get a picture of you with the Captain, please?"

"Sure thing. And please call me Alex." He lets go of my shoulder and walks away.

I let out a breath I didn't know I was holding. I start fiddling with my phone the whole time but it's no use. I can't access anything or do anything because of the damage to the screen. So that tops my to-do list. And then, I need to talk to Mac.

Everyone is starting to file out of the room. But Pennie blocks the door, her hand in the air waving her phone. "I need one last favor! Our Insta content is really getting traction guys. People love the rapid-fire questions so as you leave, please tell me what you miss most from home when you're on road trips. I'll post it when you're on the road tomorrow. Just shoot out a line into my phone camera okay? Your kids. Your wife. Your pet. Your favorite restaurant. Whatever. Make it interesting and fun."

Some of the guys roll their eyes. Others groan. Nobody likes doing social media but it's an unavoidable part of the job. Pennie plants herself against the door frame and holds up her phone. "Okay, one at a time. And let's get the coaches too."

We start to trickle through the door. Every player mumbles something to Pennie's phone. Dinner date gets said a lot because she suggested it and these guys are not wasting energy over-thinking it. I am though. I can't say girlfriend, especially after what Alex just said.

And if I wasn't one hundred percent on that hunch, I am when he slots into the line right in front of me. "I miss my family. My wife and my amazing daughters."

Yep. That's what my new coach says into the camera. I shuffle by, barely looking at the stupid phone. "Nothing."

"Not your girlfriend?" Pennie questions, and I want to kill her because she hasn't asked anyone else a follow-up question.

"Nothing," I repeat.

Pennie's eyebrows furrow momentarily and then the next guy says, "My video games" and everyone forgets my clip.

I don't stick around, heading straight to my car to find a place to get a new phone.

Chapter 29

Mac

Beckett is the first person I see when I walk out of a patient's room at the end of my rounds. He's leaning on the nurse's station, staring at his phone. Why the hell he's up on this floor I have no idea. I haven't asked Shelby about his shifts anymore because I guess I stopped caring. I've been so wrapped up with Conner that I honestly don't care if I'm working the same shifts as Beckett. That said, that doesn't mean I'm going to actually interact with the trash panda.

I turn in the opposite direction to head away from him, even if it means walking the long way around the damn hospital to get where I need to go, I'm good with it.

"Mackenzie!"

I keep walking. Sadly Beckett has legs and knows how to use them so he's beside me before I can reach the elevator. "Hey Macken... Mac. I just need a second of your time."

"What?" I bark.

He stands there staring with his big brown eyes that used to make me flutter. Now, they're just eyeballs. They lack the depth of Conner's hazel ones, with their swirls of amber and smoky gray. And they most definitely have never looked at me with the warmth I see in Conner's eyes every damn time we are in a room together.

"I just wanted to know... what with graduation happening in less than two months... I just wanted to know what your plans were," he says, folding his arms across the front of his pale green scrubs and waiting.

"Why do you think that my future plans are any of your business?" I can't help but ask.

"Because this is my town," he announces sternly like I'm a teenager who is being obtuse. "I grew up here. I'm staying. Heather and I are getting married here next summer and we've put an offer in on a house."

"And you think that means I have to move?" I cock my head at him like he's the biggest idiot I have ever known. He actually is.

"You only came to Silver Bay because I wanted you to," Beckett reminds me. "I got us into the residency program with my connections."

"I had a near-perfect GPA and top-notch references. I could have gone anywhere," I remind him because he was the one with limited options, not me.

"Yeah, but you came here and then for some inexplicable reason, you stayed when we broke up," Beckett sneers like it's the most pathetic thing ever, me staying in Silver Bay. But he knows that if I left and changed residency programs I would have had to start the year over and wouldn't be able to graduate on time. I wasted years of my personal life on him, I wasn't about to lose any time in my career because of him. "And you don't have anyone here. No family. No boyfriend because that was some pathetic lie."

The judgment in his gaze is so heavy I feel it like a bowling ball being launched into my chest. *Oof.* A tingle of humiliation tingles in the center of my chest, threatening to bloom and cover my face in an embarrassed flush. But then I remember... "Conner and I are dating. So I do have ties to Silver Bay. And we'll likely spend a lot of time here in the summer with his family."

He makes a face like I just passed gas or something equally foul. "You told Heather that was a lie."

"It was a lie. Conner's idea, but shocker, he likes me for real. And I like him. We've been dating for a while," I announce and it feels good. I haven't exactly been keeping it secret. His entire family knows, but I haven't talked about it with anyone at work other than my mentor and advisor Madeline. "Anyway, you can't claim ownership over an entire damn town, TP, and so I will likely be here in the future. Not full-time though. I've got a job lined up in Portland, where my boyfriend lives."

He blinks and sneers. "Does Conner know you're lying about this still? Again? And what the hell is TP?"

"Oh for..." I swallow down the 'fuck's sake' part of that statement because I'm at work. I will not let him take my professionalism from me. He doesn't deserve it. "You don't believe me. Cool. Spoiler alert, you don't matter. And TP is the abbreviation for everything I call you. Trash panda, toxic person, tiny penis, and more. Now please leave me the hell alone."

I walk away without looking back. God, I feel good.

* * *

The rest of the shift is uneventful. That's good on the work front but my phone is abnormally silent. Usually, Conner sends me a few texts and even a selfie while I'm working. But I haven't heard from him since he had Mae text me yesterday night. He broke his phone and is working on fixing it, but he can't call or text. Mae explained she was his 'carrier pigeon' because he had to use his teammate's phone to call and only knew her number by heart.

I can't wait until we're in the same city. I've decided to rent a place in Ocean Pines too. There are a few apartments within walking distance of Conner that I will be able to afford. I'll need a reliable car for the commute to Portland but it will be worth it to be close to him and the beach. It reminds me of my mom's vacation home in the Hamptons which is my favorite place. He wants to give me a Range Rover and I don't want to take it, because I'm still a little bit stuck on the whole worthy of help thing. I'm working on it with Madeline.

My latest plan is to ask my parents to buy the Range Rover off Conner for my graduation gift. Because it really is a sweet ride and I love it. That kills two birds with one stone. I get to accept the help from my parents I've been rejecting for most of my life and I get Conner's perfect car without feeling like my new boyfriend is bailing me out. Of course, for this plan to work, I need to tell my parents I'm dating Conner. I haven't yet. I want to do it in person, but my mom has been busy planning a charity event for her foundation, and dad is in hot negotiations with a hockey franchise, he just hasn't told me which one yet. So I've kept Conner to myself. For now.

My dad messaged me twice in the last twenty-four hours. He wants to get together and said he would come to Silver Bay so maybe I'll tell him first. I couldn't see him yesterday and he couldn't make it today so we have tentative plans next week. It's kind of weird he's coming all the way to Maine from New York, but this is the longest I've gone without seeing my family. He is the more needy parent so maybe he just misses me. The thought makes me smile.

My shift ends and I grab my coat and boots from my office and make my way out the front doors of the hospital. Shelby is at the main entrance with Heather, which stops me in my tracks. Those two are not friends, and the New Year's party solidified that. So why are they standing together?

Heather's eyes fly over to me and she shoots me an acidic smile. "Speak of the sad little devil."

"Don't be a twat," Shelby snaps at her.

"What's going on?"

"Your lies are being exposed again," Heather says. "You really should see a psychiatrist yourself at this point. You are delusional."

"Careful with your words, Heather," I warn her. "I'm not going to be slandered by the woman who fucked my boyfriend in my bed."

"Oh get over it," she snaps, her eyes fiery. "Maybe if you stopped lying about your life and actually focused on improving it, you'd find yourself a real boyfriend."

I look at Shelby. "What is she blabbering about?"

"Beckett told her you're lying about dating Conner again." Shelby rolls her eyes. "I told her she's an idiot. I know you're together."

"Can't be serious if he isn't even going to miss her," Heather counters and holds up her phone, which she'd been holding between her and Shelby when I walked up

"What?" I sputter out because I have absolutely no clue what is going on at this point.

Heather points to her phone and I see she's got the Riptide's Instagram opened. She hits the screen and one of their reels starts to play. I don't spend much time on Instagram so I don't know what they post. In this video, players are dressed in regular street clothes, not uniforms or their pre-game suits. A question is typed at the bottom of the screen, What Do You Miss on Road Trips?

And players are blurting out answers as they walk by the

camera. I watch with annoyance. I should be on my way home by now. Why am I indulging this woman and her...

Conner is walking by the camera now. He's in the same clothes he pulled on yesterday when we left me naked in his bed to go to a special team meeting. He looks hot, but... upset. His jaw is clenched. His hands jammed in his pockets and his shoulders forward. "Nothing."

Oh. Okay.

I blink. I'm not one to hinge the worth of my new relationship on an Instagram video but it does sting a little when every other player in a relationship is mentioning their significant other.

And then it shifts to another clip. Not a player but... my dad? My mouth falls open. He looks at the camera and shoots it one of his trademark cocky grins. "I miss my family. My wife and my amazing daughters."

"Why is my dad hanging out with the Riptide?" I ask Shelby but it's Heather who answers.

"He's their new coach. As of yesterday." She drops her phone and huffs out a breath of disgust. "Honestly, Mackenzie, do you even live in reality?"

"Shut the fuck up Heather," \

Shelby grabs my arm and pulls me away from Heather. But not before Heather says, "Mackenzie, Beck said you might be thinking of staying in Silver Bay. Don't. I'm not being mean but you really seem to need a fresh start and we don't want you here. No one does."

I stop dead in my tracks. Shelby is trying to tug me along but I turn back to Heather. "Does it make you feel good about yourself?"

"What?"

"Being so vicious to people?" I clarify and, although I feel humiliated, every word is giving me confidence. Standing up for myself is long overdue. "Because if that's where you get your self-worth then you've got more to worry about than who I'm dating. Also, don't look at Beckett to boost your confidence. He's not exactly an empathetic partner. Conner is but sadly for you he really is taken."

I turn back to Shelby who is smiling at me. Then she looks over at Heather again. "What she said. Also, fuck off."

Heather finally retreats, disappearing back into the hospital. Once the doors have swooshed closed behind her, Shelby eyes me with concern. "Are you okay? Did you really not know your dad is Con's new coach?"

"I... no. My dad wanted to get together but I was working. I guess he's trying to surprise me with the news because he knows I don't pay attention to the league," I shake my head. "Also, I never told him about Conner and me. So... well, this is a whole pile of confusion now."

Shelby nods. "Are you going to call Con?"

"Yeah. And my dad."

I stop and look at Shelby again. "Is it complicated that my dad is Conner's coach now?"

"Yeah. Probably a little," Shelby admits, but she gives me a reassuring smile. "But you guys seem to have it pretty bad for each other. I'm sure that you'll navigate this just fine."

"I guess I should tell my dad about Con now."

Shelby laughs. "Yeah. That might help."

I give her a quick hug and head to my car. The whole drive home I'm debating what to say to my dad. I really don't want to do this over the phone, but how long do I wait? Has Conner said something? That would be the worst possible scenario if Dad heard it from someone else. He's protective of me and he's also got a very soft heart. He'll be hurt if he thinks I kept it from him.

I pull up to my apartment and see that Conner's new Range Rover is parked by my door and my heart leaps. He's here! The idea of seeing him brings instant relief, my stress dissipates with every step I take toward the front door. He no longer has to sneak the key out from under the silly garden gnome because I gave him an extra set last week when he gave me the extra keys to his place.

But I don't find him inside. I find him leaning against the wall by the door, staring off at the vacant acres of land that someone farmed at some point a long time ago, but that Jordan and Jessie grow wildflowers and summer vegetables in now. Because winter hasn't let spring takeover yet, it's still a white tundra at the moment.

"Hey!" I smile at him and hurl myself into him, wrapping him in a hug.

"Hey," he repeats with far less enthusiasm. "Sorry to just show up. I got a new phone but we're leaving on a road trip this afternoon and I needed to talk to you. In person."

"Okay..." Something tightens in my chest. It feels like I'm suddenly in a corset and someone is tying it way too tight. Conner's got circles under his eyes. He hasn't had that since December. And he didn't really hug me back. Not with both arms. He used one dropped lightly at my waist and the other stayed in his pocket. "Is this about my dad? I just found out he's your coach."

His eyes finally find mine. "You didn't know?"

"He mentioned a few times that someone was poking around about a potential coaching job, but he never told me what team," I explain. "And I never dug for details because, for one thing, my father is super closed-lipped about work. Legal and privacy issues and also he's superstitious."

"So he's tight-lipped about work the way you're tight-lipped about boyfriends?" Conner says and that imaginary corset around my rib cage tightens half an inch.

"You told him? About us?"

Conner shakes his head, his light brown hair hanging over his eyebrows before he reaches up and shoves it back with his fingers. "No. I lied. I could tell you hadn't said anything."

"I... haven't told him," I explain because this is obviously hurting Conner and I feel like a total asshole suddenly. I didn't even think to consider if it would bother Conner that my family doesn't know about us. "I wanted to tell them in person, but we haven't gotten together yet. I wasn't hiding us. My dad is just... well, even before the whole debacle with Beckett, he was protective. I know he likes you, but when I was a teenager his only dating rule was no hockey players."

Conner snorts, his perfect mouth twisting into a bit of a sneer. "Ironic. Your dad was the biggest player in the league at one point."

"Yeah, I've heard. I made the mistake of Googling him once when I was younger," I admit and shudder. "But I'm not a kid anymore and you're not just some random hockey player. Beckett didn't play and look at how well he treated me. And is still treating me."

"Yeah, I kind of pointed that out to your dad," Conner tells me. "And he came at me kind of... growly to say the least. Basically made it clear that if you were involved with someone, especially a hockey player, you shouldn't be."

"He did what?" The wind is now whipping around us, biting at my cheeks, which is a mixed blessing because if the cold wasn't swirling around us I'd be overheating with anger.

"Yeah. Listen, Mac, this is... complicated now," Conner tells me, pushing himself off the side of the barn that he was slumped against and stuffing both hands back in his pockets. "Your dad is my coach and no coach wants their daughter with one of their players. Not a fucking one. It makes the whole work situation a ticking time bomb. I've struggled enough to last a lifetime with my coaches in the last two years."

"Look, my dad will be fine after I explain everything to him," I reply, but it feels like Conner isn't listening. He's back to staring at that stupid snowy field behind me. "He's just a little annoyed because he heard the news from someone else."

"Mmf," Conner grunts. I have no idea what that sound means.

"Your video was... a little gruff," I say as that stupid Instagram clip Heather showed me plays in my head. "You're going to miss *nothing* while you're away."

His face finally softens, and he looks at me again. He blinks and exhales long and slow. "I panicked. You hid us from your dad, and I didn't know why. I didn't want to be the one to confirm it. Hey new coach, I'm banging your daughter, but don't let that influence how you treat me on the ice."

"My dad is a professional. He's not going to punish your career," I argue, starting to get annoyed because why can't I breathe properly. Why does my chest hurt? "He likes you Con. And your family. And he will see you're treating me right. That's all he cares about. I'll talk to him."

"When? Because we get on a plane together for a week-long road trip today and I don't think this is something you should just spring on him and then leave me to deal with the aftermath," Conner replies. "I have to concentrate on being a big part of getting this team into a playoff position, Mac. I can't be wasting time kissing the coach's ass because he's pissed I'm dating his daughter."

Oh.

He looks so... distant. Like he's saying something more than he's said. Like he's made a decision that he hasn't articulated yet but no matter what I respond here, he's... ending this? I think that imaginary corset just cracked every single rib. It's impossible to fill my lungs with air at the moment. Tears prick the backs of my eyes.

"So... we should, what? End this?"

"I'm just saying it's complicated," Conner snaps, like I'm being dense. "Don't you get that? My sports psychiatrist told me to keep everything to do with my career simple. Get back to basics. Like you said, play without a name on my jersey. Now the name on my jersey is 'coach's daughter's boyfriend'. This is complicated."

"Yes, and you don't do difficult," I reply, stepping back from him. Oh God, I have been such a damn fool. "That's been your problem all this time, hasn't it? Nothing has ever been hard for you. Not hockey, not women, not anything. And so when things started getting hard in Brooklyn you turtled. Just closed up and panicked and let it all fall apart. And you're going to do that with me too. Cool. I get it. Why work at anything when something else will be thrown your way."

"What the fuck, Mac," he whispers, his eyes wide and sad. "That's what you really think of me?"

I almost smile at that. "No, actually. I can't even begin to explain to you what I really think of you because you don't deserve to hear it right now. And I'm not sure it even matters."

I push past him and shove my key in the lock. "Go on your road trip, Con. Play like there's no name on the back of your jersey. Not Garrison and definitely not the title of boyfriend."

I shut the door in his face and put the chain on the door before stomping upstairs, almost falling because I miss a step when the tears start blurring my vision. He's still pounding on the door as I drop my bag and coat in the hallway and lean against the wall covering my face with my hands, which are immediately coated in tears. That stupid fifth-grade teacher's voice fills my ears again.

'You, Mackenzie have always been and will always be a have not, not a have. And the sooner you accept that the better off you'll be.'

Conner Garrison is the crown prince of hockey so of course he doesn't want me. Not now that it takes work. I'm not the type of person people fight for.

And that's when Conner Garrison breaks down my front door.

Chapter 30

Conner

If I'm honest with myself, I think I did come over here looking for a way out. It wasn't a plan or even a clear thought, but as soon as we started talking, I could see it was headed that way. And I just stood there and let it happen.

Having a sports psychiatrist has been a much-needed humbling experience. The first couple of sessions were just me talking. A lot. Explaining my version of my entire career up until now. The next two were this man pulling at threads with pointed questions. Getting me to unravel truths behind the highlights and lowlights of the last seven years since I was drafted.

Doctor Wayne never *tells* me anything. He leads me to my own conclusions. And I've come to admit to myself and accept, that being a Garrison in professional hockey means I don't have to worry about missed opportunities. Another one will always be handed to me. Like the Portland Riptide. I've come to swallow the uncomfortable truth that they only picked me up for my name. I'm still given more slack, status, and leeway because of my family's legacy than someone else might get, on and off the ice. Am I as talented as I think I am? Maybe not. So I have decided to work even harder. Not for anyone else but for myself.

But today, right this minute, it hits me that that whole mindset should also apply *off* the ice. I remember when I had that childhood crush on Mac and why I never did a thing about it. Because there were easier options. Girls who lived closer were showing blatant interest, and were much less of a challenge, with fewer obstacles. My whole life has been about the low-hanging fruit. Sad but true.

Letting Mac go now is the easy way out.

Do I like her? Yeah. A lot. More than I have ever liked a woman before. But she's complicated now more than ever and I don't do complicated because I don't have to. So I stood there watching her draw her own conclusions, pleading with me to say or do something that didn't lead to the end of this thing we've started. But... I didn't. Until that moment when she made it official.

We end and Mac slams the door in my face and then... Well, fuck me if I don't wake the hell up. I can't possibly handle the idea of walking away from her. I pound on the door until my fist throbs. I will miss the plane, skip the road trip, whatever it takes to fix this. Not let it end. And then I remembered I'm six foot four, built like a brick shithouse, and that the landlord is my uncle. So I break the door down.

When I get to the top of the stairs, she's slumped on the floor with her face in her hands, crying quietly. I drop to my knees in front of her. "I'm sorry. I panicked."

"Leave me alone."

"Mac. Mackenzie. Princess, please."

I touch her wrists, wanting to pull her hands away but she yanks them from my grip. Her eyes are watering, and her cheeks are blotchy and wet. My heart splinters. I fucked this up big time. "You know why I dislike that stupid nickname? Because

I'm the furthest thing from a princess, Conner. I'm a dead crack-head's orphaned daughter, who ate out of dumpsters and slept in doorways. I will always be that cynical, wounded, defensive kid to some degree, no matter how much therapy I do or how many degrees I get, or who I date. And I don't even want to change that. I am who I am because of what I've survived. But princesses, aren't made up of broken parts like me. So maybe this can never work. You're right."

"I never said that," I interrupt, leaning forward on my knees and brushing my knuckles across her left cheek to wipe away a tear I don't even think she knows has fallen. She jerks back from my touch. "This *is* working."

"Boys like you aren't meant for girls like me."

"Boys like me?" I snort. Literally. "Boys like me aren't good enough for girls like you, Mac. You're right. You aren't a princess. You're a fucking warrior. I'm just a guy with a big name and a fragile ego. That's why I don't fight for things. Because I know deep down I don't deserve them. And that includes you."

She finally meets my eye, blinking as another fat tear slips free. This time when I reach up to wipe it away she lets me. "But damn do I want you. More than anything in my life right now, I want you. So please forgive me. Take me back and let's just keep going no matter how complicated it gets."

She sniffs. I gently cup her face in my hands and lean in. I kiss her softly, with all the feelings swirling inside of me, confusing and terrifying the hell out of me. And she slowly but surely kisses me back. "You can't do things like that. Make me feel like I'm not worth it, Con. Because I will believe it."

"I'm sorry." My heart is still splintering in my chest. "I promise princess I will never do that again, not even for a second."

"Can you stop with the nickname?"

"No. Because you keep calling me a prince," I explain, my forehead pressing into hers as I brush her curls back. "And you're mine baby. So that makes you a princess."

"So... now what?"

"Well, I head back to Portland and catch our private plane to San Francisco," I explain, hating that I can't consummate this reconciliation the way I want to. "And I talk to your dad. And if he doesn't throw me off the plane at forty-thousand feet, then I help win a couple hockey games and when I get back you let me spend the entire day in bed with you showing you how much I missed you, how sorry I am, and how much you mean to me."

"You mean a lot to me too, Con," she whispers.

I kiss her again and help her to her feet so I can wrap her in a hug. We stand there for minutes just holding each other. Maybe Alex won't notice if I just don't show up. Can I fake an injury or something? I don't want to leave her.

"What the hell happened to the door?" a voice booms from downstairs.

"I'll pay for it," I call back as Tenley starts stomping up the stairs.

"Jesus, I thought I was going to find kidnappers or mafia henchmen or cartel leaders or something." Tenley stands in the entryway holding a hammer in one hand and a taser in the other. She takes in the sight of Mac all teary-eyed while wrapped up in my arms. "You need me to taze him, Mac? I'll do it."

"I'll pass but thanks for the offer," Mac replies and she shoots me a small smile. "I'll take a raincheck though, in case I need you to taze him at a later date."

I laugh. "You won't princess. I promise."

"Go catch that plane," she tells me, kissing me softly but not so soft that Tenley doesn't groan in protest.

"I'm going to miss you like crazy."

"I'll miss you too. Especially if my father tosses you out of the plane mid-flight," she replies with a crooked grin.

"I'll call you tonight," I promise.

I pass Tenley and she points her taser at me. "I'm sending you the bill for the door."

"Yeah. Yeah."

I feel kind of wrecked as I climb into the driver's seat and start my trip back to Portland. I don't even care what happens next. If Alex is going to be pissed off at me about Mac or if the media turns it into some big deal that I'm dating the coach's daughter or if the players balk about it because they think I'm getting preferential treatment. I realize now that I can handle anything. And some battles are worth it. Mac is worth it.

Chapter 31

Conner

I can tell as soon as I board the plane that Mac has talked to her dad. Coach, as I will have to call him for the foreseeable future. His eyes are on me as soon as I board and he calls my name. "Garrison! We need to talk."

Okay, so much for me building up to it. I nod and drop my bag on a window seat before continuing to the back where Alex... Coach is standing next to the bathrooms. Everyone is busy getting settled in their seats and buckling up so no one is going to bother us back here. It's as private as we're going to get. I come to stand in front of him, squaring my shoulders and locking eyes with him.

I can see why Alex was such a great enforcer when he played. He can look scary as shit when he locks his jaw and narrows his eyes like he's doing to me at the moment.

"Look, I know that you don't really know me. You know my parents and my uncles, and I think you think they're good people."

"They're some of the best people I've ever known."

I nod. "Yeah me too. And I've spent my life trying to live up to that. I've been a good hockey player, a good cousin, a good son, and now I'm going to be a great boyfriend to your daughter."

"Going to be?" Alex questions folding his beefy arms over his chest. "I thought you guys were already dating."

"We are. And I was a good boyfriend, but I... I hurt her today," I admit and holy fuck if looks could kill Alex would have me plastered to the ceiling of this private plane like a coat of paint "But I fixed it. She forgives me, but I don't forgive myself and probably won't for a while. Because Mac's the most amazing person I've ever known. I figured out how awesome she was when I was a kid. But I've never been man enough to let her know until now. Like literally today. Anyway, I could have ended it today, because we both know we're gonna get a lot of media attention neither of us wants when the world realizes I'm dating my coach's daughter, but I think she's worth going through a little drama. I *know* she is. So yeah, I'm dating your daughter, and as long as she lets me I will continue to do so. Are you okay with that?"

Alex stares at me for a long time. Just stares. It's got every hair on the back of my neck standing up and a chill rippling down my spine. Thank Christ I don't play guys with this level of intimidation skills. I would piss myself right there at center ice. "I have to be okay with it because Mackenzie told me that I have to be."

I almost smile at that, but my self-preservation instincts tell me it's not a good idea. Alex finally sighs, all that animosity he can command at the drop of a hat disappears and he lets his folded arms drop to his sides. "You the reason she's chasing to stay in Portland after she graduates?"

I shake my head. "No. She really just likes the place and the job opportunity. For the record if she wanted to move back to

New York or took a job in Idaho or wherever, I would still stick with her."

He smiles. Actually smiles. And my lungs expand. I feel relief flood my veins. "She's the most amazing person I've ever known. Honestly. Since the second I saw her in that alley, I knew she was special."

"She makes me a better man," I tell him and I feel the words in my gut. Nothing has ever been more true.

"I've always liked you Con. And between you and me, you might almost be good enough for her," he says and slaps my shoulder. "Now go sit down so we can get this bird in the air."

I make my way to the seat I left my bag on. Abbott has taken the seat beside me. He moves his knees so I can slink past. "Why do I get the feeling there's an issue between you and the new coach? Please tell me I'm wrong because I really don't want bad energy in the locker room."

"You're wrong. There's no issue," I promise him, and his shoulders start to droop in relief. "But I am dating his daughter."

"Oh fuck." Yeah, even the gay guy knows that's a big no-no.

"He's cool with it," I reply. "I swear. We're old friends. He's good."

"Yeah but dude, if you fuck up just once, there's no way that stays out of the locker room." Abbott sighs and shakes his head. "Coaches with daughters are dangerous. They will always screw you if you screw their daughters. Even I know that and I don't screw daughters."

I smile at that because he's grinning at it himself. "It's fine because I won't screw up."

"So you're going to date her the entire time he's your coach, no matter what?" Abbott raises an eyebrow like he doesn't think I could want to stay with someone that long. Maybe because it took him a while to commit to Declan.

"I'm hoping to stay with her indefinitely," I confess and ignore the fear that kind of spikes in my belly. I don't know if she feels the same. I hope she does. We haven't said the L word yet.

"Well, obviously I hope it all works out, dude," Abbott tells me before he puts on his headphones and closes his eyes.

* * *

I'm in the hallway between the home team locker room and the visitor one. Tate and I agreed to this PR stunt before the game because everyone always wants pictures of the cousins together when they play each other. My dad says it's worse when it's your siblings but I can't imagine being hounded more than we already are. Tate rounds the corner. He's in flip-flops, sweatpants, and an Under Armor shirt. His sandy brown hair is tucked under an L.A. Quake baseball cap.

He smirks at me as he approaches and the press gathered at the side all start snapping photos and likely taking video. I don't look over to find out. "Ready to have your ass handed to you?"

"Language little cuz," I chastise as we hug. "You west coasters are so crass."

"Shut up. I'm a Mainer at heart, just like you," Tate laughs. "You're just jealous I don't have to shovel snow off my car after a home game."

"Your team is literally named after a catastrophic event that happens weekly here," I remind him. "I'll take the snow."

The press actually laugh. They love this, the way we give each other shit, and Tate and I excel at it. We know the game and we like playing it, on and off the ice.

We turn to face our audience now, wrapping our arms around each other and letting them snap some more shots.

"Okay." The Quake coach claps his hands. His name is Jude

Braddock and he's an ex-player just like Alex. "You guys got your *Family Ties* moment now let's go back to being opponents."

"You got it Coach," Tate says and turns to me. "Later cuz."

I turn and head back to the visitors' locker room. I have to pass the visitor's guest lounge and that's when I see her. I swear to god it's a mirage. Hallucination. I stop so abruptly that my dress shoes squeak on the polished concrete floor.

She turns away from her dad and smiles. "Surprise."

I smile so big and so fast that I might have to see a trainer about pulled muscles in my face. I walk right up to her as fast as I can and scoop her off her feet in a giant hug. "She's actually here to see me," Coach grumbles.

"No honey," Mac's mom says from where she's standing next to Coach, patting his arm. "We're here to see you. I'm pretty sure she just wanted to see him."

"My mom wanted to surprise my dad on his first road trip with his new team," Mac explains, her lips against my neck as she's still hanging from my embrace a half inch off the ground. "I couldn't resist joining."

"Can you introduce me to your boyfriend already?"

I put Mac down and she takes my hand and turns to face her family. I've met her mom before, but not her sister who has been a new addition to her family in the last decade. It's the sister who demanded an introduction and as soon as we're facing her, she steps forward and gives me her hand. "I'm Cassia."

"Cassia, I'm Conner. Great to meet you." I turn to her mom. "Nice seeing you again Mrs. Larue."

I extend my hand but she ignores it and pulls me into a hug. "Call me Brie. You used to when you were a kid and there's no point getting more formal now."

"Okay, Brie." I smile and hug her back with one hand because I don't want to let go of Mac's with my other.

"I'm still Coach, not Alex," he reminds me even though I don't need it. "And I need you to go suit up."

"Sure. Of course." I turn back to Mac and steal a kiss, hoping it doesn't get me killed. "Can I see you later? We are spending the night at—"

"The Beverly Wilshire, I know," she finishes. "Us too. We fly home tomorrow when you go to San Diego."

Brie leans in and wraps an arm around both of us before whispering. "Maybe don't plan your booty calls in front of your dad, Mac honey."

Right. Oops. "I'll text you."

I squeeze her hand and jog off.

* * *

We win the game, and much to Tate's annoyance I'm the reason why. I score both goals. He scores the Quakes' only goal so the media is eating this up. Garrison Boys Carry Their Teams on Their Backs in East-West Late Season Battle, is the only headline I see online as we're boarding the bus back to the hotel.

I'm about to settle in next to Abbott when I hear the coach speak. "Okay guys, we have hitchhikers tonight," he announces as Brie, Cassia, and Mac climb up the stairs. "My wife and kids are here."

The guys shout out hellos and I immediately move to the empty seats behind Abbott. Coach clears his throat. "My daughter Cassia, my wife Mrs. Larue to you motley crew, and my daughter Mac who is also, for some inexplicable reason, Garrison's girlfriend."

The bus erupts in a chorus of whistles until Coach's glare steals all the noise from the bus. "Yeah. So now you know and that's the last we'll speak of it. Great game guys. Thanks for pushing. One more to win before we head back home."

Mac walks right past her dad and sits down next to me. I try not to grin too hard as I lace my fingers through hers.

* * *

An hour later, after I've made her come apart on my tongue, and again on my cock, she lays curled up with her head on my chest while I wrap one of her curls around my index finger.

"So Dad's handling it okay," Mac says softly.

"Can we not talk about Coach when we're naked?" I request and I feel a laugh rumble out of her. "But yeah, I think we're going to be okay."

"We are."

I let go of her curl and pull her up, sliding onto my side so we're face-to-face, heads resting on the same pillow. "I'm still so sorry for that moment of stupidity."

"I forgive you. I told you."

"I know," I sigh. She takes one of my hands in hers and kisses the back of it. "But I just wanted to plead my case a little more because I've done nothing but think about it since. I wanted to let you know that I've never been in love before. So, like, I have no idea what the hell I'm doing. I think my brain just short-circuits a bit the closer I get to blurting out the L-word. It's closer and closer every single day. Bit by bit."

She looks... well, gorgeous, shocked, and nervous. I panic I might be scaring her off but then she smiles and nods. "Yeah, I can see why new emotions are a little overwhelming."

"Yeah. Exactly, but I want you to know." I move my hand to her waist and pull her closer. "That I intend to bring my A-game from here on out, princess."

She laughs. "I guess I better bring mine then too."

267

I graze my lips against hers. "Sounds like a plan."

And then I kiss her, long and hard, like we have forever. Because it sure as hell feels like we do.

Epilogue

Mac

Another burly professional hockey player walks by me carrying the last of my things. As he heads down the stairs I glance around the barn apartment. It looks like it did the night I moved in. So stark and empty except for the few pieces of furniture that came with it. It's kind of gut-wrenching to see it like this because it reminds me of the state I was in, emotionally, when I got here. It's also rewarding to see how different it looks because it reminds me how different I feel. This apartment started as a refuge for a broken version of me. But I'm leaving it as a new, improved, stronger version of myself. And a much happier one.

I hear footsteps and see Conner in the doorway behind me. "Is that it?"

I nod. He walks over and wraps his arms around me from behind, pulling me into his solid chest. The shaggy, unkempt beard growing on his face tickles the back of my neck. He's just finished the first round of the playoffs. The Riptide won in a four-game sweep. Now they're just waiting for the other teams to finish their first-round series so they have an opponent to play in round two.

"I can't believe how full the truck is down there," Conner comments as I drop my hands on top of his in the center of my stomach. "When I invaded this place at Christmas you could have fit everything you own into the trunk of my car and still had room for a dead body."

"And I wanted to kill you for breaking in so that would have been convenient," I snark and he squeezes me. I laugh. "Seriously though, I probably shouldn't have started accumulating furniture for my apartment in Portland while still in Silver Bay but the price of everything here is cheaper and I really loved that bed frame from the antique place."

"The guys were more than happy to earn brownie points when your dad asked for volunteers to help you move," Conner kisses the back of my neck as I keep staring at the empty apartment, trying to burn it into my memory. "You know Uncle J and Aunt J aren't going to rent it out again. We can come back and walk down memory lane any time."

"Only if you promise to drop your towel for me again," I say with a giggle.

Someone clears their throat from behind us and Conner springs back from me when we both lock eyes with Dad. He's frowning. "Everything is loaded downstairs. Anything else up here?"

I shake my head. Conner darts past my dad and down the stairs.

"What about the Hampton lamp?" Dad asks. "I didn't see it in with all your stuff."

"Oh. Yeah." I sigh. "I don't have it anymore."

Dad's dark blue eyes flare. "What? Did it break?"

"No. I didn't grab it when I ran out on Beckett and he didn't include it in the stuff he brought me," I explain and feel a bit guilty. I really did love that lamp. It had been in my bedroom in my parents' Hamptons beach house and when I got my first real adult apartment, with Beckett, they shipped it to me because they knew how much I loved it. When it was lit it cast a beautiful swirl of color on the wall and ceiling.

Dad looks crestfallen and guilt washes through me. "I'm sorry. I was in a bad place and not thinking clearly and when things got better, I just didn't want to deal with him."

Dad hugs me, pulling me against his chest and cupping the back of my head like he has done since day one. Well, since I let him, which was more like year two of knowing each other. "You don't have to apologize for anything. Come on. Let's go."

He lets go of me and heads down the stairs. I lock the door for the final time and head downstairs. Jessie and Jordan are there waiting to take my keys. I drop them in Jessie's hand. "Thank you again for helping me out when I needed it."

"Anytime, Mac." Jessie smiles at me.

"That's Doctor Larue," Conner corrects as he climbs into the driver's seat of the rental truck. He's grinning with pride and even my dad starts to smile.

"Boys, we won't need you at the Portland apartment," Dad announces to his team. "Garrison will do all the heavy lifting and my wife and youngest daughter are already there to help as well. But we have one more stop I'm going to need you to make with me if you all don't mind."

"Where?" I croak but I already know, even before he gives them the address of my former apartment. The one where Beckett still lives, with Heather. I heard through the hospital gossip mill that they had made a couple offers on houses but nothing had panned out. Also, they had pushed back their wedding date, according to Shelby.

Trouble in paradise? Maybe. I honestly didn't care so I didn't ask. I climb in the rental truck next to Conner, resigned to the fact that this is happening whether I like it or not. I'm not a fan of confrontation, but I would like that lamp back.

I explain the situation to Conner as he drives to the address, a trail of three cars full of his teammates, and my dad's car behind that, following. A deep smirk starts to spread across my man's handsome, scruffy face. He is the sexiest man ever, but I'm not thrilled he's enjoying this. "Con, I don't want my last moments in Silver Bay to be with Beckett."

"Okay. You wait in the car. I'll handle it," he replies and I scowl. He doesn't take his eyes off the road but he feels it. He starts to laugh. "Princess, you deserve that lamp. It's yours. The end."

We pull up in front of the small square apartment building and all the players get out of their cars. Jordan has caught a ride with my dad. Apparently, he didn't want to miss this. I groan as Conner gets out of the car and I watch them all lumber toward the front door. Then I quickly unlock my seatbelt and hop out of the truck to join them.

This is my problem and I should handle it.

My father has already rapped on the door and by the time I make it there, Beckett has opened the door. He's in jeans and a sweater and his eyes are the size of saucers as he stares at half the Portland Riptide and my dad and Jordan Garrison on his stoop. "Can I... Can I help you?"

"Hey TP, Mac left a lamp here. Can we get it back please?" Conner says before my dad or anyone else can speak.

"Ex... excuse me?" Beckett sputters.

"My stained glass table lamp," I call out from the back of this wall of muscled men. "It was on the hall table when I lived here. You didn't give it back when you returned my things."

Beckett's eyes find me in the group and he frowns. "My fiancée may have thrown it out. I believe she called it tacky."

"You better hope she didn't TP," Conner replies.

"Is that a threat?" Beckett tries to sound tough as he pushes out his chest, trying and failing to look intimidating.

"Kid, just go look for the lamp before you hurt yourself," Jordan says calmly.

Beckett tries to glare at Jordan but then gives up when Jordan doesn't so much as blink. His shoulders slump a little. His scowl deepens. "Wait here."

He slams the door, hard. Abbott Barlowe looks at Conner. "His name is Beckett? Why do you call him TP?"

"Because Mac does," Conner replies. "It stands for toxic person."

"And trash panda and toilet paper," I add. "And tiny penis."

"Stop talking, I beg you," Dad says and everyone laughs.

The door re-opens Beckett steps onto the stoop and shoves his hand toward my dad. My lamp is in it, looking exactly as I remember. I smile when I see it and push my way to the front of the group. Conner has already taken it from Beckett and he hands it to me. "This will look great in your new place, princess."

"Princess?" Beckett echoes but his tone is dripping in disbelief.

Conner turns to him, his hazel eyes cold and hard. "You have something you want to say?"

My father and the rest of the team had started back to their cars but now they're all frozen a few feet away, watching us with rapt attention, and tense muscles. Beckett looks out at them and back to Conner. "Nope. Not a thing. Are we done here?"

"Oh, we are so done," I promise him. Conner wraps an arm around my shoulders and kisses my cheek.

"I've got some hockey games to win and then a vacation to go on with Doctor Larue," Conner says and leads me back to the truck.

I hear Beckett slam his front door as I climb into the truck. "Vacation?"

Conner grins at me. "Not how I wanted to tell you but... I booked us a house on the beach in Hawaii. Well, I have it on reserve. The date will be set when we know how far this playoff run stretches. We'll go when I'm done. To celebrate your graduation."

"Are you serious?"

"Yes. I'm going to need some sunshine and time alone with you," Conner replies starting the truck and pulling away from the curb to start the drive to Portland. "And you don't start work until August, right?"

"Right." I am so excited I'm grinning from ear to ear. "But that's... I mean it must be pricy."

"Yep. And if you dare argue or try to pay I will spank you," Conner warns. "And not in a good way."

I laugh. "Okay fine. My boyfriend can treat me this once."

"Because he loves you and he's proud of you," Conner reaches across the seat and takes my hand in his. It's not the first time he's said I love you but it's still new enough that it makes my heart flutter and my cheeks flame. "You make me so damn happy, princess."

"It's Doctor Princess now." He laughs and I lean over and kiss his cheek. "And I love you too, Conner, crown prince of hockey and future Stanley Cu—."

"Do not jinx it!" He bellows and I giggle.

"You hockey players and your superstitions." I kiss him again and he smiles.

"Well, whatever happens in playoffs, know that I've got your back," I promise him.

"Then I'm the luckiest man alive," Conner replies and kisses the back of my hand.

I would argue with him, but it would be futile. He's earned

my love. Luck has nothing to do with it. And I finally realize that I deserve it, too. I deserve him and this life we're building together.

"What are you thinking?" he asks.

"What bikinis to pack for Hawaii," I reply with a smile.

"Private beach," he tells me. "No bikini required."

His grin is simply feral and I love it. I love him.

Acknowledgments

Thank you to the readers who have been with me since the beginning. It's because of you that I had the idea to create this series. I didn't realize how much I missed these characters and I really enjoyed bringing them back and creating this next generation of Garrisons, Richards, Larues, Braddocks, Westwoods and more.

Thank you to my agent, Kimberly Brower and her amazing team at Brower Literary. Thanks to my husband and my 'kids' Aimee and Adam who put up with my oddball hours and stress outbursts while I am in deadline-mode. Thanks to my mom for always being my cheerleader. To my friends who always have my back, including the Amigos who really supported me in 2023 when I lost my dog Gus to cancer. I can never express, fully, how much it meant. Thanks to our dear friend Novid for always being there for us in our expat adventure.

My undying gratitude goes to Brandi Zelenka at My Notes in the Margin for her editing skills and patience with my ever-moving deadline on this one. Shout out to Winona Randall Designs for the beautiful covers.

I really, truly hope that you all enjoyed Conner and meeting, or re-meeting, these hockey players and their families. I am excited to bring you more Hockey Royalty later this year.

About the Author

Victoria Denault is an award-winning Canadian romance author. Her book Dauntless won Best Queer Romance in the 2023 Canadian Romance Awards. Victoria writes both MM and MF romance in mostly the sports and small-town genres all with heat, heart and a little snark. She's a nomad at heart and has lived in three different Canadian provinces, as well as California and France. She spends her spare time at the beach, baking, or snuggling her new puppy, Maximus.

www.ingramcontent.com/pod-product-compliance
Lightning Source LLC
Chambersburg PA
CBHW071425200726
48294CB00002B/513